D1014969

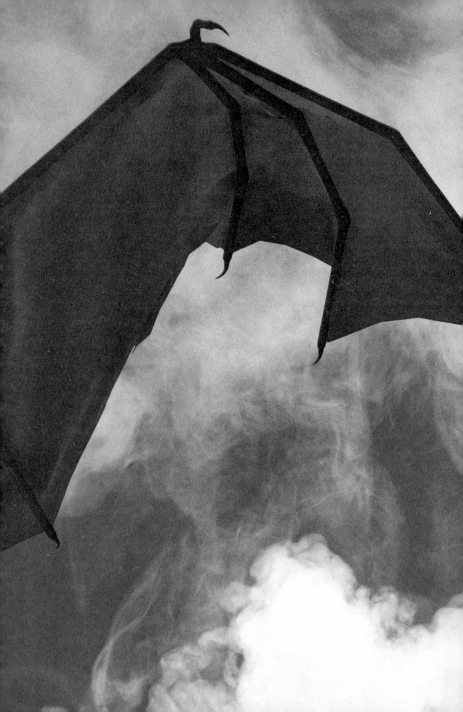

SEQUEL TO
The Story of Owen

Prairie Fire

e. k. JOHNSTON

carolrhoda LAB
MINNEAPOLIS

Carolrhoda Lab™ is a trademark of Lerner Publishing Group, Inc.

Carolrhoda Lab™
An imprint of Carolrhoda Books
A division of Lerner Publishing Group, Inc.
241 First Avenue North
Minneapolis, MN 55401 USA

For reading levels and more invormation, look up this
title at www.lernerbooks.com

The images in this book are used with the permission of:
© Corey A. Ford/Dreamstime.com (dragon wing); © Todd
Strand/Independent Picture Service (person), (bugle); © William
Langeveld/Dreamstime.com (smoke); © Algol/Dreamstime.com
(full dragon); © Badabumm/Dreamstime.com (dragon wing with
claw).

Main body text set in Janson Text LT Std 10/14.
Typeface provided by Linotype AG.

Library of Congress Cataloging-in-Publication Data

Johnston, E. K.
    Prairie fire / by E.K. Johnston.
        pages   cm
    Sequel to: The story of Owen.
    ISBN 978-1-4677-3909-2 (trade hard cover : alk. paper)
    ISBN 978-1-4677-6181-9 (EB pdf)
    [1. Adventure and adventurers—Fiction. 2. Dragons—
Fiction. 3. Bards and bardism—Fiction. 4. Fame—Fiction.
5. High schools—Fiction. 6. Schools—Fiction. 7. Family life—
Canada—Fiction. 8. Canada—Fiction.] I. Title.
PZ7.J64052Pr 2015
[Fic]—dc23   2014008995

Manufactured in the United States of America
1 – BP – 12/31/14

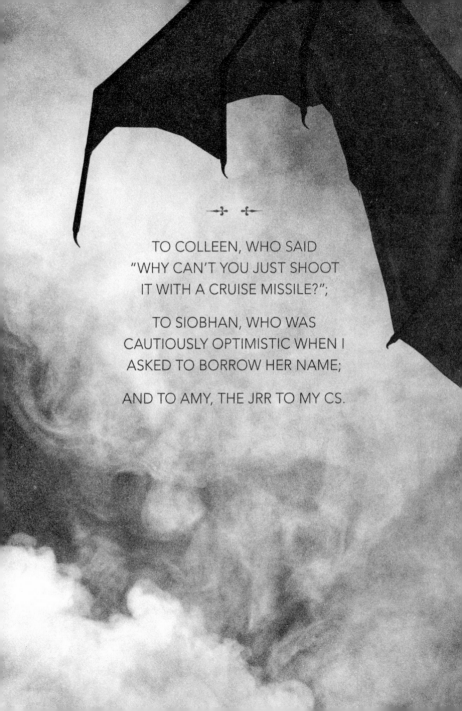

TO COLLEEN, WHO SAID
"WHY CAN'T YOU JUST SHOOT
IT WITH A CRUISE MISSILE?";

TO SIOBHAN, WHO WAS
CAUTIOUSLY OPTIMISTIC WHEN I
ASKED TO BORROW HER NAME;

AND TO AMY, THE JRR TO MY CS.

The courage of Catherine
The flames of the forge
The sword of Saint Michael
The blood of Saint George

I take what I'm given.
I follow my truth.
I shall gladly abandon
The bloom of my youth.

—*"Joan" by Heather Dale*

How I wish I was in
Sherbrooke now!

—*from "Barrett's Privateers"
by Stan Rogers*

THE STORY OF TRONDHEIM

After the Thorskards moved to Trondheim, we always had a permanent dragon slayer. It wasn't necessarily the same dragon slayer, mind, but when the great beasts threatened from the sky or the lake or their squats in the fields, help was close by. Sometimes it would be Aodhan, the gentle giant in the ancient Volkswagen, his sword and shield strapped to the roof and lights flashing to herald his coming. Sometimes it would be Lottie, the fallen one who had worked so hard to slay dragons again, and Hannah, who would walk through fire.

But most of the time, it was Owen. And where Owen Thorskard went, I was not too far behind.

It hadn't always been like that. Once, Trondheim had been left to burn. We had no factories and little in the way of industry. We could not afford a dragon slayer and always waited for the mercy of those who worked for the government. After her fall and injury, Lottie had changed that. She had come to Trondheim to train her nephew, while her brother patrolled and her wife crafted swords. We didn't pay them, except with welcome and food. But it was enough, and even the threat of a new, much closer hatching ground couldn't worry Trondheim the way it might have.

Before, we were just another small town, another second violin in the greater orchestra of Ontario. Now, we looked nowhere else for a conductor, and we wrote our own score.

And when I say "we," I do mean "me."

My name is Siobhan McQuaid of Trondheim, and I am the first true bard in a generation. Owen is my charge, and it is my work to shape his fractured notes into a logical melody. Strains of the others creep in too, of course. There's always a symphony in Trondheim now. Lottie's trumpet and Aodhan's cello and Hannah's oboe: They all work in concert. And every day, it seems, more instruments emerge from dusty cases and join.

We had one year to assemble our company before we would have to leave it. The Oil Watch had always loomed on Owen's horizon. I had chosen to put it on my own as well, and we would leave our town when we joined the Watch's ranks. Sadie Fletcher, who dreamed of fire and was born to dance with a sword in her hands, would come with us, but the others would stay and make the town safe—or go away to university in the fall.

So we worked. We rebuilt the houses burned out from when the dragons came. We trained even harder than before, knowing that Sadie, Owen, and I faced the strict physical requirements the Oil Watch maintained. And we kept one eye on the skies and one hand on our sword hilts. Just in case.

Owen slayed ten dragons that last year of high school. It wasn't a remarkably high number. He had slayed or helped to slay as many in the month before Manitoulin, and there had never been an accurate count of the dragon deaths the day we burned the island. But it was a very respectable number nonetheless.

Sadie managed three, with aid, and Lottie assured her that she would not lag behind when she reported for duty. Owen had been preparing and practicing for more than a decade, and Sadie a mere ten months. Her trumpet would soon more than match his horn.

For my part, I kept the record. I wrote the song for Sadie's first dragon and kept the details of the others. There was no need to immortalize them all in music. Owen was popular, and Sadie's notoriety was growing. I slayed no more, having already one more dragon to my name than I had ever thought I could, at the cost of my hands.

The Burned Bard, the media called me, though it was more my broken finger bones than burn-scarred skin that affected me. I'd gone to Manitoulin and left my music on its blazing shores. It wasn't the truth, of course. The music was inside my head, same as always. It was just harder for me to get it out.

Gone were the days of easy scratching on staff paper, and gone were the days of tinkering with notes on ivory keys. Even my beloved saxophone, the shape of my spirit and my indulgence throughout high school when I should have been focusing on composition, was lost to me. Instead, I struggled with software and often called on Emily Carmichael to make the little changes when I was too frustrated by my lack of finesse. I moved away from the part I'd played throughout my childhood to focus on my new responsibilities, but even the new noises couldn't fill that gaping hole.

I never doubted that it was worth the price, though. I had saved my town, my whole region. I had burned it, so they did not have to. And my neighbors, near and far, did not forget it. All through the summer and into fall and winter, the local farmers fed my family as they fed the Thorskards—the freshest and the best. My physical therapy, which would have been covered anyway, was never even billed. My high school gave me a trombone, the only orchestral instrument left that I could easily play.

Thus the vision of Lottie Thorskard was, in part, fulfilled. Trondheim, the town too small for a dragon slayer, now boasted four of them, even though two were still listed as "in training" on the official roll. And there was Hannah too, to hold Lottie's shields like the Vikings of old.

The day that Owen, Sadie, and I left for the Oil Watch, there was no parade. We left without fanfare, but with the well-wishes of the entire town. Owen and Sadie would do Trondheim proud, whether I chronicled it or not. They would be missed, but they would be welcomed home when their tours were done—on that much the three of us agreed. And while they were away, their service in the Oil Watch would honor their home. I was much, much less sure of myself.

You see, I had known since before the moment I signed my name on the enlistment papers that most orchestras have no place for a saxophone.

OWEN THE
FOOTBALL-SHOULDERED

Once he got older, they sang songs of his bravery and his heroic deeds. He'd filled out enough that I wasn't surprised to learn they'd attached names like "the Broad" or "the Football-Shouldered" to his self-effacing "Owen." Most of the time, he was kind of a legend. Right then, though, in addition to being weighed down by the responsibility for twelve people who still didn't really know him very well, and standing much too close to a terrifically poisoned forest glade, he was about to go up against a kind of dragon he'd never even seen before, much less fought. I, for one, was feeling pretty darn flammable.

Owen was a professional, though, his tempo more measured than some of the drill sergeants who had overseen our every move these past twelve weeks before turning us loose into the woods. Owen had dragon slayer singing in his blood farther back than most people kept records, and he had the training to match. He was the third generation of his family to enlist in the

Oil Watch. Though the dragon lighting aflame the treetops above our heads hadn't realized it yet, that clearing was going to be its end, if the Viking in Owen Thorskard had anything to say about it. And the Viking had done very well since he'd joined the Oil Watch and arrived at CFB Gagetown for Basic Training.

Basic Training had not gone so well for me, and I'd let my responsibilities as Owen's bard slide as a result. Where once I had kept track of all the parts and where they fit, I now had to focus solely on my own performance and ignore the orchestra around me, even if I sensed it faltering behind the beat. We'd all agreed to this, Owen, Sadie, and I, before we'd ever left Trondheim, but I still felt like I was letting him down. I didn't have a choice though. My burned hands had mostly regained their former colour, but there was no working around the angry red lines of scarring or the hardened muscles and knitted phalanges. I had no leisure for composing, which took me far longer than it used to, or even spare moments to think about songs to compose later. I spent all of my time scraping by, meeting the minimum physical requirements and trying to avoid the cold looks of the other cadets who assumed, possibly correctly, that someday my disability would get them killed.

I could have stopped. Basic Training essentially served two purposes: preparing troops for the field and identifying those who would never, ever make it. From the very first night, when I'd only managed to eat half my dinner in the time we were allotted and was berated at full volume by our barracks-sergeant for not dressing quickly enough, it was clear that I was, at best, a long shot. If I had been playing actual music, I could have just pointed my embouchure in the general direction and hit most of the right notes, but the military demanded considerably more precision.

None of Lottie and Hannah's stories had really prepared me for life in the Oil Watch. Theirs had been a different era, when gun battles with other people had been as likely—if not more common—than actual dragon slaying. They talked about the Oil Watch like it was all adventures and foreign locales. They didn't sugarcoat anything, not on purpose anyway, but I knew a story when I heard one. They did their best to tell us what to expect, but their memories were clouded by nostalgia, and I quickly learned there was nothing nostalgic about being rousted from my bed at 0400 and shouted at for ten minutes because I hadn't fastened my buttons quickly enough, before being ordered outside to run laps until the sun came up.

For his part, Aodhan reminded us that after we had done our time in the service, we would be able to return home to Trondheim, where a grateful town and familiar tune would be waiting for us. He did not tell stories about his days in the Oil Watch, which I thought was too bad. He was much more pragmatic about that sort of thing than his sister was. But I'd already heard most of the details about what had happened to him in the desert, and I knew better than to ask for any more. As the weeks wore on and I still failed, repeatedly, to keep up with my cohorts, I clung more and more to Aodhan's reminders that someday we would all get to go home.

By the time we were divided into squads—the assortment of firefighters, medics, engineers, and in Owen's case, bard, who supported a dragon slayer in the field—my place on the front line was generally accepted if not always appreciated. Sure, I was entertaining if you happened to be stuck in a shelter for a couple of hours while the more experienced troops dealt with an attacking dragon, but for the most part there was relief on the faces of those people not assigned to work with me.

For the dozen unlucky souls who would make up Owen's dragon slaying support squad, though, relief was not to be had. I tried to make myself scarce so as not to besmirch Owen's reputation any more than a solid year of news reports had already done by suggesting, not always subtly, that he was essentially an ecoterrorist. Usually, it would have been my job to sway their opinion, but this time, he was mostly on his own.

To be fair, Owen hadn't suffered that much without me to talk him up. He did come to the military with a very well established public record, for good or ill. Between my music and Emily Carmichael's Internet acumen, there weren't very many people in Canada who didn't at least know his name, if not exactly what had happened on Manitoulin Island. The other dragon slayer recruits at least respected his achievements—even if they were a bit jealous of his notoriety—and the engineers, medics, and firefighters all looked at him with something like awe. After a week, I was starting to figure out how our squad fit together, more or less, anyway. The engineers were identifiable enough, and the medics also cooked our food, so I did my best to stay in their good graces. I could only barely tell the male firefighters apart, though, much less put them into the songs I should have been writing. I felt bad, but unless one of them did something heroic or stupid, I'd end up writing them as the low bass: supportive, utterly necessary, and predominantly away from the focus of the piece.

Of course, now the engineers, medics, and firefighters of Owen's squad were looking at him with something like terror, but that was probably because the fire above us had started to burn through the trunks, and we were all in very real danger of being brained by falling treetops.

We'd been wandering around the carefully landscaped forest that surrounded the main living areas of the base for five days of drills with only each other for company. I think the general idea had been that we'd either kill each other or learn to work together, and we had chosen to do the latter. The general idea had *not* included any dragon slaying, particularly unsupervised dragon slaying, but apparently no one had thought to tell the dragon that, and it continued to demand Owen's attention, forcing him towards the poisoned ground we had been trying so hard to avoid. It was time for action, and that was the thing we had been training for all these weeks.

We were in unfamiliar surroundings, and even though there were fourteen of us, we felt very much alone. Everyone in the squad had seen dead dragons before, but this was going to be the closest most of them had ever been to a live one. Basic was for physical fitness and mental discipline. We weren't supposed to worry about dragons until we had received our posting, and then we would be working closely with a mentor, an established dragon slayer, and his or her squad. Help might arrive from the base, but it was going to take some time to get here. Another dragon slayer might have cracked, might have run.

But another dragon slayer wouldn't have had two years' experience commanding the high school soccer teams in group manoeuvers. Another dragon slayer wouldn't have grown up in the shadow of one of the Oil Watch's greatest heroes. Another dragon slayer wouldn't have been taught patience by a giant. Another dragon slayer wouldn't have had swords made for him by the woman who'd raised him from diapers. We weren't about to face the fire with just any dragon slayer. We were with Owen Thorskard, who had fought on the beaches of Manitoulin and returned home to finish the fight there as well.

When I looked at him, I saw that same reluctant smile I'd seen so long ago, half excitement and half worry. In his uniform, his shoulders seemed more square, his stance more grounded. The familiar strains of that Nordic saga came to me, not in whispers like they used to, but at full volume. If the others could have heard it, they might have smiled too.

"Send the code, Siobhan," he said, reaching over his shoulder for his sword.

That's not how it started.

ENLISTMENT AND A NEW SOUND

There were three things I realized pretty quickly after I joined the army.

The first was that I might die. This was not quite as alarming for me as it might have been for another eighteen-year-old, because I had faced down death on a pretty regular basis ever since Owen had moved to town. Even death by dragon fire was starting to lose its fatal charm. You burn down the world's largest freshwater island once, and it kind of puts the whole fiery doom thing in perspective.

The second thing I realized was that my friends might die. This was also less alarming than it might have been, since it was with my friends that I usually faced death. Owen signed up the same day I did, having waited until my birthday so we could enlist at the same time. The TV cameras were certainly more interested in him than they were in me, and I couldn't blame them. He'd grown, finally, and filled out enough that he actually looked like something a dragon might need two bites to swallow.

The third thing was that I needed to stop calling it "the army," because that's what people who aren't in it think it's called, and people who are in it can be sort of touchy about that sort of thing. I walked into the recruitment office a civilian, albeit a very unusual one, and I walked out a member of the Canadian Forces.

We didn't set out for New Brunswick right away. We still had to finish school, for one thing. The Oil Watch operated as part of the Canadian Forces, but thanks to its international influence, it also played by its own rules, and one of its rules was that all members had to have completed high school. Owen, as planned, had done well enough in his final year to squeak into the officer track, while Sadie was several steps ahead of him in that regard. I think her parents were kind of hoping that the first time a dragon died at her feet and ruined her shoes, she'd decide that she had made a mistake. I happen to know she kept those boots, looked at them often, and only worked harder as a result.

There was also the not-small matter of my physical fitness. Yes, I could do the running and the push-ups and the marching for kilometres with heavy things on my back, but my burned hands still had very limited mobility. I think, had I arrived at the enlistment office with anyone other than Lottie Thorskard, I would have been sent on my way, but Lottie had been determined, and very little could stop her when she decided she wanted something done. Furthermore, while it was common for civilians to choose the Oil Watch, I was the first bard to enlist in decades, and they weren't entirely sure what to do with me. Again, Lottie had been prepared.

"She simply won't be able to do the work required," the sergeant said. He was tall and broad and not from Trondheim, so he didn't really care about what had happened there a year ago. The Burned Bard meant nothing to him. All he saw was a girl who had to wear Velcro shoes like a child.

"She will," said Lottie, and proceeded to cite all kinds of precedents, most of which had been tracked down by Emily earlier in the week in preparation for this conversation.

Eventually, the sergeant called his superior, who conceded. He glowered all through my paperwork and barely spoke to me. I looked across the room at Owen, who was filling out his own forms quite a bit more speedily than I was. His sergeant could barely control his delight.

"That's going to happen a lot, isn't it?" I said to Lottie as we finally left.

"Yes," she said. "The military is good at a lot of things, but change comes slowly."

She opened the door for me to get in the car. I could handle regular doorknobs now, but I had problems getting my curled fingers around car latches, and even when I could, I was angled poorly to pull the door open afterwards. Lottie did all of these things for me with no attention called to them, and I knew she must have learned the trick from Hannah after her injuries. My parents did similar things, of course, but with them it was always a small production. Lottie couldn't help me sign my name on the enlistment papers, but I had been practicing for months. My signature was new, but it was mine, and even the grumpy sergeant couldn't fault it.

We watched as Owen and Aodhan spoke briefly to the cameras before cutting through the crowd to get to the car. Once, it would have been Lottie they swarmed, but Owen was younger and newer and both his legs could bend at the knee. Also he occupied that tenuous space between folk hero and government menace, and the press loved him for that more than they loved the fact that the Leafs were likely to miss the playoffs for the third year in a row. I don't think Lottie missed the camera's attention that much, but sometimes there was a hungry look in her eyes, particularly if it had been a while since a dragon had tried to eat Hannah's backyard forge.

"Well," said Owen as he slid into the backseat beside me. He didn't help me with my seatbelt, even though I was having a hard time with it. "I guess we've done it now."

"You'll be fine," Aodhan said, checking over his shoulder before pulling out into traffic. Driving in the Volkswagen with Aodhan at the wheel was commonplace for me now, but being in a regular-sized car with him still made me giggle. He had to duck to look at stoplights out the front window. "Siobhan, did you have any trouble?"

From most people, that would have been a delicately worded question about my feelings with regard to the fact that I could barely hold a pen. I knew that Aodhan didn't mean that, though. He had been there when I first saw a dead dragon, and he had defended the hospital while my mother worked inside it. He already thought of me as a comrade-in-arms. It's reassuring when a giant trusts you to protect his back. And his son.

"The sergeant clearly has his doubts," I told him. "But I do too, so I think that's only fair."

"We've still got time to work," Lottie assured me. "And I've promised your father that I wouldn't let you go if I thought you couldn't handle it."

My parents had managed to wait a whole month after Manitoulin before asking if I still planned to join the Oil Watch. They weren't surprised, I think, when I told them that I still would, if the Watch would take me, but Mum did spend a lot of time on the phone with Hannah that week.

"We've got almost a month to think of something specific for you to do if there's no need for actual music, and for me to call in every favour I have left to make sure you get to do it," Lottie continued.

Owen had his cell phone out, and I knew he was texting Sadie. Thanks to the new towers in and around Trondheim, put up once Aodhan had provided assurances that they would not be easily destroyed by dragon fire, she might actually get the text before we got home. Her parents had insisted she sign up on a different day, to avoid the news cameras. I didn't tell them that Sadie's enlistment would probably merit TV cameras on its own. Sadie's fame was entirely different from Owen's, but it was growing, thanks in no small part to me.

For the rest of the drive home, we talked about other things. The Thorskards were very good at avoiding certain topics of conversation, like impending doom, without making it awkward. I looked out at the fields, some newly plowed, some with winter wheat already stitched in green against the dark brown soil. Owen watched the skies, like always, but they were empty. His phone beeped. I did my best not to get in Owen and Sadie's way, after extracting a promise from Sadie that she would tell me if I was doing something she didn't like, because my chances of recognizing it were very low. She'd only laughed and told me I was adorable, which she did a lot anyway, and so far everything had been just fine.

Aodhan dropped me off at the foot of my driveway, and my dad waved from the door.

"It's done?" he said, when I was close enough that he didn't have to shout.

"It's done," I told him. "Is Mum home yet?"

"She got in just after you left," he told me. "But she said if you want to practice, she'll be fine as long as you keep the mute in."

One of the (very few) handy things about being forced away from the saxophone was that a trombone could be muted and made to play more softly while still using the proper amount of air. I had an electric mute, which played only for the wireless headphones I wore while I practiced, but I also had a regular mute, which served to muffle any noise I might make. This weekend, though, I didn't have the trombone home. Instead, I had another brass that I could play with a mute.

Trondheim Secondary School didn't own a bugle, but they did have several trumpets, with varying degrees of dings and scrapes. Before, I had never really used them much. Most composers feature them a lot, but after three years of watching them get all the good melodies in band, I was happy to relegate them to flourishes and counterpoint. Last November, when we'd stood at the cenotaph on Remembrance Day, one of the veterans had played the last post, and I thought of something that had, until right then, escaped me.

Before wireless communications and radios, before clocks and watches, and when flags were too untrustworthy, the military had used a series of short bugle calls to communicate things like when it was time to wake up, time to eat, and time to assemble for mail call. Most bases still used a variation of this, though the calls were all prerecorded. The Oil Watch, since it often incorporated dragon slayers who didn't speak the same language, relied on the call system even more. A trumpet and a bugle are mostly the same, and once you've developed the embouchure for a horn you can do anything, so I knew that if I practiced with the trumpet, I would be able to transfer my skills to the bugle easily enough.

And when you play a bugle, you can do it without moving your fingers.

THE BRAID

The last month of school absolutely crawled by. Sadie enlisted, with more fanfare than her parents expected, but we all still got up early every morning and ran farther than I thought was reasonable. After school there was Guard practice and then soccer. I was actually on the team this year, with no small amount of pressure from Sadie, and while I didn't get much playing time due to my extreme incompetence at kicking things in the appropriate direction, I did run. A lot.

I spent most of my evenings with the trumpet, or with whatever piece of newfangled implement my physiotherapist thought would help my hands. Most of them hurt, skin stretching and muscles trying their best to do the work with less mass, but I couldn't deny that they had improved my abilities. My right hand was still the worst in terms of looks and pain, since it was the hand I favoured, and the hand that had had the most contact with the hilt of the white-hot sword. The left wasn't much better, and I was clumsy with it besides, but it was better than nothing, I decided.

"You know," Dr. Madison had said, very early during our relationship. "Do you have access to a piano? It'll sound really hokey, but even if you can only plink out 'Mary Had a Little Lamb,' it might help you regain your range of motion."

Dr. Madison was lovely, but that morning I very nearly walked out of her office and never came back. She was from London and knew me only as a burn victim at first. I'm not even sure if my mother told her they were dragon-fire burns, though most physicians specialize in either those or mundane burns while they're in medical school, due to the specificity of chemical contamination that can infect the former. My parents still had notions of preserving my anonymity in those days, until the news cameras came back to Trondheim with a vengeance and showed no signs of ever leaving.

"No," I said. Lying for a cause was easier now. I didn't feel bad about it anymore. "I can't play the piano."

I read up on it later. Dr. Madison was right, of course. Playing would make all ten fingers operate separately and help with muscle strength. But I couldn't do it. I sat on the bench when Mum and Dad were at work, and opened the lid of the keyboard. It was dusty for the first time in my entire life, and when I hit middle C, I noticed it was out of tune. It had only been two months since I could play the masters, and now I couldn't even handle "The Old Grey Mare."

The current method of torture-by-physio involved one of those child-friendly rug hooking kits you can buy at Canadian Tire. I think this one was supposed to be a butterfly, but Dr. Madison had taken the pattern out because she knew that if she gave me details to focus on, I'd never actually get anything done. It was still very frustrating though, and by the time Sadie called at seven o'clock, I was really bored.

"There's two hours of daylight left," Sadie said, once I'd managed to get my phone answered. It was an awkward process, and I missed the days when I could just pick up the landline, but I guess progress is progress. "Please come and rescue us from calculus."

"Have I mentioned lately how glad I am that I am not taking that class?" I asked, already on the way to the door.

"Yeah, shut up," she said, laughing.

"I'll be there in a few minutes," I said. "I'm sure my keys are around here somewhere."

I slipped into a pair of flats that were very impractical for anything that might end in dragon slaying, but laces vexed me more than *lakus* these days. I retrieved my keys from the bottom of my purse with some effort. It was still really easy to forget that when I threw something somewhere, retrieving it was going to be awkward. For the first week after my bandages had come off, when I couldn't open, close, turn, or manipulate anything smaller than a loaf of bread, I'd done a lot of angry crying when I thought no one was looking. Now I just pretended that I was on camera all the time, which helped me keep it together.

Driving, mercifully, hadn't changed much. I mean, I drove with all the bad habits that would have made my driving instructor despair—palming the wheel, leaving one hand on the shift, failing to check the rearview mirror for dragons as often as I should—but I did it. By the time I pulled into Sadie's driveway, I was feeling relatively normal.

Owen was not allowed in Sadie's bedroom, which all three of us thought was both hilarious, because it's not like they couldn't manage mischief elsewhere, and insulting, because it's not like Sadie didn't have some pretty elaborate plans for the future. If I was along, they could go upstairs, but since we spent most of our time in the backyard trying to hit each other with sticks, the point was moot.

I found them hunched over the coffee table, calculus notes everywhere. Sadie was pretty much guaranteed an A at this point, but Owen needed to pass the exam to maintain his B−, so they spent a lot of time studying.

"Oh, thank goodness," said Sadie, though she must have heard me pull in. After a close encounter with a *lakus* back in March, my poor car had developed an unhealthy-sounding rumble that had thus far eluded my mechanic. My parents had offered to replace it, but we'd been through a lot together, that car and I, and I was kind of attached to its ugliness.

"What do you want to do?" I asked. "I've just moved down another handle size, so I'm not going to be good for sparring right now."

"Actually, we wanted to talk," Owen said. "About Basic."

I took a seat. I was kind of relieved that we wouldn't be practicing. Hannah and Dr. Madison had cooked up this plan where I would start with an oversized handle on my sword, and then they would gradually take me back down to a regularly proportioned one again. Every time we changed, it was like learning to hold the stupid thing all over again.

"Okay," I said. "Did Lottie tell you anything new?"

"No," Owen said. "We're just worried about you."

I looked at my hands. You spend a lot of time looking at your hands, I've discovered, when you want to avoid something. It's more awkward when your hands are what you're trying to avoid.

Emily had put in hours of research. Lottie had called in every favour she could. Hannah had pushed me harder than ever. And I was in. Now I had to make it through, and I didn't know how that was going to play out. The melody went on, uninterrupted, for Owen and Sadie—just the addition of a drum tattoo under their lines—but mine, mine had been on rest measures for months. And I didn't know for sure what it was going to sound like when it started again.

Neither of them had ever said I didn't have to do this. We all knew that it was true. We all knew that it would probably be easier if I didn't. But I was going to anyway. The fire on Manitoulin might have taken my hands, taken my music—or at least the easy parts of it—but it had left something behind. Forests burn all the time, dragon-caused or otherwise, and after, when the fire goes out, the plants and animals come back. The dead things, the unnecessary things, are gone, and life begins anew.

That wasn't exactly what happened to me, but it was close. What grew up in the space where the fire had burned was a sense of obligation. Before, I had only wanted to protect my home. After Manitoulin, I realized that things far away from Trondheim could be just as devastating as a local infestation of corn dragons. We needed oil and sugar and wood and potash. And while the island burned, I had discovered that I was one of those people who was willing to pay the price for them.

"I'm worried too." It was the first time I had said it out loud. "But we're in this together."

"That's what I told him." Sadie's smile didn't quite reach her eyes.

"What if they assign us to different places?" Owen said.

"They can't," I said. "Well, they can with Sadie. But you and I come as a pair."

"You need Sadie too," he said softly. "I can't French braid."

I had taken to wearing my hair down. It was simple enough to comb and mercifully stayed mostly straight. When we were patrolling, playing soccer, or on the training field, Sadie braided it for me. I couldn't even do a simple ponytail anymore.

"Then I'll shave my head," I told him. "We'll match and everything."

The uniform requirements for Oil Watch recruits were a bit more extreme than they were for regulars, largely because of the increased chance of burning. Lottie and Hannah had both shaved their heads while they were on their tours—I'd seen the photos—though Catalina, Owen's mother, had opted for the more complicated protective helmet.

"Siobhan," he said, "you can't joke about this forever."

"I'm not joking," I told him. "I am going to do this. And it is going to suck. But that's not going to stop me."

"Tell you what," Sadie said. "We'll borrow my dad's clippers and do it before we leave."

"We?" I protested. She'd been planning to wear the helmet.

"Sure," she said. "If you can make drastic decisions, then so can I. We'll do it tomorrow, after school."

Owen and I exchanged a glance. Our telepathy had improved dramatically since we'd met. I could tell he was thinking that there was no point in arguing with Sadie, and he knew that I was thinking it was his fault for dating her.

"Fine," I said. "Tomorrow. Now can we please go into the backyard and hit things?"

"Yes," Sadie said, and gestured to the floor in front of her.

I sat between her knees, and if we cried while she braided my hair for one last time, none of us were rude enough to mention it.

REAL PIE

In hindsight, we probably should have waited to shave our heads until after Owen's last interview with the local newspaper. Emily was annoyed. She liked having first dibs on releasing any news about us to the world at large. She'd had to give up most of her online aliases after what we'd engineered last spring. I didn't understand it fully—something about sock puppets, which apparently the Internet is desperately against—and having direct access to us was something she cherished. Usually we didn't mind letting her have the first go, but the haircuts had been kind of spontaneous.

Sadie brought the clippers over to the Thorskards' on Friday after school, as we'd planned, an hour before Owen's weekly sit-down with Sheila, the editor-in-chief (and also main photographer, copy editor, ad saleswoman, and espresso machine operator) of the *Trondheim Weekly*. I'm pretty sure we were all standing there wondering if this was a terrible idea.

"I think we should hack off most of it with scissors," Sadie said, twisting her ponytail in her hand. "That way it's kind of past the point of no return."

"Works for me," I said. "Except you'll still have to do it. I don't think I can hold scissors."

"Sit down, the lot of you," said Lottie from behind us. We'd left the deck door open and I hadn't heard her get close. "On the steps."

Lottie dragged a chair over, and sat down behind me. In a second, she had snipped off the braid Sadie had woven the night before, and handed it to me. It seemed a lot thinner than I'd expected. The clippers whirred to life and I felt the tickle as the blades ran along my skull.

"I hope your head doesn't have a funny bump to it," Owen said, running his hand over his own scalp.

"Thanks," I told him. "To be fair, I've been hit around the head fewer times than you have, so it's more likely that you'll have something weird."

Sadie laughed, pitched a bit higher than usual. The last time Owen had gone up against a *lakus*, he'd got the tail across his back as it was dying. It had knocked him into the side of a barn, and he'd ended up with a concussion. The farmer was absolutely horrified that Owen had been injured on her family's property, even though my mother ended up calling every day for a week to assure her that Owen was fine. One of the local newspapers had run an op-ed about how it was time for helmets to become standard for underage dragon slayers, but I wasn't holding my breath on any legislative change. It had taken long enough to get helmets into minor hockey.

Lottie slowed down as she went around my ears. My head felt very odd, and I twisted my hands in my lap. She ran her fingers across the top of my head, searching for any hair she had missed, but found none. She rested her hands on my shoulders and squeezed.

"Good lord, Lottie!" Hannah said from the kitchen. "Can't I leave you alone at all?"

"It was my idea," I said. Which was almost true.

"Did you tell your parents?" Hannah asked. She was the one in the Thorskard family who did most of the active parenting, after all.

"Um," I said. Because of course I hadn't. They were expecting me home with, at worst, a set of bruised knuckles.

"Oh, for Pete's sake," Hannah said. "Lottie, give me that."

Lottie managed to look a bit sheepish has she handed over the clippers, and Hannah rolled her eyes before dropping a quick kiss on her upturned face.

"Your turn, Sadie," Hannah said. "Assuming this was a group decision."

"It was," Owen said, as Sadie shifted to be better sat in front of Hannah.

Sadie managed not to flinch when Hannah cut off the bulk of her hair, but her smile got a bit watery when the clippers started up again.

"Well, it's practical," Hannah said. "If a bit showy."

"I never understood why anyone wore the helmet," Lottie offered. "It itched. And it was hot."

"We might not get assigned to the desert," Sadie pointed out. "There's oil in cold places too."

"There are pipelines in cold places," Hannah said. "But they're not usually in conflict zones."

There was a very good chance that both Owen and Sadie

would be assigned somewhere in the middle of a war. They had more experience than most dragon slayers their age, and that usually meant a ticket to a place that was hot in more ways than one. It also meant that their support crews would go under heavy arms, which I was not looking forward to. For starters, I wasn't sure I'd be able to fire a gun. And if there was a person at the other end, I wasn't sure I wanted to.

"It will be okay, Siobhan," Lottie said, looking at me. "You'll learn to do the things they ask, or you'll learn a way around them. And once you're in the field, you'll have a dozen people as backup. It will work out."

Lottie's faith was touching, but she wasn't going to have to figure out a way to get in and out of a uniform that seemed to be nothing but buttons in less than a minute, with ten fingers that refused to perform under that kind of stress.

"One thing at a time," Owen said. "We've figured out your hair. We'll figure out the rest."

Sadie's phone rang just as Hannah was finishing, and she answered it as Owen took her place in front of his aunt.

"Hi, Emily!" I heard Sadie say, and then, "Oh, no, that's just the clippers. We're shaving our heads."

I winced. Sadie was quiet for a while, presumably because Emily was yelling at her. Lottie was trying not to laugh.

"Stop squirming," Hannah said to Owen, who was also holding back a giggle.

There was the sound of a car pulling into the driveway, and I realized that Sheila was early.

Sheila was a professional—well, professional for Trondheim—and managed not to send her eyebrows into low Earth orbit when she saw Sadie and me walking over to greet her.

"Ladies," she said.

"We're around back," Sadie said, as though this was a totally normal day. "Is that okay?"

Sometimes Sheila did a video recording for the paper's Web site, and she liked us to be in the living room for that, because it looked homey. Since Emily agreed with her, we went along with it. The local municipalities had been thrilled with the outcome of the Manitoulin disaster, but the provincial and federal governments had a somewhat more adversarial response. Owen, and I for that matter, had both been painted as wayward youths at the least, and one network in Quebec had gone so far as to wonder if we were budding ecoterrorists. Emily assured us that the bulk of public opinion was with us and did what she could to ensure it stayed that way.

"That's fine," said Sheila. "Just a quick chat today. The Blyth spring fair is this weekend, so I have less space than usual."

"I hope you have room for a picture," Sadie said. "I spent forever on my hair."

I have no idea how she managed to do things like that with a straight face. It was very frustrating.

It was a medium-length interview, where Owen talked about why we'd decided to take such drastic measures.

"There's no guarantee that we'll be assigned to the same units during Basic Training," he said, which was true, though unlikely. "We've worked together for so long that we wanted to do one last thing as a set, before we take the next step in our journey." Apparently Emily's PR training had stuck.

He didn't mention me once, which was how I preferred it, but I assumed Sheila could read between the lines. Hopefully, she'd be able to keep her creativity limited when it came to writing the actual article.

When Sheila left, we went inside because it was starting to get chilly. It hadn't been a humid spring, which was odd, but since that meant the dragons were staying close to the lake, no one complained. Except the cottagers, of course, but they complain about everything. There was a message on the machine from Aodhan, who tended to forget that he could call Owen's cell if the landline went unanswered. He was bringing home dinner, though he neglected to say what it was.

"I hope there's pie," Sadie said.

"There's usually pie," Hannah pointed out.

"Real pie, I mean," Sadie clarified. "Not store-bought crust."

"You're kind of a snob about that," Owen said.

Aodhan showed up after fifteen minutes of bickering about what makes a perfect pie crust with enough food for a week of dinners. This trend had fed them all year, to the point where Hannah had stopped buying perishables at the grocery store. I went home with as much as Owen could put in my backseat, though to be fair, some of that was bound for Sadie's house.

I helped her carry it in. It was possible, if someone loaded my arms for me and got all the doors. Sadie's mother burst into tears as soon as she saw us, and it took me a moment to remember why.

"Mom," Sadie said, depositing her stuff on the table and wrapping her arms around her mother's neck. "We have to. Siobhan can't do her hair, and I won't have time."

"I know, darling," Sadie's mother said. "It's just a surprise. You didn't mention it."

"It was kind of like jumping in the lake on Victoria Day weekend," I said. "We had to do it fast, or we'd start second-guessing the decision."

"Well, you both have excellent bone structure," she said, gulping and trying to laugh. "And it'll grow back when your tours are done."

I drove home and sat in the driveway for a while before I went into the house. I ran my hands over my head. I could feel the skin with my fingers, but it felt rough because of the scarring there. If I used my wrists or the backs of my hands, it was different. Fuzzy. I looked at myself in the rearview. I was very pale, but that would change soon enough.

Lottie was right. This was one less thing to worry about now. I could practice dressing. I could practice the horn. I could make sure that I was the most over-prepared recruit ever to show up in New Brunswick. Or, at least, I could try. Lottie was so sure. And she'd done so much to make it possible. I was nervous—no, I was terrified—but I was going to do it anyway. Owen was going. And even though he'd never asked, I'd go too.

I checked the sky when I got out of the car—habit—and there were no dragons, so I went inside to show my parents what I'd done to my head.

GAGETOWN BLUES

They don't send everyone to New Brunswick for Basic Training, but they do send all the Oil Watch recruits there. Officially, this is both because New Brunswick is coastal (though the base itself is not), allowing for exposure to saltwater dragons, and because it is well-forested. Unofficially, it's because after what happened in the Battle of the Somme, the government of Newfoundland had it written into the British North America Act that only Newfie dragon slayers could be trained on the island, and New Brunswick was the next best option.

We arrived at CFB Gagetown early in the morning via train, along with approximately five hundred other recruits, less than one in ten of whom were dragon slayers. The Oil Watch employed a large support regiment, which would include engineers (both combat and smith), firefighters, medics, and for the first time in decades, one bard. I was not looking forward to being the novelty. The dragon slayers would be outnumbered, but at least they would have comrades in their work. Even if

Owen ended up assigned to a small base, I could be outnumbered one to hundreds. Notoriety was all well and good in high school or a small town. In the military, I suspected it could be drastically uncomfortable.

Our train was one of the first to arrive, straight from CFB Downsview in Toronto, but the westerners had all arrived before us, their trains taking days longer than ours had. Flying was reserved for people more important than we were, and trains were cheaper and safer, in any case. Still, after twenty-four hours, I was ready to be on solid ground again.

The arrival area was disturbingly well-organized, considering how many people were there. We found our luggage and were marshalled into lines for our lodging assignments. The Oil Watch had a marginally higher ratio of females to males than the regular forces did, but there were still few enough of us that while the male dragon slayers were billeted separately from the support crews, the female ones were all put together.

You could spot the dragon slayers easily enough. Most of them were tall and broad across the shoulders. And they often sported burn scars. My hands were clenched around the handles of my bag, and I was wearing long sleeves, which hid the burns on my arms. Soon that wouldn't be an option. It was summer, and the training uniform required a T-shirt. I wasn't worried about it, though. The T-shirt would be the least of my worries, compared with the buttons on the dress uniform.

We were sorted and shown to the barracks, where we left our things and were then hustled off to the mess hall. I followed Sadie through the line, and we took our trays to the appointed table. I couldn't see Owen, who usually stood out in a crowd due to his height, so I turned my attention to my food instead. Lottie had warned us that meals were short, and to eat as quickly as we could. I struggled with speed, but at least I could cut my own food now, not that this stuff really required it. The boy across the table from us made a face when he saw my hands, and soon after that the whispering started. I kept my eyes on my plate, but I could feel Sadie bristling beside me. Before anyone said something that might have caused trouble, though, there was the sound of a microphone coming on, and our attention was called to the front of the room.

"Welcome to CFB Gagetown," said a man I might have described as tall, had I not known Aodhan Thorskard. He was every inch cornet: compact but lacking the hard edge of a trumpet. "This is your last day of relative freedom. Finish your breakfasts and return to your barracks for tours and kit assignments. You will meet your instructors and get a taste of what the next fourteen weeks will be like. Dragon slayers, if you require an additional weapons locker, inform your sergeant."

We all stared at him, reasonably sure of what we were supposed to do next, but no one seemed to be willing to be first to do it.

"Move!" he bellowed, and move we did.

By the end of the first week, my hands ached almost constantly, except during my time in the pool. By the end of the second, I'd torn the skin between my thumb and index finger on both hands and had to forgo swimming entirely in favour of a trip to the infirmary.

"I'd say take it easy, but we both know that's not an option," said the medic as he finished winding gauze around my hands, thin, so I could still move them as well as possible. "But no swimming."

"I passed that test, sir," I said. Actually, it had been the easiest one. We'd practiced in Lake Huron starting in April, diving off the end of the pier in Saltrock while there was still ice on the beaches.

"I'm glad to hear it," he said. "I'm one of the few who had you lasting the first week."

I wasn't surprised to hear there was a betting pool on whether or not I'd make it. I didn't want to know the odds, or who had taken which dates, but I couldn't avoid the way everyone watched me. I scored very low on things like our practical weapons proficiencies. Theoretically, I knew the firearms inside and out, but I couldn't take them apart and put them back together with any speed at all. I had surprised myself to learn I was a good shot, if I wasn't moving. Apparently music had given me steady hands. I could keep up during physical drills, but I couldn't pack my own kit or make my own bed fast enough to suit the sergeants. And Quick Change was an unmitigated disaster. I was getting much better at push-ups, though.

"Thank you, sir," I said, hoping he would think I was talking about my hands and not his somewhat better-than-average expectation of me.

"That's what we're here for," he replied. "Come back if you bleed through the gauze."

He got me a note to explain that I was exempt from swimming, and I headed back out to join my training group. The sergeant read the note with a glare, his natural expression, and then suggested I use my extra time to practice in the gun range.

Well, it wasn't exactly a suggestion.

By the end of third week, I had calluses on top of my scars, and I'd gotten used to the extra pain. We started our wilderness training after that, out in all weather in the base's carefully terraformed forests. Part of this training was endurance, and included all the recruits, but mostly this was training for the dragon slayers, and since I was still attached to Owen, I went with them. Even though it was much rougher than camping with Aodhan, I still found it better than the on-base training, much to the dismay of the remaining bettors.

"I really wish you'd told me about the betting pools earlier," Sadie said one night when we were back in the barracks with almost enough time to get dry before the next drill had us at the mercy of the elements again. "I mean, I know you're not going to quit. I could have made a killing."

"They might force me out," I said. Every day the chance decreased, but it was still a possibility.

"There's a different pool for that," said the girl in the bed past Sadie's. She was a dragon slayer from Chilliwack, which put her at odds with almost everyone else on the base. British Columbia didn't send many people to the Forces, and the fact that its dragon slayers were conscripted was a sore point.

"Then I'd definitely have made a lot of money," Sadie said. "But don't worry, I won't hold it against you."

"Thanks," I said.

"Can you sing the Manitoulin song before lights-out?" the Chilliwack girl asked.

The request was echoed from all around me. It wasn't the first time they'd asked me to sing, but it was the first time they'd been so specific. That was the first song I'd written with words, on the grounds that I didn't think I'd ever be able to play it. Emily had helped, and I'd started taking voice lessons. My voice still wasn't spectacular, but since I was writing the music, my songs were always perfectly in my range. It was almost like it had been, but not quite.

Emily had also been the one to insist on a YouTube channel, claiming that it was the easiest way to go public without it costing us anything. We'd used the soundproof rooms at Trondheim Secondary to record it, and it'd gotten almost a hundred thousand hits within days of uploading. We'd also recorded my earlier works, played by the band or by Mrs. Heskie, with the appropriate footage of Owen where possible. Apparently we had a very large following, though I mostly left it to Emily to manage, because it made me nervous.

The Manitoulin song was probably the best piece of music I'd ever written at that point. After it went up on the Internet, for all the world to criticize, I had Emily go through the comments (something she had made Owen and me promise never to do), and pick out all the useful critiques of the work. Most people said it was moving, if a bit saccharine. They focused on the words, but the comments I appreciated the most were the ones that focused on the melody and the construction of the song. Emily knew that and sent them my way.

"My favourite part is when they're in the car, with the dragons overhead," Paul Anka had commented in some random interview on the CBC. "That must have been terrifying, to be so close, and you can really feel it in the notes and the pacing. Give her time to grow up a bit more, and she'll make you a dragon slayer you'll never forget."

Paul Anka knew from making people.

I looked at Sadie, who was sitting cross-legged on her bed. She smiled. Our beds lined the walls of the barracks, heads against the wall and toes pointing into the narrow aisle down the middle. There weren't any windows, for dragon safety, or decoration, beyond a Canadian flag in the corner and the articles of the Oil Watch framed in a dented brass holder beside it. I was tucked in, mercifully ready for once, but the others were still folding things to stow in their gear boxes or sitting cross-legged on their faded blue bedspreads to chat.

We didn't usually have any free time between our last assignments of the day and lights-out, but it was five minutes to eleven, and somehow there was nothing else to do. All of these girls would have heard the song on the Internet, and most of them didn't talk to me during the day unless we were working on the same project, but right now, it felt like we were a team. Like the Guard, or the soccer team. Hell, like that first Friday in history when I'd lit myself on fire.

I took a drink of water from the glass near my bed. I'd been out in the rain for two days, and I hadn't had a singing lesson in months. But this was as much part of my job as anything else I'd done since I got here. I breathed in and out, remembering the car, the sky, the water, and the eggs. The fire. I called a C to mind and found it in the same place it always was. I went up to the G where the song began, and then I opened my eyes and sang.

I had them all as soon as I started, I could tell. They could feel it, see it. Even though they knew how the story ended, they wanted me to tell it to them. They didn't get this from the Internet. In that video, you never see my hands.

SOCIAL DYNAMICS

The most dangerous place at CFB Gagetown is also the farthest hike from the barracks where the recruits in Basic Training stay. This is done on purpose, of course, as almost everything on the base is, because the danger is dragon-related, and not everyone who comes to the Canadian Forces comes from a town like Trondheim, which has trained itself to be ready for anything.

By the end of week twelve, almost everyone had lost the money they'd bet on me. There were some hard feelings about that in the barracks, but the officers seemed better equipped to move on with their lives. We started training with mixed groups, putting the engineers, medics, and firefighters together with the dragon slayers so that they would all learn to work with a team. The medics and engineers were all older than the dragon slayers, having completed their degrees before enlisting. Since Owen would theoretically be in charge of his unit, I was worried that they might balk at taking orders from him, but I had forgotten to take the training we were all receiving into account. Basic made you very good at being ten feet in the air when someone said "jump" before you thought to ask "which way?"

It turned out that both Sadie and Owen were good at teamwork, having had a lot of practice, but the dragon slayer from Chilliwack was close behind them. I heard whispers that the female dragon slayers always did better, because they were better at adapting to social dynamics than the boys were.

"Or it's because the girls have already spent ten weeks living on top of each other," Sadie had said. "If they didn't isolate the boys the way they do, they'd probably be doing better."

I liked that the strict regimen we'd been living under hadn't dulled the trumpet of her spirit.

They still weren't entirely sure what to do with me. I was attached to whatever group Owen was assigned and performed signal duties in addition to my other tasks, but I did that with flags or with shouting. There was a band on the base, but it was for officers, so I didn't play in it. Aside from singing, I hadn't done any music since I had arrived, though I continued to do my hand exercises after lights-out to make sure that I didn't lose ground. Basic had done wonders for my toughness, but I feared I was losing some of my already-limited dexterity.

The worst part of Basic Training was sitting through dragon attacks in the base shelters. There were several shelters scattered around the base wherever there was space to put them, and every time a dragon attacked, all the recruits were herded into them. I was used to hiding if a dragon attacked near my house, or if I was at Owen's and Hannah was feeling particularly protective. And I always went into the shelter at school, because the teachers relied on me for help with crowd control. But this was different. This was being underground with forty-odd dragon slayers who were very, very anxious at being out of a fight when there was one to be had.

Logistically, it made sense. If all the dragon slayers stayed above ground, they would undoubtedly be stepping on each other's feet, and some amount of chaos would result. But watching Owen and Sadie sit out attack after attack without even being able to watch put my teeth on edge, and that was before you factored in all the others. Generally speaking, we made the dragon slayers sit together by the door, where they could fret at one another and leave the rest of us in peace until the all-clear sounded.

"How do you stand having a pair of them?" one of the fire-fighters from Nova Scotia asked me one afternoon, when we were all packed into the shelter like sardines.

"Well, usually they're outside, working through their issues," I pointed out. There was a wave of nervous laughter. "It makes them nervous when they can't see what's coming."

"I don't know how you faced down dragons without a weapon," said an engineer. I think he was from Hamilton. "I mean, I know a gun won't do much, but it makes me feel better."

"City boys," said the firefighter. "You can't run around in farm country shooting dragons."

"We don't do it in the city, either," he pointed out. "We've still got sewers."

"We do well enough with swords," I said, hoping to calm everyone down. It was way too stuffy in here for an argument.

"What's it like?" asked one of the Haligonian smiths.

"What's what like?" I said.

"Slaying a dragon," she said. "There are a couple of dragon slayers here who have slayed fewer of them than you have."

Competition was inevitable, really. No one could touch Owen in terms of real life experience, and even though Sadie was miles behind him, she still had more slayings than half the others combined. There were, as the smith pointed out, a few dragon slayers with no tallies at all. And I had one whole corn dragon to my name.

"Honestly, I don't remember much of it," I told them. They looked disappointed. I have something of a reputation as a story teller, of course, but I'm never telling my stories when I do it. "Oh, fine," I said. It was very tedious down here, after all. "I'll tell you what I can."

They all leaned forward. At the other end of the room, the dragon slayers realized something was up and left off their pointless worrying to listen. I spoke louder so they could hear me.

"You've seen the clips on the news," I told them. "The burned-out beaches and the blackened trees. But all of that happened later, when the smoke cleared. When I slayed that dragon, the air was full of fire and poison."

Owen was watching me with the oddest expression on his face. We hadn't ever really talked about that day, once I'd for-given him for putting me in a position that had cost me the full use of my hands. That had been a stupid conversation, because I had volunteered and it wasn't his fault anyway. Since then, the topic had just never come up. There was always something more immediate to take care of. Always more dragons on the horizon, more fire in the sky.

"We stood on that beach together, but I wasn't there to slay dragons," I continued, falling into the style I used when I talked to reporters or elementary school students. "I was there to witness, to make sure that Owen's story would be told."

Also a lie. I had a flamethrower strapped to my back just like Owen. We weren't supposed to slay dragons at all. But no one needed to hear that.

"But dragons are fierce and hard to predict. We'd laid a good trap, but one of them hadn't fallen for it, and it was that corn dragon that found us and separated Owen from his sword."

Owen was, obviously, fine, but everyone looked at me with such concern on their faces that I felt rather proud. Basic Training had sucked for me. I was made up of nothing but shortcomings. Every time I was assigned to a squad, they drooped. We never won any of the challenges. But they were looking at me now like I was worth something, like I was someone they admired. I filed the feeling away for the next time I got stymied by the fitted sheet I had to corner perfectly every morning. This was why I was here. Everything else was just a hoop we all had to jump through.

"It was a corn dragon," I repeated. "When you're up against a corn dragon, you run. You run and you hide. But you only do those things if you're not a dragon slayer."

It was so quiet. There must have been a hundred people in the dragon shelter, and I had made every one of them hold their breath.

"My backpack was on fire," I said. "But I didn't think about that. All I thought about was that the dragon had turned on Owen, and Owen couldn't get to his sword."

They all knew what happened after that. It had been national news for weeks. But they wanted to hear me say it. They wanted to be part of the story too. And I was going to let them.

"I grabbed the hilt, even though it was heated by the flames," I said. "It was Lottie Thorskard's sword, made by Hannah MacRae. And it was mine too. It went into that dragon's chest like butter: both hearts in one go.

"You know what happened after that, of course," I said, and they all leaned back. I held up my hands, to remind them. "I screamed, because it really hurt, and then I lost consciousness. By the time I woke up, my whole world was different. I was different."

The dragon slayer from Chilliwack had pushed through until she was next to me. She took one of my hands in hers, gently, as most people did, because they thought they might hurt me. I squeezed her hand as hard as I could, which, thanks to the exercise ball, was decently hard, and she responded instinctively, pressing back. She started to laugh.

"I'm not a dragon slayer," I said, smiling with her. "And I don't want to be."

I looked around at all these faces I couldn't put names to. They fought fires and logistical problems and injuries, leaving the dragon slayer free to fight dragons. And I would do my best to remember all of them.

"But I am good at this," I said. "We will learn to be good at this together."

There was a long moment of silence after that. Sadie was grinning fit to split her face, and Owen was shaking his head. I could lie to almost anyone now, and he knew it. But I never lied to him, and the best lies were always the ones where I told the truth. I winked, and he smiled.

The all-clear siren split the thick air inside the dragon shelter, and we all spilled out into the sunlight with some measure of relief. The sergeants were barking orders, cleanup related, mostly, because heaven forbid we miss the fun part of dragon slaying, but everyone was looking at me. The cornet-sergeant was watching me too, but his face was difficult to read. Finally, the recruits called to cleanup duty mustered themselves away from the main group, and the rest of us headed for the mess.

There hadn't been any structural damage, but the south woods were on fire, and it was a while before the flames were quenched. The firefighters used a lot of chemical suppressants, which made me nervous because water seems much more natural for that sort of thing. Of course, on patrol, chemicals are much easier to carry, and if there is no water source nearby chemical suppressants might be the only option you have. Since most of the trainers were out on fire duty, we were able to take more time than usual to eat. I celebrated by cutting up my Salisbury steak instead of just eating it off the fork, like I did when I was rushed. Sadie sat with us, which only happened these days when we were assigned to the same drill, because otherwise we arrived at the mess separately. It seemed like more people than usual were sitting with us, or maybe it was just that there were more people paying attention to us. This feeling, I remembered, was why I had wanted to spend the last year of high school eating lunch in the music room, even though Sadie never let me eat anywhere but the seat she'd saved for me in the cafeteria.

I was going to have to get used to it. I'd thought I could be in the background here, like I had done when we were in school, but the Oil Watch required more of me.

For the first time, I decided that it didn't bother me.

UNIT COHESION

It got easier after that afternoon in the dragon shelter. Not everything, of course, because there were a lot of things I had to do for myself, and they were still hard, but some things, small things, were taken care of while I was busy fumbling with something else. And most people stopped looking so openly disappointed when I was assigned to their drill. All that was left to survive was two weeks of training with the group that would make up the members of Owen's support crew. I'd done this in high school, on unicorn stationery, no less. I was pretty sure I could handle it again.

Every support squad had eight firefighters; a pair of engineers—one sapper and one smith—two medics, one of whom could double as a cook if you were on patrol; and in Owen's case alone, one bard. All of them were older than Owen and I were. The Combat Engineer, Courtney Speed, was twenty-four and had a master's in engineering from the Royal Military College. This was unusual, as most people in the Oil Watch, including our smith, Aarons, had at most only an undergraduate degree. The firefighters had all completed a two year college program, and the medics had bachelor degrees in addition to their year-long medic training course. Davis, the medic who was also the cook, planned to go to medical school when his tour was up. In those first days I despaired of ever learning their names, let alone coming up with ways to write them into Owen's songs. I was more than a little bit intimidated, and I didn't even have to be in charge. Owen was supposed to be in command and would eventually be given the highest rank. It was really important that everyone got along.

"Unit cohesion," as it was called, was accomplished by a bizarrely fake week-long camping trip, wherein each squad was assigned a portion of the forest to patrol. It was choreographed so that no two patrols overlapped, and every day you had to break down your camp and move into the zone, still without contacting the other patrol. We carried everything with us, along with GPS monitors that kept us on track and let the commanders know we'd done the right amount of walking. If executed correctly, the whole exercise was entirely benign and unadventurous.

It was, to put it bluntly, the most tedious thing I'd ever done. The fire crew, who had already spent a fair amount of time training with one another, kept mostly to themselves except during meals. Davis and Ilko, the other medic, were bored because no one even got blisters, and I learned very quickly that leaving the engineers to their own devices ended badly in a hurry, even if neither of them had access to explosives.

We did get on well enough, though. Owen and I never walked beside each other during the day, though we did spar with each other because no one else was good enough to go as fast as we did. It was the sparring that finally won over the fire crew, because while I wasn't as good as Owen, I was better at instructing, and by the third or fourth time I'd called him on a mistake, the others started asking for my help in their own drills. They trained with swords for the same reason I did: in case of emergency. Also, it was good for stamina and upper body strength, and that came in handy for the fire crews and the engineers. I have no idea what the medics thought of it. In return, the fire crew helped me come up with ways to speed through my firearm practice, which I still struggled with. By the fifth day, when we reached the farthest part of the base from the main barracks, we were a team, even though I was still going to cheat and refer to the bulk of them by musical shorthand when it came time to memorialize them in music, if not make up their names outright.

I was used to farmland and being able to see the horizon most of the time. I had been with Owen when he'd slayed dragons in woodlots, but that didn't happen very often. I knew how to scan the horizon and listen for the sounds of dragon flight, even if I was in a moving vehicle. I was learning the woods, the sounds that were made, but I wasn't very good at it yet. Fortunately for us, Gratton and Parker, two of our fire crew from Northern Ontario, were used to a view blocked by trees.

"What's that smell?" Courtney asked. (Theoretically we were supposed to call each other by last name when we were on drill, but Courtney had been three beds down from me during the first part of Basic, and I figured that seeing her naked qualified me to call her by her given name, unless there was a superior officer around.)

"It smells like a dragon," Owen said. He meant that it smelled like Manitoulin, but I was the only person who knew that.

I looked at the GPS. I did most of our navigating because it was the only thing we could think of for me to do.

"We're coming up on the Orange Zone," I told them, and everyone shivered.

In the sixties, apparently before common sense was invented, Gagetown had served as a research facility in addition to being a training camp and the regimental base of the Black Watch. One of the experiments had involved the controlled slaying of dragons, mostly of the small, coastal variety—though both "small" and "controlled" were relative terms—to determine the full environmental effect of dragon death.

The experiment was never really completed, because the effects were ruled too devastating for them to continue. Most of the St. John River watershed had been contaminated, killing dozens of river fish and animal and plant species before the damage was brought under very expensive control. The ground had been left, and nothing had yet grown on it, even though it had been fifty years. I'm not sure why anyone was surprised by that. The Sahara had been a desert for centuries.

The Orange Zone was dangerous not only because of environmental contamination, which meant we had to carry our own water for most of the hike, but also because it was still an attraction to the local dragon population.

"Shush up," said Gratton, turning his head to the side. "Listen."

I could hear it, once he told me there was something to hear. It was different from the way the river ran over the stones.

It was deeper than the wind in the leaves on the trees. It was faster and more continuous than any woodland creature would be, foraging for food in the leaf litter and undergrowth. I would never forget it, any more than I could forget what made a euphonium different from a tuba. I could tell the moment the others picked it up because, except for Owen, they froze.

"Send the code, Siobhan," Owen said, reaching over his shoulder for his sword.

That snapped everyone back to their jobs. The engineers and medics fell back. There was nothing Courtney or Aarons, the smith, could do, and we wouldn't need Davis and Ilko until after. I sent the SOS code to base and received confirmation immediately. Help was on the way, but no further orders came. I'd half expected them to tell us to hide, like they had before, but there was nothing but silence. Maybe they'd decided it was time. This was, after all, what we trained for, and Owen had trained more than most.

Annie King, who'd been elected the foreman of the fire crew, marshalled the others around her, issuing orders in a low voice. They prepared as best they could, ready to focus on diversion and suppression by chemical means, since we didn't have any of the portable pumps with us. I could hear Courtney quietly adding her own suggestions with regard to the chemicals. Her specialty was oil rigs and natural gas extraction, but as a chemical engineer, she knew a bit about fire as well.

"Can you tell the species?" Owen asked, looking at Gratton.

"I'm from Kapuskasing," he said. "We have more or less the same dragons you do."

We didn't have an easterner on our crew. Wilkinson and Anderson shook their heads. They were from Montreal. You could never hear a dragon coming in Montreal.

"Perfect," said Owen. "Siobhan?"

"You'll have to get it to land, or we're cooked," I told him. "Your boots should be okay in the Orange Zone, but I wouldn't recommend falling over. Or breathing too much."

"Thanks," he said. There was a roar as the dragon passed overhead and scented us. It circled around. "Tell them the plan!" Owen shouted, the need for quiet having ended, and headed for the ugliness of the experimental glade.

They looked at me, and it was the Suez Canal all over again. I smiled, pretending a confidence I did not feel, and started talking.

"Okay, Owen's going to get the dragon to land on the government-sanctioned environmental disaster over there, and then bring it into the trees." The fire crew bristled. "I know that's a bigger fire risk, but if Owen's never fought this kind of dragon, he's going to need all the distractions he can get."

"What do you want us to do?" Mikitka asked.

"I'll let you know," I told him.

About a hundred metres away, there was a tremendous bellow as the dragon hit the ground, and then a slowing series of crashes as it pursued Owen into the trees.

"Get ready," I shouted, and the fire crew fanned out.

I had my sword in my hand now. The others all had them and could use them with varying degrees of capability if they had to, but a fire crew rarely got involved in the business end of dragon slaying. The medics and engineers fell even farther back into the woods.

"Helicopter!" I heard Courtney yell, but I knew already that our reinforcements wouldn't get here in time.

"Keep your eyes on the dragon," I said, "and keep your ears on me."

Technically, Owen was the commander of our little family, but the two of us had a system that had been born on a county highway and hadn't really varied since—though I had never had to use a hubcap for dragon distraction again. Owen slayed the dragon; I did the crowd control. His support squad seemed to accept it. Either that, or they were too scared to argue.

"Siobhan!" Owen shouted, pelting into view. "It's a Singe'n'burn."

All things considered, that was for the best. Though it was the largest dragon in the area, it was a freshwater type, and those were typically less ornery than the local salted species. It received its common name from the fact that it regularly made attempts to burn down St. John, and though it was taxonomically identical to the Newfoundland variety nicknamed Singe'ns'burn, the locals got really tetchy when you mixed them up.

I started deploying the fire crew, arranging them in a half-circle around where Owen had engaged the dragon. They coated the trees with the chemical compound that best counteracted Singe'n'burn flame, though they couldn't reach very high since we didn't have the aerosol dispensers with us.

"Next time we do this," Courtney called out from her place next to Ted back in the trees, "I am overseeing the packing!"

"You do that," I shouted back. I could understand her frustration. Not being able to help was the worst in moments like these, even though I knew, I *knew*, that Owen could handle it.

And then the dragon was on him, and the smell of burning wood and grass filled the air.

Fighting with a fire crew was exciting. Usually I had to keep moving to avoid getting lit up by incidental fire, but with eight people focused on suppression, even the grass flames went out quickly under Annie's shouted direction. I was used to watching Owen's style, so I could see the moment the dragon died. Owen got it to overextend its neck, and turned, dodging around a tree trunk. The dragon couldn't recover in time, and then Owen's sword was buried in its chest.

I breathed in, relieved, and turned back to the fire crew to help Annie with the final hot spots. Davis and Ilko raced for Owen, but he wasn't even scratched by tree branches.

"Your boots are smoking," Anderson pointed out, gesturing with the wand he'd been using to spread the suppressant.

"Orange Zone," Owen said. "I'll get my spares."

"You stay put," Ilko said, fishing out a Gatorade and all but shoving it in Owen's face like a baby bottle.

The sound of the helicopter, which had landed during the battle when the noise was so loud we couldn't hear it, reminded me that we were going to have company just before the cornet-sergeant emerged from the woods.

"It would be you lot," he said, but he sounded proud of us. "Well done."

"Thank you, sir," Owen said. "It was a team effort."

"That's why you're here," the sergeant said. "You're all coming back to the barracks. You've earned a day off after this."

The fire crew brightened at that. Now that the adrenaline was wearing off, none of us were really looking forward to another day of marching. They headed for the helicopter as the disposal squad surrounded the dragon. We could hear them exclaiming over how clean the kill was. This close to the glade, it probably didn't matter on an eco-friendliness level, but Owen walked a little straighter. I struggled with the straps of my pack, and was then nearly pulled off my feet when the sergeant lifted it for me.

"Thank you, sir," I said. My fellow recruits had done small things to ease my way lately, but the instructors had been as merciless as ever.

"Don't get used to it," he said. "But you've made me a lot of money in the last few weeks, so this one time I don't mind."

"You bet on me to stick it out, sir?" I knew that someone must have, or the odds wouldn't have been so ridiculously attractive.

"You slayed a *siligoinis* with less than a year of training," he said. "I'd bet on you if you didn't have any hands at all."

I sat next to Owen in the helicopter on the way back. It was too loud to talk, and they didn't have headsets for us, but we grinned at each other like idiots anyway.

THE STORY OF MANITOULIN(ISH)

Once upon a time, there was a beautiful island where three Great Lakes met. Named for a god, it could well have been the home of one: rolling green hills and big enough that it was dotted by small blue lakes of its own. It was the biggest freshwater island in the world, and Canada was proud to call it ours.

All was not well with this treasure of an island, though. In the early, less-enlightened days of American capitalism, poor civil planning—from which Canada has never suffered—left Michigan uninhabitable. Our island, so close to those blighted American shores, had to be abandoned for safety until a solution to the Michigan problem could be found. Two whole generations of Canadians grew up, never having set foot on that pristine sand, never staying in those quaint hotels, and never learning to swim in those sheltered bays, but always there was hope that we would someday return.

That hope is gone now. Burned in fire and destroyed by chemical warfare, without the consultation or approval of the government of Canada.

It was common knowledge, in certain levels of the government, that dragons nested on Manitoulin. Professionals had been consulted, and they determined that saving the island's biosphere was worth the risk that the newly hatched dragons would present.

And yet the island burned.

Two children, a teenage dragon slayer and his unknown companion, were convinced by their elders to go and burn our island to ruin. They are minors in the eyes of the law, yet they did tremendous damage to a natural resource. Who will be held accountable for that? Them? Their dragon slayer parents? The local politicians who spoke in their favour? The RCMD slayers who loaned them a boat and then turned a blind eye?

And, more disturbingly, what conspiracy lurks within the Canadian dragon slayer ranks?

The moral of this sensationalist little tale is this: try never to be unconscious while other people write your press.

When Owen and I got back from Manitoulin, the media storm hadn't start right away, but it was a pretty near thing. While I was confined to my bed, my mother and father went out of their way to keep me from finding out what was being said outside the slightly scorched brick walls of Trondheim General, but they couldn't keep that up forever. My room had a TV, after all, and one of the first things I learned how to do with very bandaged hands was operate the remote.

The government had declared most of Huron County a no-fly zone, which was standard procedure after a large-scale dragon incursion, even in places that didn't have much air traffic in the first place. Cars were risky enough, and putting something in the air when dragons were around was considered foolhardy, except in extreme circumstances. This limited the number of news helicopters that could hover around the hospital, school, and other buildings that had sustained damage, but it didn't stop reporters from driving into town and filming anything they wanted.

The Thorskards had spent a few days camped out at my house, because it took that long for the media to figure out where I lived. Eventually they ended up in front of the news cameras, giving interviews without me there to help them tell the story. That's when Emily had stepped in, at the cost of her online anonymity, and became their unofficial media handler. She's the one who, using the power of public opinion, made the original respondents look like Conservative lackeys who were more afraid of losing a favourite summer getaway than they were of a death toll. Which, to be fair, they pretty much were.

"She's unnerving," Lottie had told me. "You should be taller before you can control people like that."

"I think it's funny," Owen's mother, Catalina, said. "It's like watching a mouse grow teeth and take down a *siligoinis*."

"I've told you that joke's only funny in Spanish," Owen said, and his mother waved him off. "But seriously, Emily is really good at this."

"Tell me what's happening," I said. "We don't have cable in here, so I'm only getting the CBC broadcast if the weather is good."

"Aodhan's looking into that, by the way," Hannah said. "He pointed out that with regular dragon slayer patrols, he'll be able to protect the towers. We might even get cell phones."

"Put her out of her misery, love," Lottie said, her fingers linked with Hannah's.

"Fine," Hannah said, all business. "Locally, we're doing very well. The people who lost property are angry, of course, but it's a relatively small number from what it might have been, and people seem to understand that had we let the eggs hatch, it would have been much worse."

"That's good then." I hadn't been looking forward to going back to school if everyone was angry with us for getting their houses burned down.

"Nationally, it's a bit less rosy," Hannah continued. "The government is kind of put out with you."

Lottie snorted.

"I was trying to ease her into it!" Hannah said.

Every now and then, usually after a big public dragon disaster, there was talk about whether or not we should just try to force them into extinction. The debate always split into two sides: those who felt we should just do our best to get rid of the menace and deal with the fallout, and those who argued that, in addition to the environmental damage, there was no way of knowing what sort of trouble a mass extinction would cause. This invariably degraded into conversations about the fate of the dinosaurs and general name calling, and by then something else would have happened in the news cycle, and everyone would forget about it until the next disaster. The government rarely stepped in, and when they did it was usually with some fabricated science that no one could really test anyway.

With us, they had apparently decided to take another tack. MPs and MPPs across the country were either denouncing us or hailing us as heroes of a new age. There was no split by party line, though as a rule the Conservatives were generally not our biggest fans. Queen's Park, currently held by the Liberals, was taking a softer approach, questioning our ages and whether we should have been permitted such a dangerous task without supervision. But the Prime Minister cracked down nationally and cracked down hard. Our MP had already been kicked out of the cabinet, where he had been Minister of Agriculture, and relegated to the backbench because he had spoken in our defense (which, for the record, I thought was very nice of him; I hadn't been old enough to vote for his opponent, but I had actively campaigned for her). And he was not the only one to lose his seat at the big table before Emily stepped in and turned at least the Internet to our favour.

"There are really only two things holding them back at this point," Lottie had said. Her dislike of our Prime Minister was both quite personal and very public knowledge. "The first is that we are all very popular right now—not with them, obviously, but with a growing number of their constituents."

"What's the second reason?" I asked, though I had a bad feeling about what it was.

"I have to join the Oil Watch," Owen said. "So the government will have me for four years."

He didn't look at me when he said it. He didn't have to.

My hands hurt. I couldn't do buttons or use a fork or tuck my hair behind my ear without snagging it on my bandages and dragging half of it forward again. And I might never play again. But I decided then that none of that mattered. I was going to join the Oil Watch, still, even though it was going to be infinitely more difficult now. If the Prime Minister wanted to control Owen, he was going to have to deal with having us both. By the time I released the Manitoulin song on YouTube, I was, at the very least, no longer Owen's "unknown companion."

I replayed that conversation in my head fairly often as I went through my rehab and last year in Trondheim. By the time I got to Gagetown, it was part of who I was. When the helicopter deposited us back in the main base after Owen slayed the Singe'n'burn, I didn't need to remind myself any more. We only had one more week of drills, and then it would be assignment and deployment time. The cornet-sergeant was on my side, or at least on the side of bet-winning. I had learned to work with Owen's squad. The government of Canada didn't quite own us; the Oil Watch did. And we would serve wherever they needed us.

I was so innocent in those days. I thought that since we had done the right thing, since we had saved lives and prevented wide-scale damage, that we would be rewarded. Or, at the least, not outwardly punished. But our detractors were patient, and they had many more resources to draw on.

Basic wore out its last week. The girls in our squad—Annie, Courtney, and the other firefighter, Laura Josephson—all shaved their heads to match mine. The boys saved us seats in the mess, even though we weren't required to eat as a group. The others looked at us with envy. We had done something they had not, and we had done it very well. They would face their first dragon in the field, untested and possibly on enemy soil. We had defended our home, again, and we had been perfect in our execution of manoeuvers.

"I hope we get at least the same country," said Sadie, the morning of the last day. They would make the announcements at breakfast. She did the buttons on my dress uniform. I could manage them slowly by now, but she did it with much less swearing.

"You'll get the Middle East for sure," the dragon slayer from Chilliwack said. Caroline, I think, but after Owen had slayed the Singe'n'burn a lot of people had introduced themselves to me, and I was having trouble remembering all those names. "And a big fat contract when you get home."

I smiled. I knew that we didn't want that, but getting the offer, when it came, was going to be pretty sweet.

"Come on," I said. "Let's go find out."

I didn't want to say it in front of so many people, but I was looking forward to getting out of Canada for a while. I wanted to go somewhere where Owen would be appreciated, not maligned, however obtusely. And overseas they were more receptive to the idea of bards, too.

We filed into the mess and ate carefully, mindful of our hats and our white dress tunics. Then the cornet-sergeant took to the podium and began to make his announcements. His face was dark despite the fluorescents, and he had the look of a man who had fought for something and lost.

Deployments were called alphabetically by dragon slayer. We listened as our comrades were sent out to Alaska, Caracas, Kandahar, New Orleans, Newfoundland.

"Sadie Fletcher," came the call, and Sadie sat up straight. "North Sea!"

Expressions of carefully muffled outrage and disbelief warred for dominance on Sadie's face. Those were dying gas fields, and ocean rigs besides, and Canadians were very rarely assigned to them. She didn't know anything about water battles; they didn't even train us for them here because they lacked the facilities. She didn't look frightened, though. Once the initial surprise wore off, she only looked angry, and determined. I was starting to worry. Despite not being in a conflict zone, Sadie's assignment was overly dangerous because of the underwater aspect. She was good and a fast learner, but her mentor had better be amazing too, or she'd be in real trouble.

At last, it was our turn. I'd lost track of who had been sent where, of the count of dragon slayers already deployed to the Middle East. They wouldn't overload the region, but surely, surely we would be sent where the fighting was thickest. Owen had the most experience. Owen had the most training. Owen had the legacy.

The cornet-sergeant's face tightened even more. I grabbed Sadie's hand and she winced at how hard I'd gripped her. There were notes skittering everywhere across my skin. It was worse than the first time I'd sat out of dragon slaying in the shelter with Hannah. I wasn't the only one to be unnerved. Around the mess, those who had been paying better attention than I began to whisper.

"The good places," whispered Mikitka from across the table. "They're all taken."

"They can't be," hissed Dorsey.

"I think he's right," said Wilkinson.

"Owen Thorskard," said the cornet-sergeant, his voice still

ringing clear and true in spite of his distress. "Fort Calgary, Alberta."

Fourteen weeks of training was enough to keep the hall from bursting into pandemonium, but only just. Our support squad was in shock. Sadie bent my fingers back accidentally and then released me entirely when she realized she was probably pulling on my scars.

But I was only looking at Owen. And Owen didn't look surprised.

"Alberta," he said, theoretically to everyone, but mostly to me. He was apologizing. I had been so sure that we'd be sent away, made into someone else's problem. I had put too much faith in the autonomy of the Oil Watch. I had hoped we would be leaving Canada, and that when we came back, we'd just return quietly to Trondheim and save chickens and sheep.

"Alberta," I said, eyes on his. It wasn't what we wanted. It wasn't what we deserved. It was still under the watchful eye of a distrusting government. It was going to be ridiculously cold, when we weren't being lit on fire by the local fauna. But there were dragons there, and oil, and I could write songs about that.

THE STORY OF ALBERTA

Before a little queen moved a hatching ground and changed the way the British Empire dealt with dragons, there was a war. Actually, there were two wars, but in Canada, we are mostly concerned about the second one. The first war, an admittedly justified one wherein the goal was self-determination and the right to taxation with representation, saw thousands of British Loyalists retreat to Upper Canada and the shelter of the Crown. The French nationalists who supported American independence provided some dragon slayers, but many of the best trained came north with the Redcoats, rather than join Washington and the others in their rebellion against the King. The resulting American nation was woefully underpopulated by what the Founding Fathers deemed to be "responsible" dragon slayers, that is to say, dragon slayers who were neither Catholic, German, First Nation, nor Black.

For thirty years, the Americans did their best and paid for their war time and time again, as dragons flew unchecked from

New Hampshire to Georgia. A Union was formed. The new country tried to train new dragon slayers as fast as they could. But it wasn't enough.

In 1812, James Madison took advantage of pro-war sentiment and turned the fledgling American army loose on Upper Canada. Bolstered by Jefferson's assertion that conquering Canada and her dragon slayers would be "a mere matter of marching," American soldiers crossed into Canada to come face to face with the children of those they'd happily tarred and feathered only three decades before. It did not end well for the United States.

Although technically the British forces merely held off the encroaching Americans, and prevented them from making any gains in terms of land or population, the aftermath of the war had a profound effect on the American territories that were due to join the country as states. The Dakotas, less Minnesota and Wisconsin, and most of Washington Territory, less Wyoming, jumped ship and petitioned the Brits for readmission into the Empire. At the time, the Americans were not particularly sad to see them go. Those territories did not have a lot in the way of resources, and they were expensive to patrol and maintain. Also, the British were willing to pay a portion of the funds the territories had cost in the first place, and since they did that with monies taken from Napoleon, it was all deemed very cyclical and fair.

Half a century later, when oil became the lifeblood of the west, there was a bit of grumbling in Washington, DC about it, but by then the borders were solid and the citizens of the Dakotas, Montana, and Cascadon were rather happily Canadian.

Alberta, in more ways than one, came out on top. It no

longer had to defend a border against American incursion, and it became the de facto leader of the Oil Coalition, the five provinces for which oil was a primary export. Historians enjoyed theorizing that, were in not for the coalition, Canada's politics would be much more determined by the central and eastern parts of the country (by which, of course, they meant Ontario), but under Alberta's guidance, the West became progressively more wealthy, if decidedly less progressive.

The settlement of Alberta proceeded apace, led by the Canadian Pacific Railway, which laid down the tracks that made east-west transport slightly less arduous, provided you wished to travel from Toronto to Fort Calgary. From there, Alberta spread north, though the train only went as far as Edmonton before apparently deciding that it was too cold to go any further.

And then, Alberta began to dig. They dug for oil, for gas, and for potash. They clear-cut trees for lumber, though those they did replace with saplings. And the dragons came.

After the incorporation of the Oil Watch in the 1950s, Canada, as the founder, reserved the right to conscript dragon slayers for Alberta, even though there was no combat there. At the time, Oil Watch founder Lester B. Pearson was so well-liked and respected that no one was going to deny him anything, and it seemed like a very simple request. As the years rolled on, however, and conflict in the Middle East and elsewhere became more concerning, Alberta became less of a priority for the Oil Watch. Thanks to our current Prime Minister, Canada was enjoying its least popular time as a member of the UN, and as a result, only the most troublesome, most unreliable dragon slayers were sent to defend Canada's oil.

Thus it was that when Owen Thorskard left CFB Gagetown and struck out for the west, it was with considerable lack of enthusiasm on the part of his support squad. Their goodwill towards Owen, not to mention towards me, had not faded entirely, but I knew that they couldn't help but view our assignment as a punishment, and each of them was wondering how they'd screwed up to get assigned to a dragon slayer who was clearly in such bad grace.

The cornet-sergeant came to the train platform to see us off, something he'd not done for any of the other departing squads. Around me, everyone straightened in spite of themselves.

"These are difficult times," he said. "Things are changing and the government doesn't want them to. They're sending you out there because they think it's out of the way and that everyone will forget about you while you're gone. But I have been fighting dragons and training dragon slayers for a very long time, and I am telling you that Alberta is as dangerous and as important as any other place they might have sent you, and not just because of the dragons."

He was talking to all of us, which I appreciated, because he could have just spoken to Owen. I didn't think it was possible for the fire crew to stand any straighter, but somehow they did. Maybe it was because now they wanted to.

We got on the train and wordlessly sorted out who would be sitting where.

It would be days before I saw the prairies for the first time, but I heard them coming before we got there. I could feel them in the train wheels, clicking against the tracks, and in the way the carriage swayed. It was a different song—not the one that any of us had expected—but we would write it all the same.

TOTEM POLES

Fort Calgary was a hard town, between an uncaring prairie and a mountain range that would just as soon the city didn't exist at all, if the weather that rolled down the mountainsides was any indication. You could see it from pretty far away, but not as far as the jokes about the prairies suggested. Alberta was flat, but it wasn't *that* flat.

We arrived by train, all fourteen of us in one car, with the regimental reinforcements in the carriages behind us, bound for the base in Edmonton. Though Edmonton had the larger numbers and a civilian population besides, Fort Calgary was nothing to sneeze at. When it was at full capacity, it boasted twice the population of Trondheim, upwards of five thousand people, all members of the Oil Watch. At need, it could host five thousand more in emergency quarters.

The bottom berths in the train carriage folded into seats during the day, but there wasn't a lot to do besides look out the window and wonder if we were seeing the curvature of the

Earth or if we were merely going insane from the monotony. At least we slept through Northern Ontario. We traveled through Canada the whole way, because the rail lines were safer there. Since we were north of Ottawa, we were clear of most of the populated hatching grounds, whereas if we'd gone south through Maine and around the foot of deserted Michigan towards the province of Dakota, we'd have been at more risk. Furthermore, there had been a series of dragon attacks in Nebraska, along the Canadian border. There are any number of American movies about dragon slayers fighting dragons from the tops of trains, but I was quite happy not to be reenacting one. We made it all the way to Manitoba before we even saw a dragon out the window, and it was far enough away that we didn't have to worry about it.

For the first two days, everyone trod lightly around Owen, expecting him to be angry about where we were being sent. I could tell that he wasn't. Sadie had been surprised by her assignment, which should have gone to a dragon slayer who was used to the coast, but we all knew she'd be so busy learning that she'd barely have time to miss us, or me anyway. She'd said good-bye to both of us at the same time, as if she was going to see us in the morning, and stood on the train platform with her head held high as we pulled away. We were bound for Alberta, where we wouldn't even need our passports, but as the cornet-sergeant reminded us, it wasn't exactly going to be a walk in the park.

By the time we entered Saskatchewan and became more or less permanently hypnotized by the endless vistas stretching away from the train tracks, the others had relaxed. Anderson taught us to play poker, which I was wretched at, and we talked more about our lives before we'd joined the Oil Watch. Aarons took the time to look over Owen's sword and mine and lamented that he was never going to win renown by making a weapon for his own dragon slayer because Hannah's work was so good.

"There are a few of us to take care of," Annie pointed out. "Plus all of the guns."

He sighed, "It's not really the same thing."

"We didn't bring any backups," Owen reminded him. "You'll get to make those."

Aarons brightened and returned to making sketches, while Courtney looked over his shoulder and made suggestions. As our combat engineer, Courtney was the third most important person in the squad after Owen and Annie. Technically, the foreman's job had the higher rank, but it was also a great deal more straightforward. Courtney had taken over most of the logistics and was better at setting people to tasks they were good at. In the end, Annie and Courtney reached an agreement on the hierarchy, and I wondered if this was what Lottie had meant when she'd said that the Oil Watch ran differently from the regular Forces.

Laura, who was one of the tiniest people I had ever met, and who somehow managed to carry her own body weight in gear anyway, was doing a crossword puzzle. She was actually from Saskatchewan, so the prairies were less alluring to her than they were to the rest of us. Gratton leaned across her to look out the window, and she kept smacking him with the pen every time he got too close.

"Look!" Gratton said. "There it is."

We couldn't see the mountains yet, but on the ruddy yellow

horizon there stood what looked like a row of metal teeth stretching up into the air. During the day, this was the first part of Fort Calgary you could see, though at night you could see the lights from much farther away. The metal teeth were the tops of stylized totem poles, taller than the California Redwoods on which they were modeled, and thrusting jagged steel into the bright prairie sunset. Though most of the poles were around the wall of the fort, they were also scattered throughout the city itself, to prevent the dragons from dive-bombing any of the buildings. It was dramatic and, according to several European pseudo-scientists, entirely unnecessary, but since Fort Calgary was the last real stronghold between the rest of Canada and Kamloops, BC, on the other side of the John A–Zuò Tunnel, no one complained. We watched as we drew closer to the fort, though Laura kept poking at her crossword as if to spite the fact that the rest of us were Easterners.

"It's beautiful," said Aarons, who knew how to get use from metal.

"They're probably covered with bird crap up close," Parker pointed out.

The train slowed, and a steward came to let us know that we'd be met upon our arrival. We scrambled to pack everything back into our kits, and Annie did my zippers and buckles while I folded up the berth that she and Dorsey had been sitting on. The train slowed as it passed underneath the metal branches, and I watched Aarons drag himself away from the window. We'd have plenty of time to admire the sights later, so I didn't feel too bad for him. Courtney pushed his pack at him and winked at me while Owen helped me get my own bag settled on my shoulders.

"I really hope this doesn't suck," I said, quiet enough that only he heard it.

"We'll be fine," he told me. "Maybe they thought we'd done so much work already, we needed a break."

"Oh, please," I said. "Not even I am that naive."

"All right," Owen said to everyone as he pushed his way to the front of the car. "I guess we should line up. Courtney, Annie?"

They joined him at the front, and I fell back to let them. I had my bugle, one final gift from Trondheim, in my gear. I hadn't had time to play it since we'd arrived at Gagetown, but I had practiced for months before that and knew that I was as good as I was going to be. We still hadn't heard if I was going to be required to play, or if they would just find something else for me to do. I had my assignment, same as everyone else, but no official job yet besides "bard," which was very unspecific. Traditionally, I should have held the same rank as Owen did, but it had been so long since a bard had served in the Oil Watch that no one at Gagetown thought to tell me what to expect when I arrived in Fort Calgary. The squad deferred to me, or at least they did after the Singe'n'burn, but there was no telling what other, more experienced members of the Watch would do.

The doors opened, and we followed Owen off the train. The few senior members of the Oil Watch who'd come with us, bound for Edmonton, were emerging from their cars as well, but they didn't really pay attention to us, unless it was to catcall about us being new and green and dragon-bait.

"Thorskard!" came a voice that made me instantly jump to attention. "Front and centre."

By tradition, each squad was called after its dragon slayer, and since Owen was the only member of his family currently in service, we had no numerical designation. Sometimes it was odd, not knowing if we were being called as a group or if he was being called as an individual, but if the idea was to promote a cohesive group dynamic, it was working. At the sound of Owen's name, we all fell in and waited for further orders. The man who came for us was Owen's mentor, the senior dragon slayer who would shepherd him through his first few months in the Oil Watch. Overseas, this position was usually more important, like in Sadie's case, where new dragon slayers came up against unfamiliar terrain, dragons, languages, and cultures. We were only going to have to worry about the dragons. Theoretically, each member of Owen's squad would have a guide from his mentor's squad, except for me, of course, and yet the dragon slayer on the platform was by himself. Owen stepped forward as his mentor stopped in front of us.

"Owen Thorskard, sir," he said, saluting as was expected. "And squad."

"At ease." We followed the order as best we could, carrying all the gear we had.

Owen's new mentor walked up and down the line, looking at each of us in turn. He was not surprised to count an extra person. I did my best not to let my eyes wander, but it's always harder to tell the story if I haven't seen it myself. He was tall, though not as tall as Aodhan, and much narrower in build. Aodhan powered through dragons like a charging bull, all deep bass line and inevitable vanquishment. This man was like a coiled spring, something that made noise before the player began the piece. Bagpipes—right on the edge of annoying, yet oddly compelling, though you still wouldn't want more than one of them in a small room. I had no idea what he might do. He stopped again in front of Owen and didn't seem to be too disappointed with us.

"I am Lieutenant Commander Declan Porter," he said, his British accent showing through. Also, he said "lieutenant" properly, which I liked, even though it was still a beast of a word to rhyme. "It is my job to tell you all about the local dragons of our fine locale, though the irony of lecturing a bunch of Canadians on their own dragons does not escape me. We will have two additional dragon slayers joining us, one American and one from Japan. They will arrive tomorrow and shadow other mentors. It's our busy season, however, so all the classwork falls to me."

He waited, but as he had not asked a question, we weren't sure how to reply. He sighed, and I wondered if we'd just passed a test or failed it.

"Right," he said, and threw a blue beret with a tan and red stripe on it to Owen. "Follow the crowd, and you'll find your billets. I expect to see you at breakfast tomorrow, bright-eyed and bushy-tailed."

We started to move out.

"Thorskard," he said again, and we all stopped. "Owen, you and McQuaid stay here."

I fell out of line, and came to stand beside Owen as the rest of our troop filed off in search of their beds. I considered my options. English dragon slayers were usually progressives and had a tendency to be a bit wild when stationed away from home, though they had nothing on the Australians.

"Let me see your hands," he said when the others had gone. I appreciated his directness and held them out for him to look at. Owen chewed on the inside of his cheek.

"Not as bad as I was led to believe," Porter said. "You'll be slower than the rest, of course, but you've managed to get this far. I don't see what the problem is, so long as you don't get anyone hurt in the field."

"Siobhan, sir—McQuaid—is as good in the field as a dragon slayer," Owen said. It was kind of the truth, and I appreciated it. Unlike most non-professionals, I excelled at knowing when it was time to run away. Except, of course, for that one time when I hadn't.

"Noted, Thorskard," Porter said. He did not quite smile. "Now go and make sure your squad isn't wandering around somewhere, hopelessly lost without you."

We both stood at attention again, and then headed off after the others. We found them already claiming beds in the barracks. The guys only had two spare cots in their room, but ours was more than half empty because we were the first squad to arrive. It looked like, once again, the women would be mixed and the men would be separated by squad. I looked forward to meeting squads from other countries. On every pillow there was a new UN-blue beret, striped with the red and tan colors Canadians wore in the Oil Watch, and decorated in accordance with our rank as official, if very new, members. It felt the same as my old one when I put it on, digging in above my ears and scratching against my shaved head, but when I looked at the others, I thought maybe it wasn't the same at all. Alberta or not, we were for real now. The melody had shifted again.

WITH OUR BARE HANDS

When Lieutenant Porter said "it's our busy season," what he'd really meant was "Shit, there are dragons everywhere. Duck." I know this, because that's what he said the next morning, as he was hustling us out of the mess hall while the sound of alarms filled the air. That last part was directed at Annie, who was about as tall as Owen and had walked under the short part of the arched doorway into the dragon shelter without realizing she was about to knock her head.

This shelter was quite different from any I had ever been in before. For starters, it was above-ground, which I knew because there were also windows, presumably dragon-proofed, as much as that was possible. When I looked out of them, I could see the grey-washed cityscape of Fort Calgary, punctuated by the totem poles. We hadn't been able to see much of it the night before. I knew that Calgary had a strict building code: no wood, no green, no exposed lines or wires—nothing that burned—but seeing it in daylight was something else entirely. Fort Calgary was a military base, with very few non-essential personnel. Even most of the practice courts were covered. When people talk about the "concrete jungle," they usually imagine cities with interestingly-shaped buildings and telephone poles. This was more of a concrete wasteland. Said wasteland was currently under attack by a brilliant purple dragon, similar in size to a *lakus*, but apparently much faster.

"Can anyone besides Josephson tell me what kind of dragon that is?" Porter asked. Laura looked a bit put out.

"It's a Wapiti," Annie volunteered.

"Red or Blue?" Porter pushed.

"Sir, it's purple," Ilko said timidly, just as plume after plume of red fire poured out of the dragon's maw, bathing the uncaring concrete in colour. "Um, Red?"

"Very good, Ilko." Porter didn't even sound sarcastic, but that might have just been his accent. "You can't tell a Wapiti Red from a Wapiti Blue until they are breathing fire on you, but they're not shy, so it's usually pretty easy to determine which one you've got. Why are the fires different, Josephson?"

"Do you mean from each other, or from other dragons' fire?" she asked, without looking away from the window. A dragon slayer had appeared in one of the plazas and was trying to entice the Red into landing while her fire crew hung behind.

"Both, if you don't mind," Porter said.

"Wapitis get their name from the Wapiti River," Laura said. "The eggs hatch on the river banks, and the soil acidity is what determines the colour of their fire."

Everyone in the room flinched back from the windows as the Red tried to go for the dragon slayer head first, only to snag its wing on a totem pole at the last moment and pull up screaming with rage. The dragon slayer brandished her sword in a familiar challenge.

"However," Laura continued, "fire isn't exactly what they breathe. It's more of a superheated acid, which will burn whatever it touches. The blue is more acidic, but the red'll still kill you."

"Thank you," Porter said. "Speed, please tell us what you know about the totem poles."

And so it went. While Courtney outlined the practicalities of the totem pole system, including an explanation of why it was not feasible in regular towns, we watched the dragon slayer succeed in goading the Red onto the ground in front of her. From there, it was fairly straightforward and nothing I hadn't seen dozens of times, except for the colour of the flames and the part where the fire crew only had to worry about the acid eating away at the concrete, and not any trees or grass the dragon might have scorched.

When the dragon was finally slayed, Porter led us out to have a look at it. Our fire crew mixed with the more experienced one, learning what chemicals were best, and Porter showed Owen the dragon's hearts. They looked the same as any other to me, and they were located in approximately the same place. Owen, who had been his usual antsy self while we were in the shelter, calmed down a bit when he saw them, though. This was something he knew how to do.

"It's not always quite so hands on," one of the medics was telling Davis, his Texan accent so thick I could barely understand him. "But Porter likes to break you in, so to speak."

"Owen slayed a dragon during Basic," Davis said, rather proudly.

"It's 'we,' Davis," Porter told him. "'*We* slayed a dragon during Basic.'"

"Yes, sir," Davis replied, though he snuck a glance at Owen, who smiled.

While we were waiting for the cleanup crew to arrive, I related the story of the Singe'n'burn we had slayed at Gagetown. I'd told the story enough times now that it was starting to develop a rhythm of its own, and I knew that a song would show up sooner or later, if I wanted to write it down. I probably should, even if I had to lump the whole fire crew into the same theme instead of giving them their own parts. It was the first thing we had done together, anyway, so maybe I could get away with writing it in clumps and no one would realize it was because I still couldn't musically separate the fire crew.

The cleanup crew surprised me. They were not Oil Watch, as I had been suspecting, but wore civilian fireproof coveralls. Even more oddly, all of them were Filipino, or at least I was reasonably sure they were. Owen caught my confused glance, questioning, but this wasn't the time for it. Instead, we followed Porter back to the mess, grabbed whatever was still edible off our trays, and went into the training room. We didn't cover very much, because the other dragon slayers hadn't arrived yet, and since both of them were internationals, they needed the instruction more than we did. Instead, Porter told us about the dragons he'd grown up fighting in England, though I was reasonably sure he was exaggerating when he told us about the Cornish Game Hen.

"They're about the size of a Great Dane," he told us. "We SAS lads entertain ourselves by sneaking up behind them and snapping their necks, barehanded."

"Sir," said Wilkinson, "don't Cornish Game Hens have really strong fire projection?"

"They do," Porter admitted. "That's why you have to come up behind them. It's a bit messy if the dragon gets its head turned around. I don't recommend it. But it's the smallest dragon in the UK, so you can't really blame us for using it to experiment on."

"What about a Welsh Rabbit?" Dorsey asked. "It's smaller, even though it's meaner."

"The Welsh Rabbit is not a dragon," Porter said, starting the sentence as Eliza Doolittle and finishing it as Mary Poppins. Annie covered a snicker.

It was something of a sore point with British dragon experts because no one had ever been able to get close enough to a Welsh Rabbit to find out what it was. Well, close enough and *live* anyway. Popular theory was divided between those who thought the Rabbit was some kind of evolutionary hiccough, and those who thought it more likely that the Rabbit was the result of some crossbreeding between the Common Welsh Green and a local raptor species called Montagu's Harrier, which had presumably ended rather badly for the bird.

"Do you name all of your dragons after food?" Courtney asked.

"Only the ones we can kill with our bare hands," Porter told her.

It's possible that she was about to say something vaguely inappropriate, but there was a knock on the door and a messenger came into the room.

"Are they arrived, then?" Porter said, looking slightly less relaxed now that there was another officer in the room.

"They have, sir," said the messenger, a second lieutenant, now that I could see his insignia. Technically, both Owen and Annie outranked him, but while we were in training, the usual military hierarchy got a bit murky.

"All right, you lot, back to your barracks," Porter said. "The others will be arriving, and I want you to be there while they are settling in. Thorskard, the dragon slayers are Crawford and Yamamoto. Introduce yourself."

"Yes, sir," Owen said, and we were on our way out the door.

For the first couple of days, at Gagetown, walking everywhere with thirteen other people had felt ridiculous, but now it seemed quite normal. Maybe the halls were wider. I fell in beside a couple of the firefighters I hadn't spent a lot of time with yet, and they both smiled at me.

"Never a dull moment, I guess," Mikitka said.

"Only enough to sleep, if we're lucky," I replied.

Crawford turned out to be Nick Crawford, of New York City. This was of interest to me, because New York was one of the few urban areas in the world that had been able to incorporate aerial combat into their dragon slaying, and I was eager to hear about how that worked. I had imagined it with violins and piccolos, and I hoped that the reality was as intriguing as what I'd pictured. Yamamoto was Kaori Yamamoto, a powerfully-built Japanese girl from Sapporo who spoke uncertain but very good English.

"She's had a lot of training with mountains and snow, which will be handy," Owen said to me privately on the way to lunch. "And hey, we won't always be last alphabetically."

So here we were: forty new members of the Oil Watch, as international as Pearson might have dreamed. The Japanese fire crew had middling English skills, but the medics were proficient, and both their engineer and their smith had been trained in England, which Porter enjoyed when he found out about it. The Americans were from the south, mostly, though there were a couple of Californians. We met their mentors at dinner. Kaori's mentor was the Texan dragon slayer we'd seen in action that morning, a broad-shouldered woman several years younger than Porter, with hair in tight braids across her scalp. Nick's was a Maori woman who might have actually stood a chance against Aodhan in an arm-wrestling match.

An aerialist, a mountaineer, and a protector of farmlands. That wasn't how I thought of Owen, but it was how he thought of himself, so it's what I tried to convey. After three seconds talking with Crawford, I knew that he was as violin as they come: born to play the featured part and with the range to deserve it, though still skittish and playful if caught unawares. Kaori's bass clarinet rounded out the trio quite nicely, providing a calm stability that not even Owen's horn could match. It might sound strange at first, all these parts together against such a harsh backdrop as Fort Calgary. But I could listen harder, more closely, and I knew that these were people we could work with and, more importantly, live with.

Owen would learn to slay new dragons. His fire crew would see new fires and his medics, new injuries. Courtney would plan and build, and our smith would keep everything in one piece. Even if I was only a messenger, like the officer who had brought Porter notice this morning, I would do it proudly. I would be next to Owen, to Squad Thorskard, and I would be able to make sure that word got out of what we did here.

We'd been worried that Alberta would be boring. There

were two more dragon attacks, both Wapiti Blues this time, before the first day was even over. It was going to be an interesting fall.

DISPOSABLE CIVILIANS

"I have no idea why I am here," Nick said, twirling a piece of fried potato on his fork while he chewed. Usually, I was against people speaking with their mouths full, but we had to eat in such a hurry that it was better to combine eating and talking. "I mean, I get that we can be assigned anywhere. That's the point. But I thought they would at least, you know, attempt to put us somewhere useful."

"Maybe they expect you to learn," said Kaori. She did not speak with her mouth full. She was far too efficient for that.

"Easy for you to say," Nick said, spearing a new potato. "You can at least *see* mountains from here. I'm used to skyscrapers and wires, and it is *so flat*."

I looked out the window. It wasn't that flat. But then again, I had seen Saskatchewan quite recently, so perhaps I was biased.

"Imagine if you ended up in a city," Nick went on, looking at Owen now, "all buildings and people. You'd feel weird too."

Owen had never slayed a dragon in a city, or even in a really populated area. Aodhan always took care of the ones that made it into Trondheim or any of the surrounding towns. The closest we'd ever gotten to a populated area was the time a *siligoinis* mistook the model cows on the Port Albert mini-golf course for the actual cows in the fields behind it. That had been one of our better showings, actually, because Owen got to take pictures with approximately ten million children afterwards, which Emily assured us was the best kind of press, and then we got free ice cream and lifetime passes.

"I see your point," Owen said.

"Alberta is not a posting of renown," Kaori said. "We all know this. And yet none of us are particularly incompetent."

"Thanks," said Nick.

"I think she meant we can work together," I said. "Between the three of you, you can handle pretty much anything."

Both Nick and Kaori looked at me. I could tell they weren't entirely sure what to make of me, most of the time. Everyone in Nick's support squad was much older than he was, as was typical of an American team, and the majority of Kaori's didn't speak English well enough yet to really mingle. They had clearly expected to become comrades with Owen out of the gate and weren't sure what to do with the fact that he was already so close to his squad. By the time you added me to the countermelody, they felt entirely off the beat.

"That is true, Siobhan," Kaori said, nodding formally. Japan was one of the few places in the world where bards still existed, though they were not specific to one dragon slayer. I hoped that a few weeks of training would take the edge off her coolly proper dealings with me. "We do possess an interesting skill set."

"Are you going to eat that?" Nick asked me, gesturing at the overly-blackened bacon on my tray. I shook my head and motioned for him to take it while I struggled with my water bottle. Owen didn't open it for me, though he usually did when we were in a hurry. He knew I wanted to look good in front of them. While I tried to get a drink, they fell to talking about past dragon slayings, as dragon slayers usually did when other topics weren't at hand.

Meal times had lengthened a bit since Basic, but our new habits stuck hard, and our squad was usually done well in advance of everyone else. The extra time allowed me to eat in a slightly more dignified way, but I still had to rush more than was generally considered polite. It gave the dragon slayers time to talk, discovering each other's past experience and fomenting a potentially less than friendly competition among them, except that Owen and Kaori didn't care, and Nick was probably making up most of his American Basic Training horror stories. I could respect that.

"It ate all the miniature ponies?" Nick interjected when Owen got to my favourite part of that first camping trip with Aodhan.

"Well, not all of them," Owen allowed. "But most of them, yes." Living with so many farm kids as he had over the past two years, he was more or less immune to animals' unfortunate demises.

"That's depressing," Nick said. "I hate it when animals get stuck in the crossfire."

"You slay dragons in New York," I said. "What kinds of animals besides rats and pigeons do you have?"

"Well, people have dogs," Nick said. "And thanks to urban

farming initiatives, there are more and more chickens." He shuddered. "I hate chickens."

"You may have come to the wrong place," Owen said, not unkindly.

"What's wrong with chickens?" I asked.

"They have beady little eyes," Nick informed me. "Like they're planning something."

"I can guarantee you that chickens are too stupid to plan anything," I told him.

"Good to know," he said, "but I think the New York chickens might have an evolutionary edge somewhere in their gene pool."

"What happened after the miniature ponies?" Kaori asked, trying to get the conversation back on track before we ran out of time.

Owen smiled and began detailing the rest of that particular encounter. Having been there, not to mention having made up most of the official version, I tuned out. It had been a long time since I'd delighted in remembering the differences between what actually happened and what I told the press. Instead, I looked over at where our support crew was sitting. They didn't look like they missed us too badly, but Annie caught my eye and, out of sight of the American firefighter who was talking, made a slightly less than polite hand gesture that suggested her southern counterparts might be prone to talking too much. I did my best not to laugh.

"If I could have your attention," Porter said loudly from the front of the mess. He was very good at just appearing in places without giving himself away. It was probably the SAS training. In any case, we all set down whatever we were eating (except Nick, who was still working on my unwanted bacon), and turned to see him. "We are starting rotations this morning. Crawford, report to training field A. Yamamoto, field B. Thorskard, just follow along."

We knew he meant *now* without his having to say it. Nick grabbed the rest of Owen's potatoes in his hand, when Owen would have pitched them, and headed off with his squad. He was shorter than Owen but broader, and managed not to be dwarfed by his team. Kaori wordlessly fell into step with her crew as well and headed in the opposite direction. I took my usual place beside Courtney as we filed after Porter, with Owen and Annie at the head of the rank, Aarons and the crew behind them, and the medics bringing up the rear.

We followed Lieutenant Porter through the concrete corridors of the Oil Watch base. There were lines painted on the floor to help with navigation: Blue would take you to the infirmary, red to command and yellow to any of the various training fields. We headed in the opposite direction than usual though, which meant we were in for some new kind of excitement. Not everyone had the best sense of direction in the monotony of the hallways, but I could tell the moment everyone realized that we were headed someplace new. By the time we were close enough to smell the dragon, even Wilkinson, who was terrible without a map, had figured out that we were headed towards the disposal yard.

"Well, this should be fun," Courtney whispered to me, not quite quietly enough.

"I heard that, Speed," Porter said. "Mind your manners now. Not everyone is as lax when it comes to punishments as I am."

"Yes, sir," Courtney said, her tone deceptively sweet. I winced, but Porter just laughed and preceded us into the disposal area.

It was a dragon I had never seen before. At first I thought it was a corn dragon, but its tail was far too long—as long as its whole body.

"Josephson?" Porter asked expectantly.

"An Athabascan Longtail," Laura said immediately. "Commonly referred to as a 'Bascan Long."

"Thank you," Porter said. "This dragon inhabits the northern forests. It is the second-most common to Alberta, after the Wapiti; however, it is significantly easier to kill. Any idea why, McQuaid?"

Lieutenant Porter almost never directly asked me a question unless he was making a point, preferring to leave it for the fire crew to answer. I thought for a second. It did look like a corn dragon, after all.

"It's stupid," I said. "It gets its tail caught in the trees when it chases you."

"An excellent guess," he said. "And correct. The 'Bascan Long is excruciatingly stupid. Get it to land and then double back on itself, and it is yours for the slaying. This particular specimen, however, is yours for the disposing."

We all wrinkled our noses. It was inevitable that this part of our training would come. In the wild, we would have to dispose of our own slayed dragons. At least they were letting us practice where we were surrounded by concrete and couldn't do any real damage to the ecosystem.

"This is Isagani Torres, who supervises Fort Calgary's disposal efforts," Porter went on, gesturing to the far side of the area where the official disposal crew waited. "He's in charge for the rest of the morning. If you need to vomit, please do so in that corner over there."

"And they said dragon slaying would be glamorous," Owen whispered to me.

"Actually, I'm pretty sure the guidance counselor said we were insane," I reminded him.

"That's just because she's from Mississauga and doesn't understand the complexities of rural communities yet," Owen said. He was laughing now, which I was always glad to see.

"Just think," I told him. "If you'd gone where Sadie is, you'd be learning to do this in scuba gear."

"Thank goodness for small mercies," Owen said, shuddering. For just a moment, there was an odd distance in his eyes, and I knew that he missed her more than he would ever admit to me. I didn't mind. It mystified people that Sadie and I didn't get jealous of the other's hold on Owen, but I had given up trying to explain it. Some people just look for drama for drama's sake.

"Do you think it's weird that all the disposal people are civilians?" I asked.

Owen looked at them sharply, and I knew he was really seeing them for the first time. "I hadn't even noticed," he confirmed, sounding disappointed in himself. "And yes, Aunt Lottie said that disposal units were usually part of the Oil Watch."

"Maybe it's just for training," I suggested. "And the military units are out and about."

"Have you seen any?" Owen asked.

"No," I said. "And I've seen at least three different civilian crews."

"It is weird," Owen said. "I mean, I get the idea of out-sourcing, but this just seems . . ."

"Uncomfortably racist?" I suggested.

"Well, yes," Owen agreed, rubbing his face. Most people only saw his blond hair and dragon slayer shoulders. At most they assumed he was tanned from being outside a lot. But he wasn't. His skin was that colour in the dead of winter.

"What are you talking about?" asked Jeremy, appearing beside me.

"It's probably nothing," I said. "Don't worry about it."

Owen's expression was still troubled though, and I knew he wouldn't be so easily put off. Hopefully this training session would involve pairing us off with the disposal unit, or at least breaking us into smaller groups. Then I could ask some questions. Owen knew better than to poke around, I knew. He was excellent at getting people in charge to tell him things, but I was better with strangers. He nodded when I made eye contact, and I knew he already felt better having a plan.

"If you three are finished," Porter said, "you've got some work to do."

I looked at the dragon and sighed. He wasn't wrong about that.

THE VOMITING CORNER

Isagani stepped up beside Porter and began to tell us the proper way to dispose of this type of dragon. At the core, all dragon disposal is similar, though each species has a specific chemical makeup that sometimes changes the routines. I was dreading the Wapiti lessons when we got to them, because I already knew their internal chemistry was especially pernicious. After a brief lecture, the rest of the crew paired up with each of us, and we set to work.

It was easily the most uncomfortable few hours of my life, leaving aside the time I'd waged chemical warfare on a bunch of unhatched dragon eggs. I did not have to use the vomiting corner, because Manitoulin had hardened my stomach, but two of the firefighters and Courtney, to her eternal shame, did. To be fair, they were all working around the dragon's gut, which was much worse than the head, where Owen and I had been stationed.

We began by dousing the dragon's scales in water, which ran off into a drain in the courtyard floor. Isagani warned us that in the field, we probably wouldn't be using water, because there wouldn't be much on hand. Next time, we would switch to chemicals only.

My hands were already sweating under the rubber gloves we wore, and the sun hadn't yet cleared the top of the building that overlooked the courtyard. I was glad we got to do this in the morning. The idea of more chemicals on top of work in direct sunlight, even in late September, was unappealing. At least in the field, we'd likely as not have tree-cover, assuming the dragon didn't destroy it all before Owen slayed it.

After the water bath, we moved on to the truly unpleasant parts. Armed with a foaming chemical suppressant whose formula was so long it would've taken me days to memorize it, I stood by while Isagani directed Owen through the process of slitting the beast's throat. As soon as the blade cut, noxious fumes began to waft in my direction, and I laid down the foam in the wake of the blade to keep it under control. This was when Courtney puked, because she was holding the knife and Dorsey wasn't quite fast enough to put down the chemical foam.

"I'm sorry!" he shouted as Courtney bolted for the corner Lieutenant Porter had indicated.

"Keep going, Dorsey!" Porter shouted from his vantage point, well above the worst of it. He looked down at Courtney. "Speed?"

"I'll be fine," she said. Then she threw up again.

From his spot near the dragon's tail, Davis looked over. I could tell he was itching to help her. I guess four years of premed will do that to a person.

"Eyes on target, Davis," Porter reminded him. "That's not your job right now."

Privately, I thought that was kind of dumb. If we were in the field, it would be his job, and Ilko's. But neither of our medics moved from their places.

Courtney finished throwing up and moved back to Dorsey, who looked like he was expecting to get punched in the face.

"We're good," Courtney told him, and reached for the knife to get back to work.

"The first one is always the most difficult," Isagani said quietly to Owen and me. Then he spoke up so the others could hear him. "The gut is the worst place during disposal. Note how we have concentrated most of you there? That is because that is where the dragon can cause the most damage. You must always make sure to cover the gut first. We are only working on the neck and tail at the same time because there are so many of us. A single crew does the gut first."

I had an entirely new appreciation for the Trondheim disposal units by this point. They had to do this on farmland. Owen slipped the knife a bit too far and swore in Spanish. Isagani brightened immediately and asked in Spanish if Owen was fluent. When Owen confirmed that he was, the two fell into rapid-fire discussion that I couldn't follow, except I heard Owen say his mother's name and assumed he was telling Isagani why his Spanish was so good.

At last, the dragon was completely sliced from weasand to, well, where its navel would have been if it had a navel, and the body cavity was filled with foam. While we waited for the foam to disperse, Isagani described the chemical reaction that was taking place, and I started to wonder if maybe we shouldn't be wearing masks in addition to the gloves. Between dragon fire and cancer, dragon slayers rarely die of old age. When the foam finally settled, we moved on to something even more unpleasant: dismemberment. This was done by means of cleaver and two-handled boning knife. It was much like cleaning a fish, Gratton informed us, though on a significantly larger scale. By the time we were done, I was doubting that I would ever eat anything again, and the dragon was in several pieces that we could lift in teams of four.

"It is safe to burn now," said Isagani, "which is what you will do when you are in the field. Try to use the trees that the dragon has brought down, because chopping them down on your own takes too long. On the prairie, you will have to wait for a helicopter to come and take the remains back here, where we have an incinerator."

We carried the pieces to the drop for the incinerator, and then watched as Porter hosed down the courtyard, sluicing more water into the drain. We definitely would not be doing that outside of the fort, but for now I was just glad to see our morning's work disappear.

"I'm starving," said Courtney.

"I hate you," said Anderson, who had thrown up not long after she had.

Porter laughed and directed us all to a special shower room where we could be decontaminated before rejoining the others for lunch. There were extra uniforms, but they were all standard issue, none of the ones I had altered for my own use.

"I've got it, Siobhan," Laura said when I stood with a towel around me, looking in despair at the clothes I was supposed to put on. "Just do what you can."

She waited with me after Annie and Courtney left, pointedly looking at the wall while I wrestled into my underwear and then the uniform trousers and shirt. I managed the zipper and button on the trousers well enough, but then Laura came and stood in front of me, and I gave up.

"I hate this," I told her. "But thank you."

"We'll make sure you've got your own things here next time," she told me, fingers fastening the small buttons that were on the standard uniform shirt like they were nothing. God, I missed being able to do that. "And no one minds. At least, not once they know you."

"Getting to know people isn't exactly why I signed up," I reminded her.

"No," she agreed. "You signed up so people would get to know Owen. Eventually, you're going to realize it's the same thing."

I hadn't thought of that. It made me feel a bit awkward. Laura moved to my tie and smiled impishly.

"So, Courtney and Porter," she said. "What should I put you down for?"

"What?" I asked.

"You know," she said, finishing the knot and making a suggestive gesture. "Extracurriculars."

"I don't think—" I started, but then I stopped. I remembered all the insinuations Lottie and Hannah had made about their time in the Oil Watch. And, you know, the fact that Owen existed at all. "Two weeks," I told her. That would be just before the time we started actually leaving the base on missions. Team player, that was me.

"You're much more optimistic than Owen was," Laura told

me. "And the buy-in is twenty dollars."

There were thirteen of us, assuming Courtney hadn't been allowed to participate, and assuming they hadn't thrown it open to the base at large. That was not a small amount of money if I won.

"Do you want cash, or are you taking markers?" I asked. "Also, this feels a bit like I am in a terrible heist movie."

Laura laughed and told me that markers were fine. She passed me my hat, which I could put on by myself, and we headed towards the mess. Owen grinned when he saw me, and I tried really hard not to make eye contact with Courtney as I reached the trays.

Once I had my food, I sat down with Owen. It was difficult to have private conversations, but he'd secured us seats next to Kaori's firefighters.

"I talked a bit more with Isagani," he told me.

"And?" I said, clasping my fork and knife like a barbarian, but determined to at least attempt to cut something up.

"He and most of his coworkers came here for jobs, it turns out," Owen told me. "Apparently the province of Alberta is recruiting overseas to fill in some of the jobs that were left vacant by those who went to the Oil Field."

"You mean the gross jobs that no one wants," I told him, stabbing my knife gracelessly into the margarine.

"Well, yes," he said. "It does seem that way. Isagani told me he has a bunch of cousins in Fort McMurray, and they all do similar things."

"Why aren't they in the Oil Watch, though?" I asked. "It would be more efficient. Plus, I know there are Filipino dragon slayers enlisted."

"Money, probably," Owen said. He stretched down the table to snag the pepper shaker from in front of Kaori's smith, and smiled at her companionably. "I mean, the Oil Watch doesn't pay them. The province does."

"I don't like it," I said. "If they work with us, they should be part of the team too. Your dad has an arrangement with the Trondheim crews, and they only took a one day course."

"Siobhan," Owen said, and I realized that my voice had gotten a bit loud. I slouched back in my chair and gave up trying to use the knife. "You're preaching to the choir," he went on, changing the pepper shaker for the salt. "I already agree with you. I'll e-mail my aunts tonight and see what they think. And in the meantime, you do what you always do."

"Which is what, exactly?" I said, twisting my fork in my hands. "Write a song and put it on YouTube? I don't have any software to play with or record. And the Internet isn't that great here."

"Well, no," Owen said, leaning back to salt his mashed potatoes. "I meant that you would get more information about it and then come up with a brilliant plan, like in the Guard back home, but I guess there will be a song eventually. It always seems to end in singing with you."

"You're the worst," I told him.

"The worst what?" Nick said, plunking down his tray beside mine. It was absolutely stacked with food, and I knew that somehow he would eat it all and still manage to filch half of what was on my tray. I snuck a glance at Laura, who was smirking, and realized that Courtney was probably not the only one people were betting on. I wasn't sure why anyone thought Nick might try something. All he ever did was steal my lunch, but maybe that was enough to pique general interest. It wasn't like we were spoiled for entertainment. I made a note to myself to have Owen bet a lot of money on my never having a moment of weakness with Nick. Theoretically, that was cheating, or at least insider trading, but still: money was money.

"Never you mind," I said. "What did you guys get to do this morning?"

Nick launched into his morning's lesson, which had centred on forest tracking, while Kaori put in pointers about what she'd learned about prairie slaying. I took Owen's advice and put my curiosity about the Filipinos aside for now. As he'd pointed out, there wasn't a lot I could do yet, and there were plenty of other dragons in our particular corner of the sky.

SONGS NEVER WRITTEN

It was four days before we got to try our hands at a Wapiti. Dragon disposal couldn't really be scheduled, after all. Nick's team had yet to get their turn at all, because there was one 'Bascan Long for Kaori, and then our Waptiti, which Nick couldn't tackle until he'd done the first. I was a bit envious, to be honest. We did get masks for the Wapiti, but it was very unpleasant, and definitely not the sort of thing to be immortalized in song.

Lottie replied to Owen's e-mail the day after we did the Wapiti. We got thirty minutes of Internet time every second day, during the week. I dashed off a quick note to my parents the day we heard from Lottie and spent the rest of my time researching the Philippines. It was pretty easy to get the basics. Despite its relatively small size, the islands housed enough species of regular animals and dragons to qualify as mega-diverse, which meant they had a strong dragon slaying tradition. Their dragons were primarily semi-aquatic, though they did have three non-swimming species, and their dragon slayers were best known internationally for their multiculturalism. Like Canada, the Philippines was a colonial holdover, though their economy was not as stable as ours was. That explained why the province of Alberta was able to employ so many people from that country.

There was nothing—that I could find, anyway—about discontent due to their exclusion from the Oil Watch in Canada. There were several dozen active Filipino dragon slayers in the Oil Watch, with their own support squads, but if the statistics I found were reliable, then there were at least as many "independent contractors" in Fort Calgary alone. I didn't have enough time to dig further though, so I sent an e-mail to Emily. I knew she'd probably be excited to tackle it. The whole thing made me uncomfortable, though I wasn't entirely sure it was my place to judge. People more qualified than I was had passed legislation and made it possible to get visas, after all, but there was no chance at residency, let alone Canadian citizenship. Since the disposal crews didn't work for the Oil Watch, their medical coverage, which they would undoubtedly need someday, was spotty at best. It was the exclusion I didn't like. I wanted to think Canada was better than that, or at least that we were trying to be better than that.

"Aunt Lottie wasn't too helpful," Owen said to me as we filed off to the barracks for lights-out. "She said there have always been independent contractors."

"Yeah, Darktide," I said, naming the biggest firm in the United States. "But they get paid a lot of money, and they include dragon slayers. And they're mostly made up of Americans."

"Yeah, I think the point may have drifted since we were e-mailing," Owen admitted. "Did you e-mail Emily?"

"Yes," I said. "You know how much she likes a good conspiracy."

"There's no conspiracy."

"We don't know that."

He waggled his eyebrows at me. I rolled my eyes.

"Did you bet on Nick and me?" I asked him. I'd been trying to broach this for the past few days, but this wasn't exactly an easy conversation to have.

"Of course," he said. "I bet on never. Easy money."

"Good," I told him. "That's what I wanted you to bet on."

"If you give me half the buy-in, we can split the payoff," he offered. "Even though it's a bit open-ended. I think when we get reassigned after training, it'll be considered 'never.'"

"Well, that's reassuring," I said. "Did you hear from Sadie?"

"She's fine," he said. "Her mentor is some Lithuanian giant she can barely understand, but he's very good and appreciates her willingness to work herself half to death, so they get along well enough. She said his smith tends to make heavier swords than she's used to, which is taking up most of her training time, but the water stuff is going well."

"That's good." Sadie's e-mail to me had mostly been about food, and how much she missed reliable vegetables that came from someone she knew rather than all the way from South Africa. "Has Lieutenant Porter said anything to you about where his support squad is?"

We'd quickly determined that one of the reasons Porter did most of the lecturing was that both Nick and Kaori's mentors were needed to patrol. They spent most of their time outside the protective steel forest of Fort Calgary, and their support squads went with them. So far as I knew, Porter hadn't slayed a dragon since we'd arrived, though there had been several battles within the fort. Owen was itchy about it, even though the windows in the shelter let him see what was going on. Maybe Porter had just learned to cope.

"He doesn't have one at the moment," Owen told me.

"That's weird," I said.

Dragon slayers didn't always have the same squad. Sometimes people died, after all, or ended their tours and went home. The firefighters most often stuck together, only getting shuffled up for things like injury or death, but they could be reassigned to another dragon slayer. I knew that Courtney was serving out her degrees from the Royal Military College, and that Ted only intended to stay in the Oil Watch long enough for it to put him through med school, but the others—save Owen, of course—were in it for their careers.

"I get the feeling Porter works best alone," Owen said diplomatically.

"I like him, though," I said. "At least he's interesting."

"Agreed," Owen said. We stopped in front of the door to the barracks where I stayed.

"Good night," I curled my hand around the door knob. It was a pull door, which was always worse than pushing, but I managed it.

"'Night," Owen said, and followed the other guys down the hallway.

—⊱ ⊰—

Our barracks were well-ordered, all things considered, but still noisy before lights-out, especially since it was Friday night and we had most of tomorrow off from all training except sparring and firearms. Since all the girls were in the same billet, Kaori was joined by both of her engineers and one of her medics, and we had two of Nick's firefighters. I had initially felt bad for Kaori's squad, whose limited English isolated them, but it was clear by now that there were some informal language lessons going on, and Kaori was very good at rapid-fire translation. As an only child, I had been afraid that I wasn't really cut out for communal living, but at least being friends with Sadie had prepared me for the unnatural interest everyone else seemed to take in my life.

"Do you need a hand?" Annie asked as I headed for the bathroom with my pajamas and my toothbrush.

"No thanks," I said. "I'm good."

I mostly was, though the cap on the toothpaste required me to use my teeth. I rinsed my face and pulled on my hair. It was almost an inch long now, but still well within regulation. I lived in a perpetual state of hat hair, but it was still easier than French braiding it. I wiped my face with the towel and set to changing as fast as I could.

"They're breaking us in easy," Laura was saying as I came out of the bathroom in my pajamas. I didn't mind getting dressed in front of my own squad, but while the Japanese crew were polite enough to not stare at me too openly, the Americans had no such restraint. I avoided them as much as I could.

"You think this is easy?" one of the Americans drawled. "I don't think I've ever been to a place with this many dragon attacks."

"That's probably why we're here," said the other, her accent more northern. "At least there are enough dragon slayers to deal with them."

"No, I mean it," Laura said. "The Wapiti and the Longtail are the easy ones. You can actually slay them. They're saving the big one for when we've settled in."

"For the love of God," said Courtney, looking like she wanted to wring her neck. "Just tell them."

"The Chinook," Kaori said, once she finished translated for her crew. Her voice was low, almost reverent. "She means the Chinook."

The Canadians all shuddered.

"I thought that thing was a myth," said the southern firefighter.

"I wish it was a myth," said Laura. "In the meantime, just thank your lucky stars it's the only dragon in the whole damn world that we can predict."

"It's not predicting," Annie corrected her. "It's a warning."

"Close enough for me," Laura said.

There was some chatter from the Japanese crew as they conferred, and we waited until Kaori leaned forward again.

"Please tell us the details," she said. "Our mountain dragons are also island dragons, so they are small and easily dealt with. We worry that too much of what we know about your Chinook comes from legend, and we would like to know the facts."

Everyone looked at me, expecting a story. The Wapiti and the 'Bascan Long were so regional that, as a non-resident of Alberta, I hadn't really had to learn about them before I got here. The Chinook was different. Even though it was the most regionally specific dragon in the entire country, possibly the entire world, everyone knew a little about it. We didn't talk about it much, and it was certainly kept out of the mainstream media as much as possible. Emily didn't like that. She thought it was prone to cause misinformation and panic. She had a point, but at the same time, I quite enjoyed living in denial about the Chinook.

Most dragons, you see, have weaknesses. The *siligoinis* is dumb. The Wapiti has short forearms that prevent it from moving on all fours once it is grounded. The *lakus* and the *urbs* are slow. The soot-streaker can't obscure itself and light you on fire at the same time.

I cleared my throat, and they all leaned in. I trusted that Laura would correct me if I made any mistakes, but I didn't think I would. You couldn't really overstate the dangers a Chinook posed, even when you took poetic license with them. We have lots of stories, of course, about every dragon in the world. And all of them tell you how those dragons can be slayed. But the stories about Chinooks have different endings. Of every dragon to ever have lived, from the grassland giants of Mongolia to the monstrosities from the Eastern European steppes, they are the biggest. Of all the species to fill the air or sea, they are the most vicious and the best equipped to deal death in fire. You can run from them, and you can dig your shelters deep, but their hearts are so far inside their bodies that even the Royal Canadian Mounted Dragon Slayers can't reach them with their steel-tipped lances.

I haven't written songs about a Chinook. And I never will.

A MORE COMFORTABLE DISTANCE

Owen looked at the horse with an incredibly skeptical expression. I have to admit, even I had my doubts. I had been riding before, though not often. When other girls my age wanted ponies, I held out for a harpsichord.

The fireproof saddle on the horse in front of Owen looked sort of like an upholstered chair that had wandered into a bar, gotten extremely drunk, and mistakenly gone home with an equestrian. I suppose in theory the built-up front and back of the seat was to prevent Owen from being thrown, but I had my doubts as to whether or not he'd be able to kick his leg high enough to get over it.

While Owen looked at his mount, I focused on the dragon slayer who was going to teach him to ride it. It was the Texan, Lieutenant Anne Marie Beaumont. She preferred to be addressed as Amery, but Owen always called her Lieutenant and even pronounced it the American way, the better to differentiate her from Porter. Amery's dislike of Owen was plain on her face, and I didn't think it was just because of how he addressed her. I hadn't figured out why yet, because she disliked me even more.

"So you know," Porter had said the night before, when he'd informed Owen what his lessons would be today. "Horseback riding is my least favourite part of living in this abysmal place. It's worse than the weather. In England, we gave up sticking dragons with lances two centuries ago and have never looked back, but these barbarous prairies lend themselves to tilting, so you have to learn."

Amery said nothing. Just looked at us and then turned to examine her own tack.

"Look on the bright side," I whispered to Owen. "You can't possibly be worse at this than Nick will be."

"Thanks." He reached up to pat the horse's head.

RCMD horses were carefully bred for dragon slaying. Traditionally, knights had worn spurs and put blinders on their mounts to help them keep control, but unhorsing due to panic had still been very common and usually painful for the dragon slayer. Sometime just after mounted knights became trendy in Europe, an enterprising soul had noted that some horses tended not to panic when their riders had them charge down an enormous fire-breathing beast. A few decades of careful breeding had produced horses that were less likely to spook, and by the time Owen stood in front of a horse named Constantinople on the plain in front of Fort Calgary, they had it more or less down to a science. It was entirely possible that Owen's horse could trace its lineage back to the reign of Augustus, assuming the bloodline hadn't taken a detour through Spain during the Inquisition.

"Have you ever done this before?" Amery asked, not sounding hopeful.

"No, Lieutenant," Owen said. "We get to try it for a while without the lance, right?"

"Yes," Amery said. "Now stand at his shoulder—no, face the other direction, and left foot in the stirrup first."

I watched Owen scramble on to the horse's back and felt a little sorry for them both. Owen did kick the back of the saddle on his way past, and he landed rather more heavily than he should have in his seat. It was rather amusingly ungraceful, but Amery was not smiling.

"Not the worst I've seen," she said. Owen grimaced. "Now get off the same way, and we'll do it again."

I realized that it was going to be like this for a while. Amery would make Owen perfect his mount and dismount before she let him actually move anywhere (on purpose, that is, because the second time Owen landed in the saddle, the horse started and took several steps forward before Amery could snatch the reins). I didn't want to stand there and do nothing all morning while Owen was training and the rest of our squad was off doing their specific lessons.

"Lieutenant?" I asked, when there was a break in the action. "May I be dismissed to go practice bugle calls?"

Technically that was still my only real job, but since I had yet to have any reason to use them, I'd kind of fallen by the wayside, and had instead taken to following Owen around while he learned all the things that made prairie dragon slaying unique.

"Dismissed," Amery said, holding Constantinople's head as still as she could while Owen tried for the saddle a fourth time. Her professionalism was pushing through her general dislike of him. Maybe Sadie's work-until-you-drop approach would serve better at winning the American lieutenant over. In any case, Owen's fourth try was his best yet.

I straightened to attention and then turned smartly away. I retrieved my bugle case from under my bed, where it had accumulated a rather appalling amount of dust, and wondered where I was going to practice. The idea of playing where people could hear me was still unnerving, especially since all the bugle calls meant something, and I didn't want anyone to think they were getting actual signals. After a moment's hesitation, I made for one of the small indoor practice courts, assuming that everyone would be outside.

"Siobhan!" Nick said as soon as I entered the court. He was carrying his bow, and there were a bunch of supremely ugly-looking arrows next to him.

"Hi, Nick," I said. "Sorry, I didn't realize anyone would be here."

"Wait," he said before I could make my departure. "There's plenty of room. Are you shooting?"

The Oil Watch fired live rounds outside, mostly, in one of the numerous grey courtyards that dotted what passed for landscape inside Fort Calgary. When anyone else talked about shooting, that's what they meant. Nick always meant bow and arrow.

"No." I held up the hand that wasn't locked on the bugle case. "I don't think I can. I can barely manage a gun."

"It might be possible," he said, looking at my ruined fingers. "I mean, you wouldn't be fast at it, but as long as you're accurate, that doesn't matter so much."

"You're not one of those types who can have three arrows

in the air at the same time?" I asked.

"Not in here," he said, pointing at the target. "It's not far enough away."

"Is it harder than using a sword?" I asked, moving closer to him. "Slaying dragons with arrows, I mean."

"Well, you can do it from a more comfortable distance, which is nice," Nick said, with a grin. He scratched under his arm guard and fiddled with the fletching of the arrow that was closest to him. "But you still have to hit it properly, or you'll run out of arrows and have a very angry dragon breathing down your neck."

I looked closely at the points on the arrows. The largest was about the size of my hand, but I still didn't think it was big enough to get to the hearts of a *siligoinis*, let alone one of the bigger species. Nick followed my line of thought, apparently.

"We have small dragons in New York City," he said. "Not as small as Lieutenant Porter's Cornish Game Hens, mind you, but still small enough that you can slay them with these."

"And you just run around the city like Robin Hood?" I asked. I stood beside him a bit awkwardly, but his easy manner made it difficult to be uncomfortable for very long.

"I use parkour," Nick said, a bit defensively. "That's much easier with a bow than with a sword, but I usually carry both, just in case. Basically, I'm Spider-Man."

"Hawkeye," I corrected without thinking.

"Nerd," Nick said, but he was grinning again. "Anyway, I know I have all this stuff to learn, but I want to keep in practice."

"You're going to go home?" I asked. "After?"

It wasn't something we talked about, generally speaking, what we were going to do when our tours were up. Courtney was going to find a job, and Davis was going to get his own medical practice, but the dragon slayers didn't really talk about it, even though both Owen and Sadie knew their plans. I'd asked the question without thinking, and before I could apologize, Nick waved me off.

"Yes," he said. Again, his manner was easy, decided. I realized that he had a plan too. "My family has been with the New York Police Dragon Slayers since the force was formed in 1845."

"Oh," I said. If there was one thing I understood, it was family legacy. Well, legacy and the desire to go back home. Nick was tied to New York just as Owen and I were tied to Trondheim. There was no reason to start something when you could already see that the ending went in different directions.

"What are you here to practice, if you don't mind me asking?" Nick said, just as the silence was about to become awkward. I wondered if he had figured it out, as I had.

"Bugle," I told him. "Technically, the bard serves as comm officer, which means bugle calls. It'll be more useful in the forest, because radios don't always work there. There's not much use for it here, but I don't want to get rusty either."

"So play me something." He leaned against the table expectantly.

I did my best to quell the panic that welled up in my chest. I could play for my family, of course, by which I meant I played in my bedroom, and often with the mute, but that led to bad habits, and I needed to practice full volume. Lottie had heard me play all the calls, because she wanted to be sure before she expended all her favours getting me into the Oil Watch, and I kept very few things from Owen. But Nick . . . he was practically a stranger.

Just like that, the weight in my chest lifted. Nick had never heard me play. He'd never heard me play *anything*. He had no idea that I was this great musical prodigy from a small town with too few heroes to latch on to. He didn't know the hours I'd spent, from the time I was old enough to sit at the piano bench, mastering song after song. He only knew that I was Owen's bard, that my hands were burned, and that I let him steal food off my plate without punching him.

"Okay," I said. "Just give me a second."

I fumbled with the latches. A bit of that was my usual awkwardness, but some of it was that my hands were shaking with excitement. I pulled out the bugle and checked it over, rubbing out imaginary fingerprints. I took out the mouthpiece and attached it.

When I looked up, Nick was still smiling at me, patient as you can imagine. I guess he understood. He had his bow after all, and it was as much a part of who he was as my music was a part of me.

"It's going to take me a few moments to warm up," I told him. "So don't expect greatness right away."

"Noted," he said.

I took a deep breath and launched into reveille, probably the second-most recognizable of all horn calls. When that didn't fall apart on me, I switched to the long reveille. Next was mail, then meals one and two, and then the calls for all the different ranks. They were easy to switch between, and I found the up and down of the melodies reassuring after only hearing it inside my head for so long.

Nick took up his bow when I played the fire alarm, and began to shoot at the target. He only hit the bull's-eye on his first shot. After that, his shots all went wide of the centre mark. It took me half of warning for parade to realize that he was doing it on purpose. He couldn't fit all his arrows in the middle of the target, so he spaced them out intentionally all the way around.

At last, I played the dragon call, and Nick fired the last of his arrows into the target, making a pretty pattern of circles on the painted marks. He went down to pull them out—some of them had gone in so far he had to brace himself with his foot—while I played taps, the American version of the last post, which the Oil Watch used to signal end of day. It was my favourite, those long, sad notes hanging in the air like hope and sorrow all at the same time.

Buglers had fallen by the wayside as technology developed to replace them. The calls could be prerecorded and played with the touch of one button. Radios covered distances that before only those golden notes could pierce. Even at funerals a ceremonial bugle-shaped broadcasting device could be used in place of the real thing. It sounded fine, but there was no air, no artistry to the music. Nick might have heard bugle music before, but I was pretty sure this was the first time he'd ever heard an actual bugle.

"That was amazing," he said when I was finished. He was still smiling that easy smile, leaning on his bow with a rakish air that made me want to roll my eyes and laugh too.

I could have kissed him, I think. But then I would have lost the bet.

THE GENERAL

Owen did not sit well through dinner. Lunch had been fine, because he'd only just come in and his muscles hadn't stiffened yet, but by the time we were through our afternoon lecture on the forests of Northern Alberta, where we would likely be spending some quality time in the future, he looked profoundly uncomfortable.

"I was told that after a few days, the pain is less," said Kaori, who had begun her horse training that afternoon, though she seemed to be adapting better than Owen was.

Nick looked at both of them with some concern. "Well, until my mentor gets back from Red Deer, I am just happy to leave you to it."

"Your turn will come," Owen said, shifting again, even though I judged from his face that it didn't help. He looked at me. "What did you do after you disappeared this morning?"

I opened my mouth to explain, but Nick jumped in before I could get a word in.

"She came down the practice court I was using for archery and played me some of her bugle calls," he said. I couldn't help but notice that Laura was suddenly paying a great deal of attention to our conversation, though her eyes were fixed on her plate.

"I needed to practice," I said. "If we end up in the forest, you don't want me to sound like a duck."

"She's really good," Nick said, and I managed not to wince.

"She's the best," Owen said quietly.

Laura gave up trying to look disinterested, and I realized that if there was a bet on Nick and me, there was almost certainly a bet on Owen and me as well, and that Owen would rather chew out his own liver than tell me about it. I certainly had no intention of providing the entire base with drama.

"I'm getting better," I said. "At the bugle, I mean. I've only just started to play it."

"I never would have guessed that," Nick said. Now it was my turn to shift uncomfortably, and I didn't even have saddle sores to blame. I thought I had figured everything out while we were practicing, but in a room full of people, with everyone watching, somehow it was all up in the air again.

Thankfully, Kaori could read a room, and she smoothly changed the subject to the weight of the lances she and Owen had been using.

"I realize that archery requires no small amount of upper body strength," she said directly to Nick, "but perhaps you should join Owen and me for weights. I think we are all going to need it."

Nick agreed, and they fell to talking about the variety of training exercises they all used. I wished that Sadie were here.

Not only would she, as Owen's girlfriend, put to rest any doubts about his fidelity, she'd also be a person I could talk to about Nick, and how in all hell I was going to get him to keep his distance without losing his friendship altogether. She'd probably die of glee to finally talk about boys with me, even if it was only through e-mail. I made a note to send her a message about it the next time we had Internet access time, assuming I could type without someone looking over my shoulder.

A ruckus at the front of the room drew our attention. Usually, the table closest to the doors was reserved for senior officers, namely the dragon slayers who weren't in their first year of tour. Since so many of them were out in the field, Lieutenant Porter ate alone most of the time, but as we looked up, a man in a decorated uniform was taking a seat across from him.

Porter didn't stand, but he did manage to come to attention while remaining in his chair. I fought down the urge to straighten my collar, and I was halfway across the room from the newcomer. He absolutely exuded authority. It was very disconcerting.

Over the chatter in the mess hall, I couldn't hear what they were talking about, but it was pretty clear that Porter was not happy. Maybe he was getting a new support squad. I hoped he wasn't getting reassigned. He was odd and more than a little bit rude, but he was familiar, and that meant a lot. Also, I knew that Owen liked him, and that meant even more.

Porter was gesturing with his fork, arguing his point, but at a single word from the other man, he stopped. I saw his shoulders stoop, just a little bit, as he conceded whatever point had just been lost. Then he must have asked to be dismissed, because he stood and stalked out of the mess hall, leaving his plate half-full on his tray.

"What do you think that was about?" Owen whispered.

"I have no idea," I replied. "But I don't think it was because Porter's request for sticky toffee pudding to be added to the commissary menu was turned down again."

"What are you talking about?" Nick said, reaching for the rest of my green beans with his fork.

"Chickens," I said, hoping that would turn him off. Apparently it was the wrong thing to say, because he held a hand dramatically against his heart and looked at me with a most ridiculous expression on his face.

"Then I shall rely on you to protect me," he said. I was definitely going to have to e-mail Sadie.

We were all quieter than usual on the way back to the barracks. Owen was limping by then, and that made us all think about our own mortality. Courtney's face was especially stony, and I wondered if her lessons that morning had been unpleasant.

"Are you all right?" I asked, falling in beside her while Owen lagged. I kept my voice low in case she didn't feel like sharing with the entire squad.

"I'm fine," she said. "I just don't like surprises."

"Did something happen this morning?" I said. Usually we filled each other in on what we were learning separately as a matter of course. I have no idea if the people on Nick and Kaori's squads did the same thing, but we had decided that it was better for us if the whole squad knew what everyone else was up to.

"No, it happened at dinner," Courtney said shortly.

Oh God, if this was about boys I was toast. My abject terror must have shown on my face, because Courtney took pity on me.

"The general?" she said. "The one who argued with Porter at dinner?"

"Oh, you know him?" I said, more relieved than I have ever been in my entire life.

Courtney snorted. I retracted some of my relief.

"You could say that," she said. "That is General Henry Octavian Speed."

I choked. There couldn't possibly be that many Speeds in the world. Courtney looked at me grimly and confirmed, "My father."

"Your father is a dragon slayer?" I said, hoping my voice was more "politely interested" and not "freaked the heck out."

"Yes, indeed," she said. "And his father, and his father's father, and all the freaking way back to the goddamn Magna Carta."

"Oh," I said. Because there wasn't much else I could contribute.

"Yeah, it's awesome," Courtney said. "Who could have possibly dreamed that so many boys would be born in a row? And then me with two younger sisters?"

"Your dad doesn't think girls can be dragon slayers?" I asked, aghast. That was practically sacrilege.

"Oh, no," she said. "He wanted nothing more than for me to grow up and follow him right off the cliff. Provided that we don't get married, of course. Or at least don't change our name when we have kids so that the Speed line will continue."

We reached the barracks, and Courtney pulled me past the beds and into the bathroom for some privacy. No one followed us.

"I won't tell anyone," I told her.

"Oh, please," she said. "They'll all know as soon as he introduces himself tomorrow. Hell, Porter's known the whole time we've been—" she hesitated, but I finished the thought without her. "Here," she concluded.

I did some quick math, counting days, and realized I'd just won a little over two hundred dollars from the betting pool.

"So he's a hard-ass?" I asked, trying to keep my voice light.

"You could say that," she replied. "He's merciless on the dragon slayers, and he really, really doesn't like the idea of so much friendliness between the dragon slayers and their squads. He says it cuts in on their professionalism."

"Well, that's just stupid," I said without thinking.

"Choir," said Courtney, pointing to herself, then to me, "preaching to it."

"So what do we do?" I asked.

"What all good little soldiers do," Courtney said. It was easy to forget, sometimes, that that was what I was now. A soldier. If I was anywhere else in the world, I might be a killer by now too. "We follow orders."

There was a quiet knock on the door.

"I'm sorry, Courtney," said Annie. "I really need to pee."

"We've got until breakfast," I said as we opened the door. "I know it's not much, but at least it's something."

But we didn't have that long at all, it turned out, because three hours before dawn a new siren sounded. The Dragon Call that usually played over the intercom was a tinny, somewhat flat rendition of the call I'd played for Nick. This one was more like a foghorn, a single dark note, blasted against other ships as a warning to get out of the way and stay there.

Laura was on her feet before I was even awake.

"Everyone up, *now*," she shouted. This was the strength of the Oil Watch, I thought, as I hastened to obey. We were a team. We could take orders from anyone, because we knew what everyone else was good at. If it was Laura, then it was local. And probably fire.

"Annie, help Siobhan. This is no time for pride." That's when I knew it was really bad. Usually they were much better about letting me keep my dignity. "Kaori, you're going to have to translate fast, so stay close to me."

I struggled into what clothes I could while Annie dressed next to me, and then she turned and began to help me. Kaori was speaking in rapid Japanese to her crew, and Laura was helping Courtney gather her sapper kit, which she'd left spread out on the extra cot in a small show of defiance the night before.

"Sorry," Annie whispered as she tucked my shirt into my trousers and fastened the button and belt buckle. "I'm sorry, I'm sorry."

"It's fine, Annie," I said, my teeth clenched. "Just—finish."

Kaori came over to help me into my sweater while Annie got hers. There was hammering on the door just as Kaori was doing the last button, and Porter burst in without waiting for us to confirm that we were all decent.

"Move," he said, and we did, Courtney struggling into her backpack as we ran down the hall.

The guys joined us, all of Nick's and Kaori's teams too, as we followed the yellow line towards our dragon shelter. Because it had to be a dragon. That was the only reason for such a loud awakening. We'd had a couple of early morning attacks already, but they'd received the normal alarm. That difference, and Laura's fear, made me realize what we were about to endure.

We assembled in the shelter, Porter counting us in to make sure we were all in attendance. It was crowded. Usually Kaori and Nick took their squads to shelters of their own, but this time was different. It wasn't just us who needed sheltering. We had, by the longest calculation, four hours. Four hours to bring in all the roaming dragon slayers, all the passengers off any trains, and any local oil workers and farmers from the satellite communities. All of them would hide with us, beneath the shelter of our steel totem poles, but more importantly, beneath the solid concrete. There would be no one left above ground.

Before Porter closed the steel shutters, I saw it. Or rather, I saw the oncoming storm.

Owen was beside me, and he took my hand. I barely heard him whisper.

"Chinook."

THE STORY OF THE DRAGON CHINOOK

There were only two things that ever stood in the way of Canada becoming its own country.

The first was our own political disinterest. The Victorian era was good to us, and we were happy subjects of the Crown. The Americans had rebelled and had paid a high price for it. We were mostly untroubled by Napoleon. We did not seek sovereignty, not until it became absolutely necessary.

The second was the dragon called Chinook. Unique in its size, and in it inexorability, the Chinook had more than enough power to drive politicians to horrible compromise and dragon slayers to terrible choices.

When John A. Macdonald fathered confederation, he dreamed of a country united from coast to coast. Aware that he would have to woo the West, he promised them a secure rail link from Halifax to Vancouver. And everything went well until the builders reached Fort Calgary.

From that open plain, the railway men looked up and saw mountains. They knew what lurked there. Settlers to British Columbia went south, always south, to the Wyoming passes, where the wagons were easier to defend. But America was creeping westward too, and Macdonald was determined to cede no territory—or any more tolls—to them.

The death toll was obscene. Even with the early warnings provided by the clouds of smoke that preceded a Chinook's appearance, the railway men had nowhere to hide, and the newly created North-West Mounted Dragon Slayers could not protect them. They retreated to the safety of Manitoba, where rebellion was already on the horizon, and Macdonald resigned in disgrace over the tragedy he had caused. Canada, it seemed, would be split after all, and might even lose the territories it had won from America during the War of 1812.

But the westward dream persisted. And the empty rails called for trains.

Mackenzie followed as Prime Minister and came down hard on the Red River Rebels in Manitoba. He encouraged the recruitment of Chinese workers, bringing them to Canada in ships and paying them just enough that they might forget about the dragons in the sky. It was those Chinese workers, and the dragon slayers who came with them, who made the railway possible, though it took Macdonald's reelection for anyone to listen to what they had to say.

From Fort Calgary stretched a short and nervous railway spur, until Hinton, when the mountains loomed too large on the horizon and the warning hours were too few. There, the rails went underground. Thousands of men moved acre upon acre of solid stone, excavating the very roots of the Rocky

Mountains. It was called the John A–Zuò Tunnel, for the man who paid in coin and the workers who paid in blood.

Because the Chinooks did not stop coming. They sat upon their mountaintops and waited. When they grew hungry, the spread their wings, breaking rock and tree and all else that might get in their way. They did not use stealth in their approach, because they did not need to. Great clouds heralded their approach, giving precious hours of warning to those below. And they didn't care who had a chance to hide. They simply descended, and everything with any sense at all ran away.

Fort Calgary tunneled too, building in concrete and steel. While the towns and cities outside the Chinook hunting grounds grew, cautiously turning prairie grass to house and school and business, Calgary closed in around itself, providing shelter to all who might need it when the dragons came.

There were small mercies. Their range was quite short, not stretching as far north as Edmonton, nor as far east as the Saskatchewan border. Chinooks were also the only dragons to hibernate, which meant that the deepest parts of winter would be untroubled. But the mountaintops on which they lived caught sunlight well, and sometimes even in the dead cold of the frozen months, a Chinook would wake and turn its fire towards the east.

But progress, or whatever name you might call it, does not stop.

More tunnels were dug, connecting British Columbia and Cascadon to the rest of Canada at multiple points through the mountains. More tunnels meant more trains and, in the north where Chinooks were less worrisome, trucks and cars. More carbon, more people. More food.

Their small number and limited range had once kept the Chinook at bay, allowing Canada to carve out a country instead of settling for a wall to forever split it in twain. But as a result, the limitations were gone, and the Chinooks spread east and south, leaving ash and devastation behind them as they flew.

It was in Kansas that disaster truly struck.

No one knew what drove the dragon from the mountains so far across the plains. Kansas was completely unprepared for such an onslaught, even with the warning a Chinook provides. There was a small Oil Watch outpost there, to protect the coal beds and the trucks and trains that serviced them. There was one dragon slayer and one support squad. Usually they only dealt with local variations of the corn dragon, or the occasional blue-grey Motherlode that had flown up from Texas.

As the sun dawned that fateful morning, though, the dragon slayer looked up, saw the clouds. He knew his dragon lore well, and despite how far he was from the mountains, he knew that his doom was upon him. It wasn't his death—because he wasn't going to die that day—but his fate, his fate would be changed forever.

There were a lot of people in Kansas. Farmers. Miners. Teachers. Children. The Chinook didn't burn the ground as it flew, staying above the storm of clouds that preceded it. It held back all its fire for when it reached the refineries around Lawrence. And in the face of that storm, the dragon slayer made a choice, and he chose to save as many lives as he possibly could, no matter what the other costs might be.

You do not shoot a dragon, ever. This is engraved upon the heart of every dragon slayer while they are still in their cradles. But there was one missile, left over from an administration more likely to take unpopular risks than the current president. The dragon slayer wasn't even sure it was going to work. His squad mutinied and left him alone at his post. He didn't care. There would be no trial for them, he knew. He would bear the blame for this.

The firing mechanism was almost distressingly straightforward, even for someone who didn't have the level of training the dragon slayer did. It was meant to be braced by a truck or small munitions tower, but the dragon slayer had neither of those. Instead, he used his left shoulder, not his sword arm, and held off firing for as long as he could to be sure of his aim. It wasn't like he could miss the Chinook, but he had to kill it, and he only had one chance.

The missile caught the dragon in the air, its wings spread so wide that a man would have to turn his head to look from wing tip to wing tip. It cut into the Chinook's chest, filling the air with dragon screams, and exploded. Such fire and waste rained down on Kansas that day as has not been seen since Hiroshima. The coal beds took flame, and burn to this day.

But the people evacuated.

If you ask him why he became a dragon slayer, Declan Porter will tell you stories about slaying small ones barehanded as a sign of strength. If you get him really drunk, which is not an inexpensive process, he will tell you the truth of what happened on the Kansas plains. And he will look you in the eye and tell you that whatever the consequences, he has no regrets.

"I pressed the button," he said to me years later when I asked him, soldier to soldier, about that day. In the yard, his daughters fought with tiny swords, while his son hammered

red-hot steel alongside their mother in the forge. "I pressed the button. And I would do it again."

I might die of old age, in the end. And when that time comes, Kansas will still burn.

THE ONE AND ONLY

They had turned the siren off, thank goodness. My ears echoed for a moment after the sound was cut. It wasn't exactly a melodic way to be jerked out of sleep, and the longer we listened to it, the more I found it sinking into my bones. This would be a terrible song. It began too abruptly, proceeded in a discordant fashion, and then faded to nothing but low murmurs that lasted too long to be interesting. Owen stared at the shutters, and I stared at him.

"He won't open them," Courtney said to me, leaning close to whisper. "Porter, I mean. Not unless he's ordered."

"Why not?" I whispered back. "Shouldn't the dragon slayers at least see it?"

Now that the sirens had stopped, it was deathly quiet. I knew that soon it was going to get deathly loud.

"That coal bed near Lawrence?" Courtney's voice was so quiet now she was practically breathing the words into my ear. "The one that's still burning."

"That bed will burn forever," I told her. "It's not like it's going to run out of fuel."

"True," Courtney allowed. "But anyway, my father was the commander of that zone when the Chinook came. He ordered a full evacuation of Lawrence, but there wasn't going to be enough time. The official policy with Chinooks is only to run, but one of the dragon slayers serving under him broke orders and fired on it."

"I've heard the story," I said.

"Yeah, well, I've lived it," she said. At my startled look, she continued. "Not in Kansas, no. I've never been. But Dad was livid for months. He wanted to nail the dragon slayer's hide to the wall, but since so many lives had been saved, he had to settle for giving him the crappiest assignment he could think of."

"New Zealand?" I guessed. It was so small and transportation was so difficult that dragon slaying there was the end of the line for the Oil Watch. Plus, the only export was wool, and by then I'd been in the military long enough to know what rumors would follow any dragon slayer who ever managed to serve in New Zealand and then leave it.

"Alberta," Courtney said, and turned her head very subtly to where Porter was sitting, his hands on his knees and a very strange expression on his face.

"Porter?" I said, only remembering halfway through the word that we were whispering, and thus ending the word in a squeak. Courtney looked around to see if we'd drawn too much attention.

"The one and only." Courtney's tone was almost fond. "Anyway, Dad couldn't even make an example of his support crew, because Porter made them leave before he fired."

"I thought they mutinied," I said.

"Siobhan," she said. "You do this professionally."

Of course. Porter had made them leave, and then told everyone they'd mutinied to save them from court martial. Dragon slayers are always doing silly things like that. Things like jumping off bridges. Like reaching into fire. I looked at the lieutenant, trying to imagine him as something besides the brash, barely-contained soldier that he'd become. I assumeded his tendency to be a smart-ass had come from surviving his training in the SAS, but maybe it, like my hands, had been tempered with dragon fire.

"Don't stare," Courtney said. "And for the love of God, tell Owen privately."

I could understand the lieutenant's desire for privacy. Something occurred to me then. "Wait," I said. "Are you just, you know," I made a vague gesture, "with Porter, to piss off your dad?"

"No," Courtney said sharply. Then she considered it. "Well, maybe. But to be fair, I do a lot of things to piss off my dad."

"Like become an engineer?" I said.

"With two university degrees at that," she said, clasping at imaginary pearls around her neck. "I am so high above my station."

"My parents wanted me to be a doctor," I told her. "But I think they'd have been happy with an engineer too. I'm not switching, though. I don't imagine that the general is a fan of bards. Or Thorskards."

"You're probably right," Courtney said. "He's never approved of Lottie, and he's only met her twice. He considers her a poor example of a dragon slayer. Says she thinks too much. And he thinks only the worst of Aodhan."

"No opinion on Hannah?" I asked, though I was pretty sure of her answer.

"He doesn't pay attention to support crews," she said. "Not even his own, when he has to have them."

"Has to have what?" Owen said. I guess he had finally stopped trying to see through the shutters.

"Breakfast," Courtney said, her eyes shining with sincerity. "It's the most important meal of the day."

Whatever Owen might have said to that was swallowed up by the loudest sound I had ever heard. It was like a train crashing through a hundred timpani, skin after skin giving way with a tremendous boom that echoed in the kettles even after the drums had been smashed. It was wings, I realized half a breath after Owen did, huge wings that rent the air in swaths so thick, a soccer field might fit inside them. I knew that between those wings hung a monstrous body capped by a head full of teeth, the smallest of which was bigger than the car I had left in Ontario. I could only imagine the fire.

Fort Calgary did not break, though we heard the scream of metal and knew that the Chinook had tried to rip out one of the totem poles. Kaori sat in the corner by herself, her hands on her knees with her eyes closed, and breathed as steadily as she could. I could see her shoulders shake. Nick paced, twisting his fingers in delicate motions I knew must have some real purpose, but couldn't identify. Owen was beside me, and it might have looked to anyone else like he was standing still, but I could tell that he was bursting at the seams to be this close and not even get to see the beast.

I risked a look at Lieutenant Porter. He stared hard at his knees, fingers stretched out over his kneecaps and white at the knuckles. This is what he saw, I knew then. Aodhan saw the oil rigs burn, and Lottie saw a long fall onto hard cement. I saw egg shells shattered and Owen defenseless. And Porter saw this. This room full of recruits, only a month off the trains and under his protection, even though he was forbidden from doing anything to protect us. I had a great deal of respect and friendship for Courtney Speed, but right now I thought her father was kind of a douche.

"Lieutenant?" Nick said, and I realized that he probably knew exactly who Porter was, whatever Courtney thought. He might be from New York, but the American press was as attached to their dragon slayers as the Canadians were to ours. "I'm sorry, Lieutenant, but we need to see it."

"Go ahead, then," Porter growled. I don't think he was angry; he just couldn't talk.

Nick went to the shutter controls and took a deep breath. Owen and Kaori came to stand beside him, and the rest of us fell in. I would have stayed at the back, but Owen took my hand and pulled me forward. He wanted to see it with me.

Nick pulled the shutters open, and one of the Japanese girls screamed. I very nearly did too, except I was too busy trying not to faint. Courtney's hand closed on my shoulder, the one opposite from where Owen stood. She squeezed so hard it hurt, and snapped me back to myself. We all gaped out the window clinging to one another for strength.

In your dreams, when you're chased by monsters, you don't usually see them. They are these big things looming in the corner of your eye. If you see them, make them stand in front of you, or chase them down, you know them, and they lose their power over you.

That is not how it works with the dragon Chinook.

It wasn't in the sky when Nick opened the windows, it *was* the sky. I didn't know if it would smother us or burn us first. The totem poles kept it in the air. If it landed, it would be like when a person lies back on a bed of nails. Presumably the dragon would not be hurt, but at the same time, neither would it sink to the ground. The totem poles would bear its weight. I forced myself to think of that, just as the sky cleared. The Chinook had passed overhead and had gone to breathe fire on another part of the fort. Out of our sight line, it was even worse. Now we knew what it looked like, we'd seen its teeth and fire, but we didn't know what it was doing.

We all jumped back from the window as sheets of orange flame burned down from above. The Chinook flew back into sight, and it was too hot to stand close. It flew up into the sky, thwarted again by the solid concrete it could not break, and trailed back towards the mountains. We watched it go for a long, long time.

After the all-clear came, the only sound in the shelter was the rumbling stomachs of the hungrier members of Nick's fire crew. The all-clear was followed immediately by the call to breakfast, and we knew that we were about to start our day as if nothing had happened to put us behind schedule other than a regular dragon attack.

"Will there be a cleanup?" Kaori asked.

"The fire crews will be called out, and maybe the engineers," Porter said, looking at Courtney. Try as I might, I could not find one iota of unprofessionalism in the way he looked at her. "Depends on the structural damage."

We didn't say anything else as we filed into the mess hall. The older dragon slayers and their more experienced crews looked just as rattled as we did. I wondered if they had watched, or if they'd closed their shutters against the one thing they could not fight. There were no civilians present, which I guessed meant that they were being debriefed separately.

General Speed was already sitting at the table Porter usually ate at, the other dragons slayers taking seats around him, and the lieutenant left us to head towards them, squaring his shoulder like a man who is about to walk into something unpleasant. No one spoke to him, though. They let his ghosts be. We ate, and then the general stood up to make an announcement. He didn't need a microphone. His parade voice was just fine. "First of all, I would like to commend you on your expert handling of this morning's exercises," he said. Exercises. Like we'd gone for a run. "You are a credit to the Oil Watch."

He didn't look at Porter, though his gaze swept the rest of the room when he said it. I wondered if he'd looked at Courtney for a fraction of a second longer than the rest of us, but I don't think he did.

"Furthermore, it is time for the new dragon slayers among us to receive their winter assignments," he continued. "Crawford, Thorskard, and Yamamoto companies, stay behind. The rest of you are dismissed."

The older officers and crew filed out, already talking to each other like nothing had happened. We sat as straight and as still as we could. I didn't have to look at Porter—and I could tell that Owen didn't either—to know that whatever was coming, it wouldn't be good.

DISMISSED

I had only a very short time to fill Owen in on what Courtney had told me. I was unsurprised to find out that Lottie had already told him a bit of it; he knew the story of what had happened, anyway, even though he hadn't known it was Porter who'd done it.

"She mentioned it before Manitoulin," he said. "Half cautionary tale, half how-to. You know how it is with Aunt Lottie sometimes. I'm more surprised she hasn't said anything about the fact that we're working together."

"I don't think it can be good," I told him. "I mean, Porter's already on the low end of the food chain in terms of what the Watch thinks of him, and there's at least one world government that hopes you fade into obscurity."

I could have said "die," but I really didn't think the government of Canada wanted Owen dead. They wouldn't mourn him too much, but I was pretty sure they'd just settle for him doing fewer things that made him look cool on the Internet.

"Maybe they thought we cancel each other out," Owen said.

"That doesn't even make sense," I replied, but before I could really get on a roll, General Speed was on his feet again.

"Right, Crawford!"

Nick's squad was quick to get to their feet. I wondered if any of them were from Kansas. "Sir!" Nick replied, his spine as straight as one of his arrows.

"Your squad is deployed to Grande Prairie," the general said. His snare drum was so tight that it didn't rattle at all. There was no room in it for anything but a military march. "Your mentor will join you. You will be in charge of monitoring the town itself, in particular the mills."

"Yes, sir!" Nick said, and his squad chorused behind him.

"Yamamoto!" The general moved on, not even pausing long enough to hear Kaori's reply. "You are being stationed in Edmonton, where you will serve as liaison to the regular Canadian Forces stationed there."

Kaori acquiesced without question, but I had a few. Sending the team with the least experience in North America, not to mention the team with the least proficiency in English, to work alongside regular Canadian soldiers as they drilled with live artillery seemed counterproductive. There certainly weren't mountains in Edmonton that would make Kaori's specialties useful. I was suddenly profoundly uncomfortable about what would happen to Owen.

"Thorskard!" General Speed said. "You and Lieutenant Porter will be decamping for Hinton tomorrow morning."

That wasn't a complete disaster, I thought. Hinton is the eastern mouth of the John A–Zuò Tunnel. It's a key strategic base, and it's much closer to the shadows of the mountains than

Fort Calgary, though it often goes untouched by Chinooks. Unless there's a train derailment, Fort Calgary is a much more tempting target. Hinton, the joke goes, is so unpleasant that even the dragons don't go there, but at least it would be relatively safe.

"Yes—" Owen started, but Speed put up his hand.

"I'm not finished," he said. Beside him, Porter ground his teeth. "Your squad stays here. You don't need them in Hinton, and they'll be assigned to the Chinook cleanup as needed here. Your bard too."

We were completely silent. The squad might not have been instant fans of Owen, but he was their dragon slayer. We'd been a team for more than a month now, and we slayed a dragon together. That sort of thing sticks with you. And yet here it was, barely Thanksgiving, and we were being separated. It was as good as if they'd told us flat out that we weren't passing muster, except that we clearly were. The Oil Watch was supposed to be about teamwork too, and it looked increasingly like someone had forgotten to mention that to General Speed.

We had mastered disposal much faster than Kaori had, even though the Wapiti we'd dealt with had been twice as large as hers. Nick's squad had failed entirely and nearly contaminated the base sewage system in the process. Owen's seat was much better in his riding, and while his accuracy wasn't as good as Nick's, he could complete more passes than the American due to his greater strength. He was the one who should be slaying dragons, and while they were sending him to a place where he would probably get some, they weren't sending the rest of us with him.

I realized that Owen was looking at me with a concerned expression on his face, and a second after that, I realized that his concern was not for himself. It all crashed in on me then. I'd spent the days since we got here learning all the dragon lore I could and shadowing the others as they trained, but I still had no specific job. I spent most of my logged call time in the communications office, practicing the bugle and painstakingly making notes about what everyone else was up to. Once Owen and the squad had gone their separate ways, though, I had no idea what I'd do.

General Speed didn't give us long to mull it over.

"I expect you to be packed and ready for inspection before dinner, and all drills except riding are postponed for the day," he said. "You're all dismissed."

He turned on his heel and strode out of the mess, not even checking to see that we were moving. Porter rose to his feet, slowly, like Lottie might have done when she was stiff. He always wore long sleeves, and the uniform had long trousers anyway. I wondered what burns they hid.

"You heard him," he said, his voice almost soft by comparison, even though bagpipes don't usually have that in them. "Get a move on."

Packing didn't take very long since we weren't going anywhere, so we went to the rec room that was allotted to the junior dragon slayers and waited for the others instead of just sitting around in the barracks getting depressed. Kaori and her two-female fire crew came in first and veered off to the corner, where they sat and talked quietly to one another. Nick was next and installed himself in the activity area, throwing darts at the dartboard with disturbing accuracy. I stared at him while everyone else trickled in. No one spoke.

Finally Aarons couldn't take it anymore and stood up.

"Okay, everyone just stay here for a moment," he said. "I'll be right back."

It wasn't like we had anywhere else to go, and none of us had really moved by the time he got back, carrying Owen's practice shield in one hand and a bag of white powder in the other. There was a hot plate in the rec room, theoretically for boiling water for tea or coffee while you were on downtime, and a sink beside it. Aarons turned on both burners and laid the shield down across them to heat. Then he measured water into the bag before sealing it and shaking it up.

"Legend tells us," he began, "that one day on the field of battle, a Viking war band fared ill. They did their best, but the results did not come, and at the end of the day they were exhausted and forlorn. When they sat down to make dinner, they realized that the griddle had gone missing, and then they were really extra sad, because they thought that meant they couldn't have a hot meal."

His timing needed some work, but he wasn't a bad story-teller. I listened carefully in case we ended up writing a song together.

"But all was not lost," he said, grinning a bit now, "because their clever smith had a solution."

"I'm sure he did," Courtney said, smirking, but the American smith laughed and, once Kaori translated, the Japanese smith smiled as well.

"He got the dragon slayer's shield, and he held it over the fire," Aarons continued. "And he poured in the batter he had made."

There was a sizzling sound as Aarons opened the bag and poured the newly mixed batter on to the shield.

"Ew," said Annie, wrinkling her nose. "Do you have any idea where that's been?"

Owen hadn't been using that shield to tilt, so I wasn't worried. I trusted Aarons. Trusted the story he was telling.

"Anyway, the shield was dented from the fight," Aarons continued. "The batter ran into the dents, and instead of flat pancakes, a new cake was invented."

All of the Americans were leaning forward now. The cakes smelled very good. I wondered how long Aarons had been carrying that mix with him. I filled in the story myself. His father had packed it in his suitcase when Aarons wasn't paying attention, and when he'd gotten to Gagetown and found it, he'd smiled and known that he was loved. I shook my head. It wasn't my story yet. I forced myself to pay attention.

"They called it *eibelskiver*," Aarons said, using a piece of flat steel to flip the round cakes over. I didn't remember Owen's shield being that dented. In fact, now that I was close, I didn't think I'd ever seen Owen practice with this shield at all. "And they ate it together—and remembered for all of their days."

He turned the little cakes onto a plate and poured more batter in. None of us said anything, and at last there was a pile of cakes on the plate and an empty bag. Aarons turned the burners off, leaving the shield to cool, and walked around the room, passing the *eibelskiver* out to every one of us.

As we ate, Annie asked Nick's fire crew foreman what it was

like to work in cities. He was from Miami, so they always had plenty of water available. From there they fell into one-upping each other. The Japanese fire crew joined in as best they could, one of the engineers translating, and Kaori came over to me.

"I think I have eaten these cakes before," she said.

"You know a lot of Vikings?" I asked.

"No," she said, and laughed. "Owen is the first. But these cakes are much like something I ate when I was in Hong Kong. I think your Vikings may have stolen them, not made them on the field of battle."

"You're probably right," I said. "But it makes a good story."

"You ought to know," she said and frowned. "You should know?"

"Yes," I said. "Well, both are correct, but the second is more idiomatic."

"I hate idioms," she said, but I could tell her heart wasn't in it.

We listened as one of her fire crew, through the engineer, told a story about racing a dragon's fire down a mountainside. It sounded terrifying, and also remotely possible, which just made it worse.

"Myself, and the others," Kaori said. "The girls. We will shave our heads tonight."

I looked at her. She had short hair already, but I could tell from the way she carried herself sometimes that she used to wear it long. She held her head like I did.

"Kaori," I started, not sure what I was even trying to say. She shook her head.

"Siobhan," she said. "We are part of your story now. The world should know that if it sees us."

I ran a hand through my close-cropped hair. It was long enough to tuck behind my ears again. I could use a haircut too, and said as much. Kaori smiled, and soon after that all the girls, even the Americans, retired to our barracks to take care of it. They could split us up and send us all over the province, but we had lived together this long, in a way that the guys hadn't, and that had made us into a team in a way the military hadn't predicted. The general was trying to limit Owen's influence on his own squad, but because of the billet assignment, his story would spread to the US and Japan. It was too late to stop it. All he could do now was chase the fire down the mountainside.

In the mess hall at breakfast the next morning, General Speed looked out over a row of newly shaved heads and frowned.

THEIR LIAISON

I was lonely with Owen and the other squads gone. It was so strange. There were only four of us in the barracks now, which meant more than half the beds were empty. Courtney took advantage of the space to requisition a large drafting board to sketch on. I had no idea what she was designing, but I gathered pretty quickly that she sketched things the way I sketched music, which is to say she did it all the time. But having paper handy made it much easier to remember what she had already done. Annie and Laura had work constantly. And I had nothing. Just endless days in the comm office, listening to radio chatter and feeling like I wasn't contributing anything to the Oil Watch at all, let alone to Owen.

The fire crew was sent out of Fort Calgary on a regular basis for that first week, putting out the fires the Chinook had started and treating the ground with chemicals in the hope that next planting season something would be able to grow on the razed ground. They told us what they saw outside the walls, and it was pretty grim. There were four small satellite farming communities that sheltered under the Fort's totem poles when the dragons came, and though three of them had escaped with minor damage, the fourth had been nearly leveled. That, of course, was the town where there was also an oil refinery. The cleanup crews our team worked with said that they had seen worse, but not by much. The only mercy was that, thanks to the Chinook's extreme visibility, the evacuation had prevented a death toll.

The thousand or so people who had lived in this unlucky town were now semi-permanent residents of the fort. They would live here at least for the winter—because we couldn't start reconstruction until the ground thawed in spring—unless they had somewhere else to go. By the time the first week wore down, almost all of the children had been sent to relatives back east, and only the adults remained.

It was an odd Thanksgiving and a colder one than I was used to, but that's par for the course for October in Alberta. We didn't have real turkeys, at least not the kind that you can carve, but there was enough food for everyone. When the train left the next morning with the last of the departing children on it, I couldn't quite shake the feeling that this winter was going to be entirely stranger than any I had ever experienced.

Emily, who was rather morbidly pleased to learn that I had been serving under *the* Lieutenant Declan Porter, sent a flurry of e-mails detailing her most recent ventures into perceived government conspiracy. The wave of Filipino workers had begun in the late eighties when it became apparent that the number of dragons slayed in Alberta (and Saskatchewan) was about to increase exponentially. They were brought in as experts in those days: Due to the number of dragon species on the islands in comparison to their relatively small land mass, the Filipinos were by necessity very good at cleaning up. Soon enough, though, wages had been cut, and before long the cleanup crews handled the worst jobs with no guarantee of long-term security.

The government of Alberta had been sanctioned by the UN twice, yet no one had ever recommended that the cleanup crews be incorporated into the Oil Watch, which made Emily think the sanctions were more a formality than anything. She also noted that Filipino dragon slayers were never posted to Canada, which meant that they never witnessed the conditions their compatriots worked under. Owen and I might tease Emily quite regularly for her ability to see conspiracies where there weren't any, but even I had to admit that this whole situation smelled pretty lousy.

Emily had no solution, though, which was unusual for her. She said that there were a few groups, both in and outside of Alberta, that were trying to get things changed, but they weren't making any progress. She thought this was largely because Alberta kept electing Conservative governments both nationally and provincially. This meant that the few members of the New Dragon Slayer Party who managed to get elected tried to make inroads, but their bills were always shot down on the floor. She did say that she would keep an eye out, and mentioned that the NDP had managed to get a member of Parliament elected in Strathcona, so perhaps there was hope. For now, though, it looked like we were at a dead end.

I was used to problems I could solve. I was used to support. Instead I monitored the chatter of the cleanup crews while they were out in the field and tried to ignore the impractical little voice in my head that insisted on whispering, "What would Lottie Thorskard do?" This was, I was pretty sure, a situation where she couldn't help.

As the cleanup operations wound down and the fire crews returned to their regular drills, it became apparent that someone was going to have to deal with the oil workers and farmers who would be staying with us for the winter. General Speed—who didn't really trouble himself with the small details, I'd noticed—flagged me down at breakfast one morning not long after the last trains departed with family members aboard.

"Bard McQuaid," he said, spitting the words out like gristle. "You will report to the mess assigned to the refugees."

"Sir?" I said, shifting my tray in my hands. I could hold it, just, but if my muscles spasmed, we'd both end up with egg on our faces. Literally.

"As their liaison, McQuaid," he said. "You will ensure that lines of communication remain open between them and the Fort quartermasters, and you will deal with their problems, unless they are so large that you cannot handle them."

He looked down at my tray, which was shaking slightly despite my best efforts, and made no effort to conceal his scorn.

"You have your orders, bard," he told me. "Go sit down."

I did, as quickly as I could, my milk carton listing dangerously close to the curled edge of the plastic before I managed to set the whole thing down on the table. I was very well aware that General Speed thought he was insulting me by giving me this assignment. He hadn't even bothered to speak quietly about it, so the entire mess had heard my orders. I didn't really care. I wanted something to do, and this was better than the comm office.

Since they'd been out in the field aiding the cleanup crews, I had yet to manage a proper conversation with any of the refugees. They didn't even eat with us, which annoyed me to no end, and I wasn't sure where they billeted either, though I assumed that if I followed the orange line painted on the floor in the hallways, I would find them soon enough.

"And then we had the dragon over for tea and scones, and it agreed to pay for my PhD," Courtney concluded, and I realized she had probably been talking to me for a while. "Earth to Siobhan! We're starting to feel all neglected here."

"Sorry," I said. "I was thinking."

"Obviously," said Aarons. Now that the dragon slayers were gone, I sat with the fire crew again. That helped stave off my loneliness, at least when they were in the mess for meals. I had missed them, though I didn't miss the way Davis's fingers itched towards my knife and fork every time I struggled with something. I didn't really blame him, though. Some people were just born to help.

"I asked if you were ready for your big meeting," Courtney repeated.

I grimaced as I wrestled with the carton of milk before Wilkinson just reached over and took it from me. He didn't make a big production of it, and he didn't seem to expect acknowledgment, the way that some of the others might. I missed milk bags, though. With large-handled scissors, I could open those.

"I'm trying not to worry about it," I replied, pouring milk as deftly as I could. "I mean, it's me and a room full of grown-up farmers and oil workers. What could possibly go wrong?"

They stared at me for a second before they realized that I was actually concerned. Without meaning to, I had become the reliable one. The one who was always self-assured. And now that I had no idea what to do, now that I had remembered that I was the youngest and the least likely to be taken seriously, they were spooked and didn't know how to offer help. The silence stretched uncomfortably between us for the first time since the early days in Gagetown, until Aarons finally elbowed Annie and she leaned forward.

"Just make sure they don't get bored," Annie suggested. For something she was making up on the fly, it was actually pretty good advice. "I mean, we're probably going to go stark-staring bonkers in here all winter, and we don't spend quite as much time outside as they do."

"They do still have jobs," Parker pointed out. "Courtney managed to get the rigs back in shape, and what else do farmers do in the winter anyway?"

"You have clearly never experienced a prairie winter," Laura said.

"I'm from Northern Ontario," Parker reminded her. "I'm not sure how much worse it can get."

"You guys are really not helping," I told them.

"Hey, a lot of them are from Ontario anyway," Gratton pointed out. "Maybe they're already fans of yours."

I hadn't even thought of that. Suddenly I really wanted to throw up. But I didn't, because General Speed was on his feet to dismiss us, and we had to move. Porter had been much more relaxed about that sort of thing, leaving it to the bells and calls to remind us when it was time to go. Speed liked us to be halfway there before the signal was given. Fortunately he didn't jump the gun by too much, and I was able to finish eating without rushing like a fool.

"Have a good day," I said as the fire crew, already carrying their outerwear, headed to the caravan.

"Shut up," Anderson said, but he was smiling.

"At least we're not going to get rickets," Dorsey pointed out. "Or whatever it is you get when you don't get any air or sunlight."

"Thanks," I said, and they were gone.

Courtney and I walked towards the forges, where she'd been spending her days with Aarons and the other smiths. I wondered how much that pissed off her dad, but a few nights ago, Aarons had caught a glimpse of her drafting board and declared that it was time they both starting cross-training. Courtney had been making nails ever since, which she hated, and which we didn't even need, but Aarons assured her it was a time-honoured tradition.

"Nails," he said, "are where you start. They are what hold the whole craft together. Like a house."

"Aarons, you are so full of shit," Courtney said, but she went every day, and every night she passed him the drafting board and made him design something so that she could point out its flaws in a loud voice.

After Courtney turned off down the hall that led to the forges, I continued on my own to where the refugees were living. I hoped that none of us would be too disappointed with this arrangement. I stopped outside their mess and took a deep breath. Then I pushed through the door.

The mess was more than half empty, thank goodness, since

all of the oil workers had gone for the day, and even some of the farmers had left to finish what late harvest the Chinook hadn't burned. But there were still a lot of people.

"Imagine them in their underwear," I heard Sadie whisper. That did not help. "Imagine they're the Guard," Emily suggested. That made much more sense.

"Good morning!" I said, not quite shouting, but definitely louder than usual. Once I had their attention, I quieted a bit. "My name is Siobhan McQuaid. I am part of the Thorskard squad, and I am going to be your liaison for the winter, or until you leave us."

I paused, and there was no general outrage at my presence, so I took heart and kept going. If this was a story, I could do it with no problems. And it kind of was: This was the first time I'd done something useful as a member of the Oil Watch. This Siobhan didn't exist yet, and I could make her be whatever I wanted her to be. I made her taller and as authoritative as possible.

"If you have any issues or requirements that are not being met, please feel free to approach me," I continued. "I know that circumstances aren't exactly ideal, but I think we should be able to do all right for ourselves this winter, as long as we talk about it. I will come down every morning after breakfast, and if you need me outside of that time, you can leave a message in the main communications office."

Another pause. This one slightly more awkward. I dropped into parade rest and did my best to look unthreatening, though I couldn't imagine that I had been threatening at all.

"Any questions?" I said.

"Just one," said a voice from the back. I couldn't see him, but he sounded young.

When I'd entered the room, before I called for attention, I had heard them talking among themselves. For the most part, they were exactly what I had expected: low brass and the odd bassoon. Common sense and hard work, and a fear of nothing except fire from the mountains. They were flexible, and they were willing to rebuild. They were exactly the sorts of people I liked to work with. They reminded me of home and of the people I wanted to protect when our time in the Oil Watch was done. Suddenly, I wanted to win them over, not just cohabitate. I wanted them to see me as home too, even if it was just something that reminded them of how life should be, not how it was.

This voice was different. He was practical, or he wouldn't be here, but there was movement in his tone that I hadn't encountered in anyone except Nick since I'd enlisted. Nick was controlled, his violin classically trained, like you'd expect from a dragon slayer. This was something else. This was five finger picks and the ability to play all the notes together, rapidly, one right after the other.

"Just one," the banjo repeated. I looked for him through the crowd, but I still couldn't see him. "Can you tell us about the time you burned down Manitoulin Island?"

THE BANJO

If I had a party trick, telling the Manitoulin story would be it. Whether I set it to music or chanted it like the Viking bards of old, it came out of me as easily as water flowing downhill. Even before I had registered surprise at the request, I could feel my diaphragm getting ready for it; I heard the music in my head. The request was repeated from around the room, and I decided that if this was to be my way in, I would take it. Maybe, as Annie had said, they were just bored. Maybe they didn't respect me or the Oil Watch, but they just wanted a show. I could do that. I was a bard, and the Oil Watch was supposed to be flexible when it came to civilian relations. I wouldn't always concede, I decided, but if they opened the door first, I was sure as hell going to let them hold it for me while I went through.

"Could I get a glass of water?" I asked, every inch the small town country girl. I didn't have to worry about rank in this room. I had to worry about experience. "I walked here kind of quickly, and I don't think you want to hear me sing like that."

There was some laughter, and an older woman passed me a cup. I still couldn't see the banjo, and I stopped scanning the crowd for him so I could focus on the song. I drained the cup and tried to think of fire. As usual, it wasn't very far away. The smells, the way they clung to my hair even after I'd gotten out of the hospital. I hadn't been able put that in the music, how it felt to burn, but I'd never forgotten it anyway.

Like always, they were leaning in before I was through the first few bars, and by the time I got to the part where the dragons flew over the car, they were mine entirely. They all joined in on the last chorus, the one about waking up in the hospital to find out that the skies were safe again. That was new. I'd written this song as a solo, like I did with anything that wasn't orchestral. Yet here were harmonies and counter-melodies I hadn't written, merely laid the path for. I thought about the cold October sun on Kaori's newly shorn head. Maybe this was what being part of the story was all about.

They applauded when we finished, and I clapped too. I wondered if they knew that this was the first time I'd actually sung this song with other people. When the clapping faded, they asked me questions for a while, mostly directions and who to talk to about certain requirements, and I promised them better maps than the ones they'd been given so they'd be able to find their way around. I moved from table to table, both professional and approachable, and trying desperately to remember everyone's names. Even with most of them gone for the day, I knew it was a lost cause. But it was a start. At last, I made it to the back of the room and looked around again for the banjo.

"Man," he said, sliding down the bench to sit directly across from me as the two men I'd been speaking with got up to leave. "That song is really not the same without you to sing it."

"You sing it without me?" I asked. I knew we had a pretty decent number of YouTube subscribers, and Emily had told me that there were a few video replies of people singing their versions of my songs, but I never imagined it on a larger scale.

"Do you mind?" he asked, elbows on the table.

"Of course not," I said. "I'm just a bit surprised."

"That a bunch of farmers sing a song about a dragon slayer who went over and above the call of duty to defend another bunch of farmers?" he said. "Yeah, I can't imagine why that song would speak to us."

"I'm used to writing for a very small audience," I told him.

"What, like the busts of Beethoven and Bach that sit on top of your piano?" he said.

"How do you know about that?" I said, shocked.

"Because it's a piano," he said. "What the hell else do you put on a piano?"

"Fair point," I said. It was a little bit unnerving how quickly we fell into rhythm. Maybe I was getting predictable. "Though you could make a strong argument for Liszt and Mozart."

"I'm Peter, by the way," he said, extending a hand across the table. I shook it, and he didn't even look down to see my scars. "And I think it was kind of adorable how you introduced yourself to a room full of people who already knew who you were."

"It's the training," I said, putting my hand back in my lap. "It encourages redundancies."

"Don't I know it," he said. He was, I decided, much more gregarious than Owen, even more so than Nick. Maybe that's what was throwing me off. I added it to my ever-increasing list of questions to put to Sadie at the next opportunity. "Do you have any idea how many forms I've had to fill out since I got here?"

"Yeah," I said. "What do you think I spent last week reading?"

"My condolences," he said, but he didn't look sorry at all. Then he leaned forward with an overly eager expression on his face. I braced myself. Emily looked like this sometimes. It could be exhausting. "So," he said. "Thorskard and Porter banished for the whole winter. That's gotta suck for you."

"We go where we're sent," I said. It was the unofficial motto of the Oil Watch. Well, the unofficial motto of the Oil Watch that was fit for print.

"That's all you got?" he said. "I thought you'd be writing angry emo music about it by now."

"Excuse me?" I said.

"You know." He gestured vaguely, like he was playing a piano. "Like you do."

"I record what Owen's done," I told him. "And he hasn't done much lately, because he's been busy training."

"Right," Peter said. "Training."

"Besides," I went on, "I can't play my own stuff anymore, and this place doesn't exactly have a recording studio."

"Yeah," he drawled, "it's too bad that a few dozen farmers with nothing better to do in their spare time than learn to play the fiddle couldn't just wash up at your door."

"You play the fiddle?" I asked. He really didn't look like the type.

"Well, no," he said. "But I know at least three guys who do."

I considered this. I'd tried to tell myself otherwise, but I missed music so profoundly that it hurt sometimes, almost as much as it hurt to try playing something only to be reminded that I couldn't.

"I can't write it like I used to, either," I told him. "Do you have a friend who can take musical dictation?"

"No," he said. "I'm not even sure I have a friend who can read music. Not that that stops us from playing it."

"Somehow I don't think this is what General Speed meant when he told me to liaise with you people," I said.

"What do you think he meant?" Peter asked. He had that look in his eyes. That Emily look.

"I gave up trying to figure that man out almost immediately," I told him. "It's too depressing if I look at him too long."

"Well that's uplifting," Peter said. "I'll tell you this for free: wintering here isn't exactly a great option for us, but it's the only one we've got right now, and when we thought Lieutenant Porter was going to be here, it was a lot more appealing."

"Why?" I asked, even though I had a feeling I already knew the answer.

"Did you know that in the entire history of dragon attacks in Western Canada, there have been thousands of dead people and only one dead Chinook?" he asked rhetorically. Of course I knew that. "And the Chinook wasn't even slayed in Canada."

"But it was slayed by Declan Porter," I finished his thought.

"Exactly," he said. "We felt safe here. Like someone cared about more than oil and wheat for a change."

"Owen cares about more than oil and wheat," I said, without even thinking about it.

"We know that too," Peter said. "And look where that got him."

I shifted uncomfortably. I had grown up admiring the Oil

Watch for what it did around the world. Meeting Lottie and Hannah, and even Aodhan, hadn't damaged my perceptions of it either, but ever since I'd joined, it was like I was overturning stone after stone and nothing good was ever beneath them. I wanted to love the Oil Watch. I wanted to be proud to put on my beret. And usually I was. But here was yet another sign that something, either in the Watch itself or in the government, was working against Lottie's plan. Against Owen. And it didn't seem to care who got in the way. The notes tugged at me, stronger than they had in months.

"It's just for the winter," I said, even though I knew as I said it that I sounded hopelessly naive. I needed time to think, time alone with a lot of staff paper to sketch out all the notes that pulled at me. It was time to sort them into the tunes they went with. It was time to write music again, even though I had thought until I walked into this room that there was nothing more to write music about.

"Of course it is," Peter said, but not unkindly. Maybe he could tell I was thinking. Maybe he just thought I was stupid. He smiled. "You know," he said. "I play the mandolin, and you sing. You know what this means."

"I already have a YouTube channel, Peter," I told him. But I could feel the music pulling at me, and I couldn't help but smile. I hadn't felt like this in months, not since I'd arrived at Gagetown. It was nice to have a musician around me again.

"Yeah, but you haven't posted anything in months," he said.

"I've been a little busy," I reminded him. "Serving my country and all that."

"Uh-huh," he said. "And how's that working out for you?"

"All right," I said, holding his gaze. "We'll give it a try."

"Excellent," Peter said, and I held up one curled hand.

"Don't tell too many people," I cautioned him. "This is an experiment and possibly outside my orders, and I really don't want it getting out of control before I know what it is."

"All right," he said.

"I have time for music between two and four o'clock, unless there is a dragon attack," I continued. "I'll get you directions to the room that are easier to follow than the map they probably gave you."

"I look forward to it," he said. "And I'll get you that list, so you'll know what else you've got to work with."

"Thanks," I said. "I have to go now. I've got a duty shift."

"It was lovely to meet you," Peter said as I stood up.

"Likewise," I told him. "See you tomorrow."

He nodded and I headed for the door. I was more than half-way to the comm office before I realized that I had just agreed to write music with a veritable stranger. For me, that was practically second base. It was entirely possible that Sadie was never, ever going to stop laughing at me.

THE FAMILIAR CEILING

There's not really a lot you can say about winter in Alberta. It snowed right after Hallowe'en—but not as much as I had expected—and then it got really, really cold. It was a different kind of cold than I was used to. The sky stayed mostly blue, and the sun on what snow we had was blinding. If you sat next to a window, you'd boil with the heat. And if you opened that window, not that many windows in Fort Calgary could be opened, you would freeze to death in fairly short order. At least it was dry, and the snow stayed light and fluffy instead of getting weighted down with slush. Peter and Laura tried to explain what the difference between thirty below and forty below was to the rest of us.

"If it's thirty below," Laura said, "and you leave the milk in the car, you can just run out and get it."

"Yeah," said Peter. "At forty below, you have to put on your coat, hat, mittens, scarf, and boots, and by the time you get to the car, the milk is frozen."

I didn't have to go outside very often, for which I was profoundly grateful, but on the rare occasion that I did venture out, the cold took my breath away and I could feel my nose hairs freeze.

"Why the hell does anyone live here?" I asked, standing next to my bed, peeling off layer after layer of clothing and still feeling like I'd never be warm again.

"Same reason they brave the dragons," Laura told me.

Oil. The answer was almost always oil.

"And it's going to be like this until March?" Annie said.

"If we're lucky," Laura replied. "If we're not, May."

"As long as the snow melts by itself, I don't really care," Courtney said.

I nodded. Fort Calgary did get early thaws sometimes, but they were always the result of a Chinook attack. The dragon could raise the temperature in a matter of hours. The record was minus 45 to 26 in four hours. I wasn't in a hurry to see it happen for myself.

Two weeks before Christmas, we drew lots to see who would get to go home for the holiday. It was a weeklong leave, and the first proper one we had had since we'd arrived. Fort Calgary was so isolated that on a 24- or 48-hour leave, all you could really do was ignore the calls. It wasn't enough time to go anywhere besides Edmonton, and there wasn't much in Edmonton to see. The only problem was that we couldn't all be spared, and thus we decided to let random draw decide.

I drew Owen's lot and my own, announcing which was

which when Courtney passed me the hat she'd used to hold the tags. Mine was the pass, and Owen's wasn't.

"Don't you even think about it," Anderson said when he saw the expression on my face. He'd drawn a stay too. "You drew your own pass fair and square."

I had a phone call scheduled with Owen that night. We spoke once a week, as per Porter's request. Since Owen was separated from his squad, Porter felt he deserved to be kept up to date as to what was going on. I was pretty sure the calls were recorded, so I hadn't told him about Peter and the music we'd been writing together. I wasn't sure how General Speed would react to my writing music again, and I wanted to be sure I had a whole piece written and recorded if he decided to shut us down. The next time Owen and I got to talk, I might have taken the risk, but I only had enough time to tell him that he'd lost the draw.

"You can have mine, if you want," I told him.

"Your mother would kill me," Owen said. "Besides, then I'd have to leave Porter here by himself, and I think that would make him even more off-kilter than he already is."

"He's that bad?" I asked.

"He really hates the mountains," Owen said. "Though he does appreciate the fact that it's too hilly to practice tilting."

"Constantinople is desolate without you," I told him.

"Horses can be very emotional, but our relationship is nobody's business but the Turks'," he said, and we both laughed. The horse probably didn't miss him at all, but I did. Even with the liaising and the music I wrote with Peter, there was always a twinge where Owen should have been, a feeling that I wasn't doing my job. Also, I missed my friend.

"As far as I know, they don't make fireproof snowsuits for horses," Owen said. "We spend all our time in the forest with the logging crews. It's about a million times worse than camping with Dad."

"But you're doing okay?" That was about as personal as I could get. For all I knew, General Speed was listening live right now.

"Well, I'm getting plenty of exercise," Owen said. "We had a 'Bascan Long last week, and Porter and I got it in the woods outside of town. He was not kidding about the part where you can tangle them in the trees. It was a fucking mess."

"I'm glad to see he's rubbing off on you," I said. He laughed. Owen didn't usually swear much.

"Do me a favour, would you?" he said.

"Of course," I told him.

"Bring back some kind of British food if you can, and send it to Porter on the train," Owen said. "I think it would make him feel a bit better."

"You know what they say about Trondheim," I said. "It's pretty much a centre for culture like that."

"Sadie can bring souvenirs," Owen pointed out. "And if you tell either your mother or Hannah, I am sure they'll help you find something."

"Good point," I said. "Any requests for yourself?"

"Surprise me," he said.

"I'll do my best," I told him. I already had several ideas, but I wanted to clear them with Emily first.

"Say hi to Sadie for me," he added, his voice a bit quieter. "Tell her I miss her."

"You can do that on the phone," I pointed out.

"Yeah, but it's not the same."

"I don't think hearing it from me is going to be quite the same," I said.

"She'll understand," Owen said. "Just don't kiss her. That'll only confuse the issue."

"Right," I said. "And I was so looking forward to that part."

"I think we should hang up now," Owen said, "before this gets any weirder."

"Merry Christmas, Owen," I said. "If I don't talk to you before then."

"And a Happy New Year," he said back. "Now go catch your train."

Technically, we were still on duty when we were on the train, which was just as well or we'd use our entire leaves getting to and from Toronto. It meant that I had files to read and official e-mails to send, and also that we had to stay in uniform, just in case one of the lieutenants traveling with us decided to make an inspection. Peter had sung Christmas carols nonstop for the three days leading up to our departure, and I had so much music in my head that I thought I was ready to burst. Playing with him was fun and an interesting change, but it was slow, even by my new standards, and I was itching to get to Emily and our recording software.

And, you know, see my parents. And sleep in a room by myself.

It's possible that Mum and Dad had meant to pick me up by themselves, but since Sadie's train from Gagetown was getting into Dansworth at approximately the same time mine was, there was quite the welcoming crew for us. We weren't the only ones, I was happy to note. I'm not sure how many people even live in Kapuskasing, but then when we'd stopped in Thunder Bay, which was the closest the train went to the town, and Parker and Gratton had gotten off the train, we saw their welcoming parties through the windows, and it looked like the entire population had made the trek. In Toronto, Mum and Dad were on the platform with Sadie's parents and Sadie, whose train had arrived ahead of schedule, along with all of the Thorskards and, much to my surprise, Catalina. There was a lot of hugging, basically, is what I am saying.

Once we'd finished and gotten everyone into their cars for the drive back home, I finally let myself relax.

"They're not throwing a party for us, are they?" I asked as we passed the "Welcome to Trondheim" sign. I was tired, and my uniform was wrinkled.

"Not today," Dad said, rather unreassuringly. "But there are a lot of people who are excited to see you while you're home."

"Great," I said. "As long as I get to sleep and take a bubble bath first."

"You take bubble baths?" Mum said.

"Well, no," I said. "But I don't see any reason why I shouldn't start."

"The military has changed you, darling," Dad said.

"You have no idea," I told him.

And, really, they didn't. When I had left them in June, I'd been uncertain and still not very good at doing things for myself. Now I was more confident and much more able. I was also, thanks to the squad, better at letting other people help me do the things I couldn't. Annie didn't do my buttons unless I asked, but she tied my tie most mornings, and the boys always seemed to make sure that the lids were off everything on the table before I needed anything. Even Peter, new as he was, would have my bugle case open for me when I was ready to put the horn away and turn to composition. It had become second nature, and I didn't even mind. Of course, I had a whole assortment of new problems that my parents wouldn't understand, let alone help me solve. Not even Hannah, the most thoughtful of the Thorskards, could fix those for me. It kept me from getting full of myself.

"The Thorskards are coming for dinner tonight, though," Mum said. "And Christmas Eve as well. We thought it was fair."

"They're practically family anyway," I said. "Did you invite the Fletchers?"

"Yes," said Dad, "but I think they want Sadie to themselves for a while before they start letting her out into the wild. At least you and Owen have each other, and you're in Canada. Sadie's very far away, and I think they're feeling it."

"Did Aodhan talk to them?" I asked.

"They don't really talk to the Thorskards much," Mum said. Her face was a bit hard, I thought, but maybe she was just focused on the road.

"Oh, and Emily is coming for brunch tomorrow," Dad said, seamlessly changing the subject. "She seemed to think you had a government to overthrow or something?"

"You know how it is with her," I said. "There's always something."

We pulled into the driveway and got out of the car, and I was surprised to find that the house didn't look smaller. I had wondered if it might. I hadn't done a lot of traveling before I'd left for Alberta. We'd gone to Florida, of course, but not that often. In stories, whenever the hero comes home, things always look a little smaller. The comforts of home are welcome, obviously, and much needed rest is had, but the horizon always beckons.

I paused in the kitchen while Mum started dinner and Dad set the table, watching them go about their tasks like I'd just come home from school instead of halfway across the continent. Their rhythm hadn't changed, any more than the house had. Dad set the extra places as if he did it all the time, and Mum was already humming tunelessly to herself while she measured and chopped.

"Go on up," Mum said. "We haven't made your room into a Zen garden or anything."

"I'm glad to hear it," I said.

"Have a nap, if you want," Dad added. "I'm jumping the gun a bit setting the table. They won't be over until six. You've got plenty of time."

Plenty of time. Seven days. I shook my head, laughing to myself as I pulled my kit behind me up the stairs to my room. I was better traveled now, sure, and probably more jaded too, but I wasn't the hero of this story, and I had no plans to be. I was the bard, and home would be what I made it, wherever Owen led me, because I was the one who told everyone else what home was.

Seven days. I lay down on my bed and looked up at the familiar ceiling. I didn't nap right away, though. I had too much to do. I thought going back to Trondheim would be like stepping back into a bubble. I would be with my parents again, and even though my car was waiting for me in the driveway, full of gas no less, I was still back in the place where I had been a child.

What happened was almost exactly the opposite.

NARY A BUTTON

My parents woke me up after two hours of sleeping so that we could have dinner, but there were no bells or calls. No one yelled at the Thorskards for arriving late. When Mum finally finished putting all the food—all my favourites, I noticed—on the table, there was no rush to eat. And the conversation wasn't exactly regulation either.

"I can't believe Speed thinks that putting Owen and Porter together is solving a problem," Lottie said. Hannah rolled her eyes. I could imagine that they had already had this conversation ten times. Still, Lottie had a point. If Speed had wanted to crush Owen, he would have assigned us to Amery and let the American lieutenant's disdain do his work for him. Instead, we got Porter, who didn't precisely encourage us to colour outside the lines, but who didn't complain when we did.

"The refugees were upset that Lieutenant Porter was gone," I said. "It was their first official complaint. The general just told them it was military deployment and none of their business."

"Which is true," Aodhan put in.

"Could you pass the broccoli?" Hannah asked. Mum handed it over. "And Siobhan, it sounds rude when you call them refugees."

"I know," I said. "But it sounds extra dumb when I call them farmers or oil workers, so I just stick with the word they gave me."

"I'm sure that's very comforting," Hannah said. Lottie snorted.

"But aside from the political shenanigans, everything is all right?" Dad asked.

My e-mails home had been pretty brief and possibly not private. Mostly they were a general summary of events. I had yet to really tell them about Peter and the fact that I was writing music on a regular basis again.

"Everything is fine," I said. "We're literally burrowed in for the winter. I don't have to go outside unless I want to, and from what Owen tells me, he's got more field practice in since moving to Hinton than he did the whole time we were in Fort Calgary."

"That's good news," Catalina said. She had already booked her ticket when Owen found out that he wouldn't be coming home, but hadn't canceled because Lottie had talked her into visiting anyway. She saw Aodhan infrequently enough as it was, Lottie reasoned, and just because Owen wasn't there was no reason to forget she was family. "Now, tell us about the Singe'n'burn."

I did, thanking my lucky stars she hadn't asked about the Chinook. I was still sorting out how the story came together. It resisted my efforts to put it to music. Peter had tried to help, because he'd lived through the attack too, but his lack of technical proficiency made it difficult.

By the time I was done telling the story, Mum was serving dessert and I was nearly asleep in my chair. The Thorskards didn't stick around for long, and while my parents were doing dishes in the kitchen, I went and sat on the piano bench. The lid was closed, and there was a layer of dust on it. My sheet music was gone, some packed away in the bench with the overflow in the small filing cabinet that sat beside the piano. Back in its place was my grandmother's hymnal, opened to a random page as it had been before I'd learned what music was.

"Siobhan?" I turned around and saw my Dad standing in the doorway to the kitchen with a tea towel thrown over his shoulder.

"I'm fine." I was surprised to find out that I was telling the truth. "I'm going to bed."

"Sleep well, darling!" Mum called from the kitchen. Dad came over and ruffled my very short hair.

"See you in the morning," he said. "If Emily gets here before you're awake, we'll hold the food until you're ready."

"Thanks," I said. "But if I sleep past six, I am going to be really surprised."

"You know," he said, "now that you're not on duty, you could always just roll over and go back to sleep."

I felt a bit silly. That thought had never even occurred to me.

I got out of bed at eight o'clock, unable to stand being still for any longer. While I waited for Emily, I started sorting through the few things I had brought with me from Fort Calgary.

I didn't really have presents for anyone except Sadie, who was getting a bundle of handwritten notes from Owen. I hoped no one would mind too much. I had an abundance of papers packed in my kit, though. About half of them were the files on which I'd spent my train ride working. I should be receiving another bundle by courier before I left, for the ride back. The rest were all my attempts at music, and they were a mess.

I'd given up trying to teach Peter proper notation almost immediately. Instead, I told him the letters to write down. This meant that I had sheets of what looked like code, and none of the music it produced had any shape at all. Fortunately, I had the shape—the rhythm and the dynamics, how the notes were to be played—in my head. When Emily got here, she could help me make all the conversions, and then we'd have actual playable music. I sorted the sheets into piles on my bed in the order of how important or complicated I thought they were, and stopped to add to them where I noticed gaps.

"Siobhan!" Mum called from downstairs. I looked at the clock and sighed. Off duty for fewer than twenty-four hours, and I was already lacking discipline. And I was still in my pajamas.

"Be right down!" I said. I could hear Emily chatting to them as I dressed. It was a relief to wear these clothes. Nary a button in sight.

"Hi, Emily!" I said as I pounded down the stairs. I gave her a quick hug. "How are you doing?"

"I'm good," she said. "Dad's Christmas presents came in the mail this morning, and he got to them before I did. But I managed to snag the DVDs I ordered for him, so at least that will be a surprise."

"We all know how much your father likes surprises," Dad said. "Now sit down, the bacon's ready."

"Well," Emily said, taking in the mess of papers on my bed and floor. "You've been busy."

"I'm playing to my strengths," I said, and winced. "No pun intended."

Emily laughed, and we started to work. She dug the staff paper out from the drawer in my desk and started writing everything down. It was so much easier this way. Peter was fun to work with, but he got distracted very easily, asked a lot of questions, and didn't know how to draw a quarter note. Emily could get distracted and ask questions, to be sure, but that didn't stop her from writing things down. Gradually, she filled the staff paper with recognizable music, and I filled her in on everything I had been up to in Fort Calgary.

"General Speed has quite the reputation online," she said.

"I'm not surprised," I told her. "Do they talk about his daughters at all?"

"They know he has some, but not much else besides," Emily said. "I haven't brought them up."

"Thanks," I said. "I really like Courtney, and I'd hate for the Internet to get a hold of her before I've warned her about it."

"Seems fair," Emily said. "Anyway, Speed is as old-guard as they come. He doesn't like the idea of support squads at all. He claims it leads to fraternization."

"He's . . . not wrong," I said, thinking about how easily my own crew helped me get through meals and, of course, what the general's own daughter was up to. "But I think that would happen anyway."

"Of course it would happen anyway," Emily said. "But he thinks that the Oil Watch should be for dragon slayers only, and that the cleanup should be done by private contractors."

"And I assume he doesn't mean Darktide?" I looked down at what she was writing. "The guitar rests for four bars after that, by the way."

"Nope," Emily said, marking off a measure of rests with a flourish. "Man, your Peter really sucks at this."

"He's not my Peter," I said. "And he's doing his best."

"You should probably nix the defensiveness before you talk to Sadie about him," Emily said, grinning like a fox. "She'll eat you alive for that."

I rolled my eyes, but I knew that it was true.

"I like the turn to guitars and fiddles, though," Emily said. "It's a bit more country than usual, but I think it will be easier for people to play on their own."

"It's still really weird to think about playing with anyone else besides the TSS band," I admitted. "The first time the refugees joined in with my Manitoulin song, I almost forgot the words."

"I wish I'd heard it," Emily said. "Not the part where you panicked, but the part where they all sang. It was probably wonderful."

"It was pretty good," I admitted. "Maybe I'll figure out a way to record it. Some of the guys have laptops with mics, but the recordings sound pretty wretched."

"I don't suppose if you requisitioned something, Speed would get nervous," Emily said.

"I don't think General Speed gets nervous," I said.

"He sent Owen and Porter to the sticks," Emily pointed out. "That sounds like nerves to me. In any case, I'm glad you have time to record while you're home. We'll dole the songs out over the next few months, and it'll be like you're here all the time."

"I'm glad to know you miss me," I said. "Do you think I should wear my uniform?"

"No," Emily said. "But I think we should hang it up behind you, so that people remember what you're up to."

"Good," I said. "I don't mind it, but I'm really enjoying wearing my own clothes again."

"I love the hat, though," Emily said, plunking it down on her own head. "Do you think if I asked nicely, they'd send me one?"

"Nope," I told her. "You're probably on too many watch lists."

She laughed, and we turned back to the papers that were scattered all over my bed.

A PERFECTLY LEGITIMATE
FORM OF CAKE

Sadie came over on the morning of the twenty-third. My parents were excruciatingly polite to her while she was standing in the kitchen taking her snow boots off. That's when I realized that there was something she hadn't told me.

"So?" I said, once we were safe upstairs in my room. "What's up?"

"It's my parents, obviously," Sadie said, flopping gracelessly down on my bed. I still found myself sitting at attention and straightening every time someone said my name. I'm not sure I could have slumped if my life depended on it.

"They're not pleased you went to England?"

"I think they were hoping that I'd go overseas and finally get away from Lottie's influence," Sadie said. "But then my mentor had to go and be nearly as crazy as the Thorskards. They think I can't make my own damn decisions."

"What do they have against the Thorskards?" I asked. As

far as I knew, the whole town loved them.

"Well," Sadie said. "In theory, nothing. I mean, they're thrilled to have local dragon slayers and all, but Dad's always been fairly active in local politics."

She meant Conservative politics. We'd had the same MP for our whole lives, but he was getting older. It was a very ill-kept secret that Sadie's dad would be our next candidate. Mum said the Health Unit had a list of extra dentists on standby, just in case they had to replace him.

"Won't having a dragon slayer daughter help?" I said. "I mean, that's usually pretty good press."

"It would if I were a normal dragon slayer," Sadie said. "But I have known ties to radical thinkers. And I'll never be a normal dragon slayer anyway. I'm not born to it."

"You really think Trondheim will invest in a scandal?" I asked. "Most people just vote for the person they went to high school with."

"The Conservatives favour a more American approach," Sadie said. Her voice sounded like Hannah's. The one that was always sad and a little bitter when she talked about our neighbours to the south. "They won't nominate Dad when his daughter is a de facto poster girl for the NDP."

"Is he really upset?" I asked. My parents didn't even like to attend school board meetings, but they had voted for the New Dragon Slayer Party since its inception. I planned to follow their example, now that I had reached voting age.

"I think it's just that he doesn't understand," Sadie said. "Which is totally fair, because I don't understand him either. We're both doing what we feel is right, and it unintentionally crosses paths."

"I hope it doesn't get too awkward," I told her.

"You and me both," she said. Then she sat up, a bright smile on her face. "Now, tell me about the boys."

"Oh, God," I said. "What did Owen tell you?"

"Something about an American who thinks he's a super-hero," Sadie said. "And you've mentioned a Peter."

I explained Nick as quickly as I could. With him gone on assignment, he was the less immediate concern.

"Sounds to me like he's a good guy," Sadie said when I was done.

"Well, yes," I said. "That's the problem."

"Because he's a dragon slayer?"

"Yeah," I said. "Well, that and he's set on returning to New York and joining the NYPD after his tour is up."

"That's four years from now," Sadie said. "You plan way too far ahead."

"Someone has to," I pointed out.

"What's your concern, then?" she asked.

"I like being his friend, but I don't want him to think I want to be more than his friend," I said.

"Right," Sadie said. "That is not your problem. That is his problem. You be as friendly as you want, be as *you* as you want, and don't let anyone trick you into thinking you've made some kind of promise. Because you haven't."

"I'm not sure that's how it works," I said.

"That's how it should work," Sadie said. "Aren't you sup-posed to be some kind of trailblazer?"

It was my turn to collapse back into the pillows now. "I didn't think it would be so constantly exhausting."

Sadie laughed and lay down beside me. "Okay, so that was

the easy one. Now tell me about Peter."

"I think he's the easy one," I said. "I only see him professionally."

"Siobhan, you write music with him," she said. "For you that's practically second base."

"You know, I thought that at first, like those exact words," I said. "But I don't think it's like that after all. We have music, but aside from that there's nothing to really talk about. He doesn't understand us, not really. I don't think he'd buy in long term."

"Uh-huh," Sadie said. "Well, when the dam finally breaks on all this denial, I'm only an e-mail away."

"Tell me about the North Sea," I said, suddenly desperate to change the subject.

"It's freaking cold," she said. "The scuba training was miserable. But aside from that it's kind of fun, unless we've got rig duty. Then we just sit out on these enormous metal platforms and wait for the dragons to come get us."

"You're actually slaying dragons?" I said. She hadn't mentioned that in her e-mails.

"Of course," she said. "What else did we sign up for?"

"We get to spend all of our dragon attacks in the shelter," I said.

"Yeah, but your dragon slayer is gone," she said.

"Even before that," I told her. "Except for the dragon at Basic and the Athabascan Long he got with Porter, Owen hasn't slayed a dragon since he left Ontario."

"But he's the best," Sadie said. "For his age, I mean. And Porter's a fucking *legend* in the UK."

"That may be," I said. "But they're not really well thought of in Alberta."

"I wonder why he stays," Sadie mused. "Porter, I mean. His contract has come up a couple of times since Kansas. Why doesn't he just leave?"

"Owen thinks he doesn't know what else to do," I said. "He's been out of England a long time, and he's old to get a starting contract with a corporation."

"Maybe he'll settle down with your engineer," Sadie said. She was smiling like she used to when we were in high school and she was trying to pair me off with Alex Carmody so that we could all go on double dates.

"At the rate Courtney's going, it's a distinct possibility," I allowed.

"Is it safe there?" Sadie asked. "I mean, as safe as you can get when you're staring down an oil field?"

"Are you asking me if I think our own military is trying to get your boyfriend killed?" I replied. It was something I had considered, in my darker moments. I figured I'd get really concerned when Emily started talking about it, and so far she hadn't brought it up.

"I guess I am," she said. "I was really hoping we'd both end up overseas. I thought the furor would quiet down while we were gone, and then we could all just come back here and save chickens from premature barbecuing."

"The weird thing is that I think they are actually trying to sideline him," I said. "They shunted him off to Alberta in the hope that he would disappear, but he's in Canada, so everyone knows who he is. And they gave him a semi-disgraced mentor, but the local civilians think that he's awesome too. They've done the opposite of what I would have done, if I'd wanted people to forget the name Owen Thorskard."

"If you wanted people to forget the name, all you'd have to do is stop writing music about it," Sadie said.

"Maybe that's what they're doing," I said. "They're not trying to get rid of him. They're trying to make sure that I don't have anything to say."

"That sounds more reasonable to me," Sadie said. "You haven't written anything in a while."

"I have, actually," I said. "Emily and I spent most of yesterday working on it. She's coming back on Boxing Day and we're going to start recording so that she can upload them a few at a time after I go back west."

"What are you singing about?" she asked. "The price of wheat?"

"Not in terms of money," I said.

"Remember when our only problems in life were accidentally ending up at field parties where people had lit fires?" she said.

"Yes," I said. "Someone died that night. I'll probably never forget it." I had that song still, even though I'd never written it down and Owen was the only other person who would ever hear it.

"Let's go downstairs and make cookies before we murder the spirit of Christmas entirely," Sadie said, sitting up.

"I don't know if we have stuff for that," I said.

"I brought most of what we need," Sadie said. "Mom's gone all healthy since I left, so there're no cookies at all at our house. What's the kid of a dentist to do?"

"Eat sugar and develop radical politics at the neighbours', I guess," I said, laughing.

"You betcha," she said, and we went down to the kitchen.

"What is that?" I asked after we had the trays cooling on the sideboard and went into the living room to sit down. Sadie had brought a large bag with her from a store I'd never heard of and put it under the tree.

"Oh, that's the British food I brought home for Owen to give to Porter," Sadie said. "He mentioned he'd asked you to get something, and I had the luggage space."

I looked at the cans and packages. Some of them looked familiar, or at least comfortingly normal.

"Chocolate cake in a can?" I asked. "Made by the same people who make ketchup? That can't possibly taste good."

"You'd be surprised," Sadie said. I looked back in the bag.

"I can't give my commanding officer something called spotted dick. It sounds like an STD."

She looked affronted. "It is a perfectly legitimate form of cake."

I don't know who I was channeling at that point, but I replied with: "That's what she said."

Sadie laughed so hard she had to sit down.

"Honestly, I don't know how you get on without me," she said. If she was still angry about her assignment, she wasn't letting on. Maybe the adventure was winning her over. She was actually getting to do what we all thought we'd do once we'd enlisted: see the world and slay dragons. And besides, it was only four years. We had all the time in the world to change it.

"It's pretty awkward," I admitted. I missed her a lot, but I knew that she and Owen missed each other more. Or at least in a different way. "But I manage."

"Soon it'll be over," Sadie said. "And we'll all come back here and raise baby dragon slayers together."

"Now who's planning too far ahead?" I asked, but it made me feel better to know that she and Owen were of like minds when it came to the future.

THE STORY OF YOUTUBE

Once upon a time, if a bard wanted to spread word of her dragon slayer's accomplishments, she would require a lyre and a stout pair of shoes. Her meals and board would be covered by whoever's house she stayed in, paid for with stories or with a dragon slayed. She would wander the countryside, and if she was talented, she would find welcome where ever she went, and her dragon slayer too, even if there were no great beasts in the air.

There is the story of Richard the Lionheart, who was more interested in slaying dragons than he was in ruling his kingdom. He was caught and held for ransom, and it was not his soldiers or his brother, John, who found him, but rather his bard. Legend says the bard traversed hither and yon, singing the king's favourite song. One day the king heard him and answered back, and he was rescued. There are other tales, of course, of wandering bards who saved children from wells or stole them from their beds in the middle of the night, but they are only tales.

Soon, the days came when bards no longer traveled. They lived in stone houses with solariums and sitting rooms, and in the evening, people would come from miles around to hear them sing or perform. Soon, bards lived in cities and had the patronage of princes. They took students and taught at universities, or ventured out into the wilds to take their chances in the new countries being founded all over the world.

At last, there came the radio, the record, the cassette tape, the 8-track, the CD. And, finally, YouTube. Most bardic practice had died out somewhere between the record and the cassette tape, but there were still a few musicians who came together online, and as Internet traffic increased, so too did the number of videos on YouTube.

Traditionalists dismissed the online community at first. It was, they argued, just a bunch of kids with Wi-Fi and microphones. They hadn't fought their way through the music industry. They hadn't auditioned or, in most cases, written the songs they sang. They just did covers. But what the traditionalists neglected to realize was that some of them were very, very *good*. It was only a matter of time before those kids got a little bit older, a little bit wiser, and started to write their own stuff. It still wasn't bardic, but it was good music, and the fans came online in droves.

Into this scene came Emily Carmichael, Internet personality and social media savant. She correctly concluded that Twitter was a terrible medium for a dragon slayer. No one really needs live updates of a dragon slaying, and she felt that it would set a bad example. We wanted people to put their phones away and run, not make a few updates while they tried to video us. She dismissed Facebook because of the layout and Tumblr for much the same reason as Twitter. But YouTube, she decided, had potential.

It was easy enough to get started. We had most of the equipment at school. We didn't have to record in the bathroom for good acoustics, though I applauded the inventive nature of those who did. Our gear wasn't top of the line by any stretch of the imagination, but it was good, and it meant that we didn't stumble through our first few dozen videos figuring out how to get the right aspect ratio. The first videos were simple, just me talking and then introducing Owen. By the third week, when we started releasing songs, we had more followers than Emily had projected, and by the time we posted the Manitoulin song in week five, we were getting so many comments and video responses that Emily wasn't sure how she was going to deal with all of our traffic once school started again.

We hit the expected roadblocks. We were banned in a couple of countries almost immediately, and the videos that featured songs I had laboured over inevitably received fewer views than the video of the Battle of Manitoulin as reenacted by Sadie's family cat. But Emily assured me that we were doing well, and a couple of our teachers had allowed us to use the videos to count towards course work, so it wasn't even eating into our homework time too much. And soon there was ad revenue.

By the time we filmed our final video with the three of us together, heads shaved and ready to head off to Basic Training, I had stopped paying attention to the metrics. I could never remember what CPM stood for, but Emily knew. Emily told me what I needed to know, and I didn't like reading the comments anyway. She was always the most interested in the video replies and made sure to link to them as often as she could. It took me a couple of months to realize it, but eventually I understood what she was doing. We didn't need her help to build a community in Trondheim or Saltrock, so she built us one online.

It didn't matter what time zone our viewers were in or how far away they lived. They could communicate with us whenever they wanted. There were hundreds of covers of my songs out there now, converted to synthesizer music, performed *a capella*, translated into other languages. A prominent American young-adult novelist and his brother (who seemed to harbor bardic aspirations of his own) talked about us on their vlog and actually invited Emily to speak at their conference. There was fan art, videos of Owen and Sadie's TV clips set to whatever love song was currently popular (they didn't like that, but Emily and I thought it was hysterical), and something called OT3 fanfiction, which Emily made us all promise never to read.

And yes, our viewers and those people who made art in response to us were mostly kids. But so were we. We were a whole year older now. Owen and Sadie were better at slaying dragons. I was better at writing music in spite of my new situation. Emily was better at whatever it was Emily did. And those other kids, people I'd never even met—they were getting older and more talented too. I didn't know their names, let alone their plans for the future, but I knew that they supported us, that they had carved out their identity using us as a backdrop. We gave them something to aspire to, whether it was Sadie's fashion sense or her tai chi lessons. And they gave back.

I had to take time off when I first joined the Oil Watch, but after Christmas at home with Emily, the videos started going up again, each one winging its way across the world without government oversight or parental supervision. That was the future, I supposed, and we could be patient, because someday it would be ours.

A TO Z

Owen was waiting on the train platform, along with Nick and the rest of their support squads, when we got back from Christmas leave. I was certain he'd stopped growing before we'd gone to New Brunswick, but he seemed taller. Maybe working with Porter had filled him out a little more. Maybe it had just been a while since I really looked at him. Emily and I had spent days in my room recording songs, and it had made me think about everything Owen and I had done since we'd left home together at the end of the spring. I had worried we might have grown apart, but when I saw him, I knew that we were still a team, even with the new additions and the forced separation. Courtney was there too, with Porter standing as close to her as he could without actually standing close to her at all, and she smiled and waved when she caught sight of us in the crowd.

"We've got a bloody assignment!" she said, almost jumping up and down. "They've brought Owen and Porter back to travel with us and Nick's crew down to make it a party."

"Really?" I said. "And you don't hate it?"

"Well," she said, slinging an arm around my shoulder and taking my bag, "it's still tedious, but at least it's out of Fort Calgary."

"She says that like she goes to British Columbia all the time," Anderson said, bumping fists with Parker in what passed for greeting.

"I've been twice," Courtney said. "It's not like it's some grand adventure."

"It's the A to Z!" Nick crowed, pronouncing the Z incorrectly as Americans do. Courtney rolled her eyes. She was not the only one.

"The John A–Zuò Tunnel is good practice for shepherding convoys," Porter said. We all straightened. Apparently Christmas hadn't been enough to break our good habits. He handed me a file. "McQuaid, you're going to want to read fast. You have a meeting with the refugees after dinner."

It was nearly impossible for me to read and eat at the same time, but the documents weren't classified at all, so Annie read me the salient points while we ate. It turned out that Peter's family had invited everyone he worked with to stay with them until their fields were back up and running. Our assignment was to accompany them as escorts, in case of dragon attack.

"Peter's family knows how many people they'll be dealing with, right?" I interjected once Annie got through the basics. There were almost a hundred farmers, and even if only half of them wanted to go, that wasn't exactly a kitchen party sort of number. Plus they would have to host all twenty-eight of us for two days.

"Let me get to it," Annie said, skipping ahead a few pages.

"Peter's family has a lot of land and housing up around Prince Rupert. It's all forestry work, but at least it's probably better than sitting around here until the snow melts."

"Are you talking about them or us?" Nick asked. He hadn't really been prepared for what winter in Alberta would mean, and the others in his support squad, who were mostly from southern states, were even more miserable.

"Pack warm, darling," Laura said unsympathetically.

"Keep reading, Annie," I directed, but from there on out it was mostly scheduling and details about the train lines that would only be important after we crossed the border.

I had never been to British Columbia, which isn't unusual for most Canadians. It isn't exactly a safe trip. The Rockies are riddled with dragons, even leaving the Chinooks out of the equation, and use of the A to Z Tunnel is carefully controlled by the Oil Watch. The isolation of BC, and of Cascadon to the south, is a sore point in the Watch, which feels it provides enough dragon slayers to keep the two provinces safe. While not directly separatist like parts of Quebec, the two westernmost provinces had been trying to pass legislation to control their own dragon slayers for almost a decade, but the bills never made it off the floor.

"I still think it'll be fun," Nick said. "Even with your ungodly weather."

"We'll start packing for you," Courtney said, picking up her tray after the general dismissed us from the mess hall. "And I want to see everyone's kit before we leave."

"Yes, ma'am," Nick said, saluting.

"I don't care so much about you," she said.

"I'm hurt," Nick replied. "But I'll live."

"Thank goodness," Owen said. "I'd hate to miss your first

view of the Pacific. You would not believe the *nature* they have over there."

Nick laughed, and everyone but me headed for the barracks. I made my way to the mess where the refugees ate. It was one of those pointless meetings that I've learned the military is so fond of. They knew most of what I told them already, but they listened politely anyway. I could tell that they were as excited at the prospect of seeing the A to Z for themselves as we were.

When I was done, Peter came up and asked if I could spare a moment.

"Yes," I told him. "I don't have much packing to do. I only just got back before dinner."

"I won't keep you long," he said. "Did you have a good Christmas?"

"I did, actually," I told him. "Emily and I recorded a lot of the songs we'd been working on."

"She's uploaded the first one already," he said. "I guess you didn't have Internet on the train?"

"Not for that sort of thing," I said. "How is it doing?"

"You have a lot of hits," he said. "And no real criticism yet. Just the usual yahoos."

"Emily will be so pleased," I said. "You never mentioned that your family was in BC."

"You were always all business," he replied. "I didn't think to share."

"Sorry," I said. "I didn't mean to be."

"It's fine," he said. "But, yeah, my family has the title to a lot of the forestry around Port Edward, near Prince Rupert. We've been there a long time. I'm Haida."

"Really?" I looked at him more closely. He had very dark

hair, but Owen had blond hair and his mother was Venezuelan. And I'd never met someone from the Haida nation before.

"Just enough for tax exemptions," he said in an overly cheerful tone. I realized I was staring and shook my head.

"Owen will be thrilled," I said. "Lottie mentioned Haida dragon slaying at one point, but our library was foggy on the details and the Internet sites we found didn't look terribly reliable."

"Oh, it's all true," Peter said. "That's what makes it so excellent. But I won't tell you any more. It's better if you see it for yourself."

"I'll take your word for it," I said.

"And that's not even what I wanted to talk to you about," he said. "My mother is a locally famous drummer, so we have a soundproof recording studio in the house. It's not much, probably not even as good as your high school's, but I thought maybe we could record some of the songs with both of us? Don't get me wrong, I like the one you posted, but it's not the same without the mandolin."

The prospect of drumming was almost more exciting than the idea of getting out of Fort Calgary, though that was probably because I had only just returned. After Manitoulin, I had made a list of all the musical instruments I would never play again. It was a long one and included all of my favourites, all the ones I was familiar with. I hadn't had a lot of time to experiment and, to be honest, I'd been more than a little bitter about my loss, but in addition to the trombone, the various forms of First

Nation drumming were still left to me. There wasn't a lot of it in Trondheim, of course, but getting to meet a drummer in person was exciting. I could move my hands enough to play now, thanks to my therapy and my refusal to let things like buttons and milk cartons get in my way.

Someone, probably Annie, had my bag open on my bed when I got back to our room. Courtney had a sheaf of papers in her hands and was divvying out extra supplies based on who had what room left in their kits. Some of the items looked a bit odd, but after the Singe'n'Burn, Courtney was determined never to be caught wanting in the woods again. I couldn't say I blamed her.

"We liked your new song," one of the Americans said when I walked through their section of the barracks to get to ours. Their packing process was much less orderly than ours was, I couldn't help but notice.

"Thank you," I said. "I hope you like the others as well."

"You know who loved your song?" Courtney said, once I was close enough that she could speak to me without raising her voice.

"Oh, crap," I said.

"Oh, yeah," Courtney said. "The general particularly liked the part where you weren't wearing your uniform so he can't discipline you directly, but the beret is clearly visible over your shoulder, so everyone remembers what you're up to now."

"That was Emily's idea," I said.

"Good call," Courtney said. "Still, he's angry and can't officially do anything about it. I'm glad the orders for BC had already come down by the time he saw it, or we'd probably never again see what the totem poles look like from outside the walls."

"Sorry, guys," I apologized to the room at large.

"We all knew what it meant when we drew Owen in the first place," Laura reminded me.

"Also, now half the planet knows that we nabbed a Singe'n'Burn before we left Gagetown," Annie added. "I swear, we've been getting better desserts all week because of that."

"Well, as long as there's dessert." I pulled out the bugle and wondered if I should bring it. The trains in the A to Z Tunnel were different from regular trains, because they shipped so many necessities to BC. Space was key, and Peter and his comrades were moving a good portion of their lives. I didn't want to be the reason one of them had to leave something important behind.

"That counts as an essential," Courtney told me. "I made a list."

"Don't ask about the lists," Laura said in a desperate stage whisper when I opened my mouth to do just that. "Just pack exactly what she tells you to, and we might get to bed before midnight."

"I'm efficient," Courtney pointed out.

"That's one way of putting it," Laura replied.

The Americans laughed along with us. It was well before midnight when we turned the lights out, and well before winter-sunrise when the train slid away from the platform at Fort Calgary and headed for the mountains. It was a tense ride at first. Owen, Nick, and Porter took turns looking out the windows and fretting, but we reached Hinton without so much as a candle's worth of flame spotted. The sun was just starting to rise when we reached the mouth of the John A–Zuò Tunnel, and before it had fully cleared the horizon, we had already gone back into the dark.

STRONG FEELINGS
ABOUT RAISINS

The John A–Zuò Tunnel was a remarkable feat of engineering, but it wasn't very interesting to look at, even if the meagre glow from the far-spaced lights had allowed for a close examination of the hewn walls. Courtney, Aarons, and Nick's two engineer-smiths clustered together near the rear of our car, poring over the schematics Courtney had brought with her. I had to admit, their enthusiasm was infectious, and I found myself listening to what they were saying and composing without even meaning to.

It would be a dark song, obviously, with spots of light to match the panels we passed at regular intervals. It should feel safe, or at least safer than the alternative, and yet there should be something to account for the feeling of having all those metres of rock above our heads. Annie, far less sanguine about the trip than I was, had taken a Gravol and was doing her best to fall asleep as quickly as possible. I noticed that Ilko and a couple of the American firefighters were uncomfortable too, but they'd been too tough to follow Annie's commonsense example. That would be where the strings came in, I decided, to give that uncomfortable edge to the dark.

"The American tunnels were laser-cut," the American sapper was telling Courtney. I didn't for a second doubt that Courtney already knew that. "So they're much straighter than this one."

"True," Courtney allowed. "A couple of our northern tunnels were made that way, and so was the tunnel that connects Montana to Cascadon. This one is older though. And they had dynamite. It's not like they carved it out with their teeth."

"I can't believe they managed the whole thing with only six cave-ins," said the smith. "And even those were the result of blasting, not of striking blind and hitting a flaw."

"Can we not talk about cave-ins?" Annie requested. She didn't even sound groggy.

"I was about to tell you that this area of the Rockies is very stable," Courtney said. "So don't worry. I can explain to you how it works, if you like."

"I'd rather not," Annie said. It might have been the pale light, but I thought she looked a bit green. "Understanding it just means I can think more creatively about things that might go wrong."

"Go to sleep," Owen said. "We'll be through it soon enough."

"I heard from Caroline before we left," Laura said. "She said to tell you that we will be seeing all of the terrible parts of the province, and that she can't recommend any places to eat in Port Edward, because she's pretty sure the only thing they eat there is fish."

My confusion must have been apparent, because Laura sighed.

"Caroline is the name of the dragon slayer from Chilliwack we lived with for fourteen weeks," she explained. "Seriously, Siobhan, aren't you supposed to be the one who remembers these things?"

"There were a lot of people at Basic," I told her. "And many of them were kind of jerks to me."

"Fair enough," Laura said, and then raised her voice to be sure that Courtney overheard her. "I'll make you a list, if you need it."

"Efficient!" Courtney called back, without looking up from the discussion she was having, which had become so technical I'd stopped trying to follow it. For a moment, I just listened to the train.

"So," Owen said, leaning towards me across the aisle. "My name's Owen. Who are you?"

I laughed—quietly, in case Annie was making any headway. It had been a while since we'd really had a chance to talk in person. I missed him. It was one thing to write songs about a dragon slayer, and quite another to remember the boy who'd stood so awkwardly through the national anthem the day we were both late for English.

"Your mother says hello, and your aunts send their love," I told him. "Aodhan too, obviously, but I didn't want to overwhelm you with all their admiration at the same time."

"Good plan," he replied. "I'm feeling very unadmired these days. It's probably best to break me in gently."

"Was Hinton that bad?" I asked.

"It was kind of nice, actually," he said. "Nobody cared that

I was a Thorskard. Porter was a bigger deal than I was, and I could just sit in the background and not worry about living up to Lottie for a while."

"Laura seems to think that Hinton is the rear end of the universe," I told him.

"Oh, that it is," he said. "Cold, grey, full of trees. But the people weren't so bad, once they got used to us. A 'Bascan Long attacked one day while we were patrolling in the forest and burned down ten buildings in town before we could get to it. I thought for sure the locals would be angry that we were more concerned with the forestry zones than with their houses and shops, but there wasn't even a sarcastic editorial in the newspaper afterwards. Our billet didn't have much of a kitchen, so we ate out a lot, and I don't think Porter paid for a meal or a beer the whole time we were there. After your song went up, neither did I."

"Yeah, Porter's surprisingly popular. Peter's friends all like him a lot. I spent my first week as their liaison ferrying their complaints about his reassignment back and forth."

"He's actually kind of fun, once he managed to relax a bit," Owen told me. I tried to imagine Porter relaxing. It didn't work. "I get why Courtney likes him, anyway," he continued. "And he seemed interested in how Lottie's arrangement with Trondheim works."

"You think he's eyeing retirement?" It wouldn't be too surprising. I got the impression that the Watch envisioned Porter leaving Alberta one of two ways, the first of which involved a body bag.

"He misses his support squad more than he lets on," Owen told me. "Not that he said as much, obviously."

"He did a good thing protecting them, but I can see how it would be lonely," I said. "Did you give him the food Sadie sent?"

"Oh, yes," he said. "He was very happy. And then I had to try something called spotted dick, and I may never forgive you."

"Apparently it's a perfectly legitimate form of cake," I told him.

"It has raisins." He wrinkled his nose. "I have strong feelings about raisins."

I realized that Nick, who was sitting in the window seat next to Owen, had yet to interject himself into the conversation. I looked over Owen's shoulder, wondering if he had fallen asleep. He hadn't, and was instead looking out the window with a mournful expression on his face. I very nearly asked him what was wrong until I heard a voice in my head that sounded a lot like Sadie's, reminding me that I might not want to know.

"What about Grande Prairie, Nick?" I asked. Work was probably a safe topic.

"It's not a prairie, really," he said. "I was disappointed. It was barely flat at all."

"I mostly meant the dragons," I told him. "We already know that Owen didn't see much action in Hinton, but you must have seen something up there."

"Wapitis, for the most part," he said. "Blue and Red, though we managed to kill one before we found out which. I gather that's something of an accomplishment. And there were a lot of eggs."

I couldn't help the shudder or the way I curled my hands into my lap. Dragon eggs were such a stupid thing to be afraid of. Most of the time, you didn't get close to them because of the adult population, and if you did get close to them, they were absolutely harmless and easy enough to break. But every time I thought about them, I thought about fire, and then I couldn't stop.

"It's okay," Owen said, so quietly I wasn't sure Nick could hear him.

"Did you get to shoot any of them?" I asked.

"What, like you think some magic bird is going to tell me about the magic place where I can shoot a dragon the size of a Wapiti with a magic arrow?" he said, grinning. "No, I used a lance."

"Are you over your fear of horses, then?" Owen asked.

"I was never afraid of horses," Nick said in a grandiose tone with all the wrong parts of Lieutenant Porter's accent. "I merely hold them in the highest regard."

"Sure you do," Owen said. "And do you have the same feelings for chickens?"

"Hell no," Nick replied. "Those things are terrifying."

My hands uncurled as they talked, and the fire dimmed behind my eyes.

"I thought the prairies were boring," Gratton said from the seat in front of us. "But this." He looked out the window into the dark. "This is extremely tedious."

"I bet you it's nice and exciting if you try to go over the top," Laura replied.

"Did you know that fewer than fifty people have ever survived going that way?" Gratton said, a morbid grin on his face. "Officially, anyway? I'll take my chances with the cave-ins."

"Stop. Talking. About. The. cave-ins," Annie growled.

"Someone go and get that Peter guy," Parker suggested. "I want to hear the Singe'n'Burn song played properly—no offense, Siobhan."

"None taken," I assured him as Wilkinson got up to go see if Peter wanted to come back and sit with us for a bit. "It's meant to be sung with live accompaniment. The synth can do a lot, but there's something to be said for live performances."

Peter was interested, it turned out, because he was just as bored as we were, and his fellows just as claustrophobic. Porter left the door open between the cars, because we couldn't all fit in one even if everyone stood. Owen gave up his seat and moved forward to sit with Ted, and Annie stopped pretending to sleep so that she could listen. I didn't blame her. As the foreman of the fire crew, she'd been fairly central to the Singe'n'Burn fight, and the song reflected that.

I'd written it without a percussion part, but the sound of the train on the rails below us provided one anyway, and both Peter and I followed it without discussion. The song and the tracks were the only sounds; even the engineers quieted to hear us. This was different from singing in the barracks or in the mess when the refugees requested it. This was performing, and it had been a very long time since I'd done that for an audience I could see.

It was a happy song, the Singe'n'Burn, and so it was fitting that I couldn't stop smiling as I sang it. Peter was smiling too, adding all sorts of little flourishes that hadn't been a part of the original arrangement, and joining in to harmonize during the chorus. I didn't mind. This song was as much his as it was mine or Owen's, because he'd been the one to help me piece it together.

Beside Peter, Nick had gone back to looking out the window into the darkness. I was worried that he was moping, mostly because I had no idea what I was supposed to do about that, even though Sadie had told me it wasn't my problem. I could see his reflection in the window, though, between the lights that flashed past as the train sped by, and he was smiling. I sang until we got to British Columbia and the sun was high above our heads. I sang until the dragon dropped out of the sky and landed on the railway tracks right in front of us.

LESS THAN TWO PERCENT

"Courtney!" Porter and Owen said in the same breath, but she was already moving.

Like she promised that day in Gagetown, Courtney had masterminded the packing of each kit. In my case, and in Aarons's, she simply packed for us. With Owen and the fire crew, she worked from a list Annie gave her and Owen's suggestions. Ted and Jeremy did their own packing, but Courtney watched them do it. I didn't understand at first, but I soon realized that she did it so that in an emergency, she would know not only what we had with us, but also who had it and where in the pack it was. Accordingly, she had both Owen's and Lieutenant Porter's swords and shields out of their wrapping before the train had slowed down enough for them to jump from it, Nick right on their heels.

"We are really lucky that thing wasn't closer to the tunnel entrance," Laura said. "There's no way we'd have stopped in time otherwise. And it looks big enough to derail us."

"It's not a species I recognize," Mikitka said.

"Okanagan Greenback," Peter said, looking out the window. "It's a bit like a Wapiti, but without the acid."

"Does Lieutenant Porter know that?" Wilkinson asked. His face was glued to the window. Last time we'd done this as a team, at least we'd done it together.

"And hey, if there's fire, shouldn't we be out there?" Annie said.

I could hear Porter yelling at both Owen and Nick, who ranged out on either side of him with swords at the ready and shields up in the fire position. I couldn't make out the words, but he didn't look out of sorts.

"He's been here before," Courtney said. "He'll be fine."

Sheets of fire billowed from the dragon's mouth, and the snow steamed around it.

"Are you sure we shouldn't be out there?" Annie said. "It's wet now, but the dragon's got to be hot enough to dry the grass, and then it'll burn."

A tree caught fire and went up almost immediately, flames licking along the boughs and reaching for the trees nearby.

"We don't have enough supplies on hand to deal with a forest fire," Courtney said. "Not unless you give me thirty minutes and I can get to the cargo cars safely."

"It should be okay," Laura said. Peter was also nodding.

"Yeah, the train engineer will have radioed ahead to Kamloops," Peter said. "They'll be sending their own fire crews."

"They won't get here in time either!" Courtney protested.

"They're flying," Peter said. "Small planes are fast enough to outrun anything but a Chinook, and those don't usually come down on the western side of the mountains."

"How will they land?" asked Nick's smith. He was holding Nick's extra swords in his hands, ready in case they were needed.

"They won't," Peter said. "Smoke jumpers. Parachutes."

Annie's face lit up despite the danger. "That sounds exciting," she said.

"Yeah, it's all fun and games until a dragon snags you midair," Parker said.

"That almost never happens," Peter said. "They won't make their jumps until the dragon's dead."

I turned my focus out the window while Annie continued to ask questions about the smoke jumpers.

On the ground, Owen and Nick were busy making trails in the snow. This served two purposes, I saw, in that it confused the heck out of the Greenback, and also meant that whenever Porter got close enough to take a swing at it, he was standing on beaten-down snow instead of fresh snow. I watched Porter set himself and wait for the dragon to extend its neck after Nick, who was much better at moving on the uneven ground than Owen was. When the opportunity presented itself, he slashed along the dragon's neck. It was a shallow cut and didn't do much damage to the dragon (or the ground on which the blood landed), but by now I'd seen enough of these to know the blow's intent. Porter was trying to make it turn, make it show its belly, and then he'd go for the hearts. Once I realized that, I knew how the battle would unfold, and I stopped focusing on the details. I could always make those up if I had to write a song about it later, and it helped me keep my cool if I didn't have to watch Owen's every move. That's part of the reason Hannah and Lottie had started me off by watching him train in the backyard. I knew what he'd do just as he did.

"Porter's very good," I said to Courtney, who had come to sit beside me. She was uncharacteristically nervous, not having seen as many of these as I had. She knew now how dragon battles were supposed to go, but she didn't trust the dragon slayers as much as I did. If I could help her feel better about how her dragon slayers were doing, I would.

"He really is," Courtney said. There was a fierce light in her eyes. She might not know Porter as well as I knew Owen, but she was proud of him regardless.

It was freezing cold outside the train, and none of them were wearing particularly good footwear for this kind of activity, yet Porter might as well have been on the practice field, he moved with such surety. I was used to watching Lottie, who always had to limp, or Aodhan, who always worked with Owen and paused to teach. This was the closest I'd been to a dragon slayer in his prime, and the difference was clear. Someday, I could only hope, Owen would be this good.

"You know," I said cautiously, wondering how far I could distract her, "your dad thinks dragon slayers should work alone." I gestured out the window. "Isn't that pretty compelling evidence to the contrary?"

"Of course it is," she said. She leaned back against the seat without taking her eyes off the scene. "But the general thinks that dragon slayers should practice and work alone just in case they ever are alone. He thinks if they work in teams, they'll get used to each other, and if they have to work alone, they'll be incomplete."

"Porter was alone in Kansas," I said. "And look how that went."

"That was a Chinook," Courtney said. Her tone wasn't overly defensive, and I knew I hadn't misstepped. "And all things considered, it didn't go that badly."

I looked at her quizzically. It had gone badly enough.

"No, I mean it. Kansas is over two hundred thousand square kilometres in size," she explained. "The stories make it sound like the whole thing's on fire but it isn't. It's less than two percent. And there's a company in Switzerland working with a lab in Japan that's close to figuring out a way to put the fire out."

"They can't do it without losing the coal bed," I guessed. You talk about the oddest things when you are trying not to panic on the sidelines of a dragon battle.

"Correct," Courtney said. "Porter's just the guy they blame, and people from Kansas think he's the freaking second coming, because he managed to do it with such a low death toll. They were predicting deaths in the hundreds. They got away with only a few dozen, and most of those were the people who were too stupid to abandon their houses and get out of the way."

"So why doesn't he retire?" I asked. "Go to Kansas and be a hero or something."

"He doesn't want to," she said. "He wants to slay dragons, and the Oil Watch is the only way he knows how."

A flurry of activity drew our full attention back to the window, and Courtney leaned forward again, though this time she didn't grip the armrests quite so tightly. We watched as Nick led the dragon past Porter. Porter looked fine, but Nick was clearly starting to flag. He'd done most of the distraction runs because he was better at it than Owen was, but he only had a few more passes in him. The Greenback's neck was as green as its back now, as the scales bled poison onto the winnowing snow. The trees burned, and even the grass was starting to catch. Annie was right: the dragon had been enough to dry it.

"Is the plane with the smoke jumpers close?" I asked. Watching the fight, I'd lost track of them.

"Look." Courtney pointed out the window, and I saw six dots on the horizon. They were circling us, and I knew that they were ready for when the killing blow landed.

Owen was running now, and this time Porter's sword bit a little deeper into the dragon's neck than it should have, spilling too much poisoned blood on the newly-exposed grass. He was clearly frustrated, but it was enough to finally get the beast to turn, and when it did, Porter's blade slid home so quickly I barely saw it move. We heard cheers from the car where the refugees sat, and the support crews relaxed too. Davis and Ilko were out of their seats in an instant, with Nick's medics close behind them.

"Here they come!" said Annie, pointing up.

The blue winter sky was speckled with white dots, shifting in the wind as they steered down towards us. The planes turned and headed back for Kamloops, fading before the parachuters made their landings. Soon enough, they were working to bring the fire under control.

"You might as well go," I said to Annie, who was clearly dying to see how the smoke jumpers worked.

She led the rest of the fire crews and Aarons, who never let anything pass by without looking at it, out of the car. The Americans could be heard protesting the cold, but it was more habit than anything else. Courtney hadn't moved from beside me. Neither of us were really needed right now, and I could tell it wasn't a position she particularly liked.

"I swear, I didn't mean for it to get serious," Courtney said, once we were alone in the carriage. "I thought it would be fun and make my dad see spots for a good bonus."

It took me a moment, but I figured out what she was talking about before I said something that would embarrass me.

"I thought he'd be a mess," she continued. "And I didn't want to fix him. That's not how I work."

"You build," I said. "With whatever you've got."

"That's true," she said. "I figured I'd do a tour and then leave dragon slaying behind. I still might."

"You might stay for a second go?" I said, surprised.

"Hell no," she said, smiling. On the newly exposed grass, Porter was clapping Owen and Nick on the shoulders and trying to wave off Davis, who was attempting to check him over for scorch marks. "But if he would come with me, I'd learn to make swords."

"Not for nothing," I said, "but I think I know someone who'd be happy to teach you."

The dragon slayers managed to get free of their medical team and talk to the chief smoke jumper. Nick apparently had as many questions as Annie, because after a few moments, Porter just pushed him towards a discarded parachute and headed back for the train, Owen trailing behind him.

"All clear?" I said as they boarded.

"More or less," Porter said, collapsing into a seat. "It bled a bit more than I'd like, but there was no help for it. They'll do what they can for the ground once they're done with the fire, and that's mostly under control."

Courtney passed them both water bottles. It might have been my imagination, but I thought Porter's hand lingered on hers for just a fraction of a second longer than he really needed to.

"I'll see to Nick," she said, and hopped down into the snow.

"I hate British Columbia," Porter said to no one. "I swear, the farther west you go in this country, the worse it gets."

"You need to come back in the summer," Peter said. He had

returned from the refugee car just as Courtney left. "It rains all the time. Not only would you feel right at home, it keeps the dragon activity down too."

"I don't think so," Porter said. "I've been here in the summer too."

"How are you?" I said to Owen. He was still red from all the running, and his shoulders moved steadily as he regained his breath.

"I think I've been letting Constantinople do too much of the work," he replied. I knew he was joking, because he hadn't taken the horse with him to Hinton. It was always best when he could joke after slaying a dragon. "But I'm fine, I promise."

"Good," I told him, "because you have to tell me all the parts that happened up close."

That was a joke too: I knew what had happened. If the dragon was slayed and Owen was talking to me, I could piece together the battle whether he filled me in on the close details or not. We had had a lot of practice.

"It's always work with you two," Peter said. His tone was mild, but there was an edge to it that I didn't entirely like.

"Sometimes there's spaghetti," I said, a bit more peevishly than I'd intended.

Peter threw up his hands in defeat, though I wasn't quite sure what I had won, and headed back to the other car. With the fire out, the crews came back too, including the smoke jumpers. Parachutes being something of a one way trip, they needed a ride back to Kamloops.

The scenery grew monotonous after a while, but no one requested a song. We were all too busy watching the sky.

PAY SPECIAL ATTENTION TO THE DANCING

The dragon didn't actually land right in front of us. If it had, we'd all be dead. Going that fast, we needed a couple hundred metres to come to a complete stop, and even that pretty much ruined the train we were on, though we did avoid both derailing and warping the tracks. The dragon had been on the ground when we came out of the tunnel, yes, but it had gone aloft again almost before the engine driver could throw the e-brake. We would have been better off if his instincts had been a little slower. Committed, we had slowed until Porter, Owen, and Nick could get out, even though at the time, it had felt like everything was happening very quickly. We should have kept going, even if it meant leading the dragon all the way to Kamloops. The engine driver's panic had made the isolation of the dragon fight inevitable, and even though the dragon slayers had responded well, it was mistakes like this that led to things like falling off the Burlington Skyway.

The driver should have known better.

It took Courtney, Aarons, and Nick's engineers almost an hour to work out a way to release the emergency brake so that the train could go forward again. There was no train that could come and meet us, due to the existing schedule, and an airlift was too dangerous unless it was a true emergency. By the time we limped into Kamloops, hours behind schedule, we were hungry and tired. I don't think Porter stopped swearing the entire time. The engine driver did not come back to check on us. I don't really blame him.

We switched trains in Kamloops and headed north towards Quesnel and Prince George. Though we were in the mountains, we saw no more dragons, and by the time we turned west to Port Edward and the Pacific coast we had almost managed to relax again. Well, that or we were so bored that even cribbage couldn't keep us from falling asleep in our seats.

"Did you ever make any headway with Amery?" I asked Owen, once the shine of crib had worn off.

"No," he told me. "I mean, I assume it has something to do with Porter. She's a bit more by-the-book than he is."

"Lottie is more by-the-book than Porter is," I pointed out.

Owen laughed. "Kaori seems to like her," he concluded, as though that was good enough for him.

"Kaori likes everyone," I pointed out. "Or at least she's too polite to complain. She's the most professional person I've ever met."

"Did you know that some of her ancestors are actual gods in Japan?" Owen asked. "I mean, I'm not sure exactly how it works because Emily is usually the one who does the research, but it kind of puts Aunt Lottie's commercial endorsements into perspective, eh?"

I hadn't known that, actually. It's not the sort of thing Kaori ever would have said to me herself, and I wondered how Owen had learned it. The selfish part of me, the part that told stories people wanted to hear instead of the truth, rather liked the idea that a girl with divine ancestry had chosen to shave her head like mine, to show her support for Owen. Kaori explained it to me later, about how ancestor worship worked and how she happened to be from a very large family, but that certainly didn't lessen the story.

The train lurched and began to slow normally. I noticed that we all looked out the window anyway, but there was nothing but clouds between us and the sun.

"Enjoy it while it lasts," said Peter, who had joined us for most of this leg of the trip and sat beside Laura. "We mostly get grey skies here in the winter."

The town—or village, really—of Port Edward sprawled along the coast. White clapboard houses stood on stilts to keep them above the tide, while the houses further inland looked more like the sort I was used to. The air was clear: The cannery was long gone, and the forestry all took place inland, near Prince George. It was a bit of a commute for those who lived here, but it was better than having dragons on their heads all the time, so I supposed it was an even trade.

There was quite a crowd of people waiting for us at the platform.

"Are they all related to you?" I asked Peter, who was glued to the window with a beaming smile on his face.

"More or less," he admitted. "Sometimes it's very distant,

though, or just through marriage."

"Trondheim is a lot like that," I said. "Or, at least it was. People are starting to move away more than they used to."

"Well, I did go to work in Alberta," Peter said. "But it's different in BC. There's isn't as much 'away' to move to, and it's nice to come home."

I couldn't argue. I hadn't been homesick, not really, since leaving, but every now and then I felt a twinge. Seeing Peter light up, seeing all those people come to meet him, reminded me what I was missing. This wasn't even my home, and I was looking forward to spending time here. We only had one night before we had to head back to Fort Calgary, but it was a night in a real bed, one that didn't sway back and forth, and I was looking forward to it.

Peter was engulfed in hugs as soon as he stepped onto the platform, and it was a while before the mob cleared enough for us to unload the train. We'd brought supplies, contributed by the Oil Watch, to help the village sustain the extra workers through the rest of the winter, and then the workers themselves had brought a lot of their belongings. I waited until the last moment. It took me long enough to carry my gear that I didn't want to get in anyone's way. Finally, there was space for me to move, and I flipped my kit onto my back. I made it about three steps before Peter's arm came around my shoulder, and he pulled me off-course.

"And this is Siobhan McQuaid," he said, presenting me with a flourish and a bow to a silver-haired woman. "Siobhan, this is my mom."

"Pleased to meet you," I said, extending my hand. Peter's mother shook it firmly and didn't even blink when she realized how damaged my fingers were.

"Peter's mentioned you a few times," she said, and I knew that it had been a lot more than a few. "I like the music you've been working on."

"It doesn't sound quite as good when it's just me," I told her. "Peter's been very helpful."

"I'm sorry you can't stay as long as you originally planned," she said. "You had trouble in the mountains, I hear?"

"Just after we were through them, thankfully," I told her. "And the dragon wasn't as much trouble as the train."

"McQuaid!" shouted Porter from up ahead, cutting off any further explanation. I excused myself to go and see what he wanted.

"Yes, sir," I said.

"Dinner is in an hour," he said. "Full dress uniform is required."

"Yes, sir," I said again. "Anything else?"

"Tell Owen to pay special attention to the dancing," Porter said. I hadn't the foggiest idea what he was talking about. "He might learn something."

I nodded, mostly because the idea of saying "yes, sir" out loud again felt ridiculous. General Speed would have objected, but Porter just smiled sarcastically and waved me on. I passed Porter's instructions along to the rest of the squad, and by the time we reached our billets, I realized that Porter had just used me for my actual job, which was kind of nice.

Except for Porter, who got a separate billet on account of being the ranking officer, we were all staying in what I would, for lack of a better term, call longhouses. As usual the women all ended up together: the four of us in Owen's squad, those from Nick's, and eight farmers who had decided to become foresters until the reconstruction was completed. Meanwhile, the men were separated based on whether or not they were in the Oil Watch.

Annie was just straightening my tie when Peter came to fetch us.

"You all clean up nicely," he said.

"We'd better," Courtney said. "Carting these things around is kind of a pain."

We followed Peter across a paved road to the large building that served as the community centre. They'd put down boards across the hockey ice, and we all sat up in the bleachers, the cold from the cement seeping through our clothes. I sat next to Owen, and Peter sat on my other side.

"In summer, we do this outside," he said. "We have an amphitheatre that seats more people, but it's a little snow-covered right now, and I know you all just shined your shoes."

"Thanks," Owen said dryly. I looked at his feet and saw a tiny scuff mark that he'd missed. He saw what I was looking at and sighed.

"You're still pretty," I told him, and he laughed.

Peter's mother was sitting on the ice level, along with the other town leaders, but it was an older man who approached the microphone.

"This whole production is mostly for you guys, you know," Peter whispered to me. His breath was weird against my neck, like a buzz that escaped from the trumpet mouthpiece.

"We appreciate it," I said back as quietly as I could without breathing on him.

"That's my uncle," Peter said. "Well, kind of. Anyway, he

represents the chief's council on the mainland. Most Haida live on Haida Gwaii, in the bay, but it takes too long to get from the island to the mainland for work every day, so we keep this as an outpost. Or inpost. Whatever."

"That makes sense," I replied. I wished he would sit a little farther away, but if he did, it was possible he'd fall off the bleacher.

"Welcome to Port Edward," said Peter's uncle. "We are happy to welcome friends to our shores."

"This would be the part where you'd ask permission to get out of your canoe," Peter said, still too close. "But we're skipping that."

"We are now a people of trees, but we have not forgotten that we were a people of the sea," Peter's uncle continued. "Please join us as we honor our ancestors who slayed dragons on the ocean to keep the mainland safe."

I wasn't entirely sure what he meant by that, and for once Peter didn't offer an explanation. His mother stood and went to one of the large drums near where the blue line would be, if the ice was visible. Three others joined her there. They began to beat the drums, and when I heard this entirely new kind of music, I stopped worrying about how close Peter was sitting.

HAIDA WELCOME

It's difficult to describe, the way a drum sounds when you can't say they sound like your heart. Because these drums didn't. They were irregular and too unlike my heartbeat for me to make the comparison. I couldn't say that they were like someone else's heart either—like when you put your hand on someone's chest or borrow your mother's stethoscope. That's still like you. That's still human.

And these drums were not human. They were a dragon's hearts, both of them beating in that scaly chest, an inhuman tattoo that pushed cold, dark blood around a massive body. I'd touched that sound once, and it was the last thing I'd touched before fire changed my hands. Beside me, Owen tensed, recognizing the sound, the rhythm, for what it was. I could hear Porter's short breath behind me, just barely between the beats, and I wondered if Nick could tell too.

One of Peter's cousins stepped forward, dressed in a T-shirt and jeans, but with his hair spiked on his head like a dragon's spines, and a cape that flared out when he pulled on it. He wove back and forth across the stage with heavy, measured steps. I could feel the squad straighten as they realized what they were witnessing. Lights came up on a row of miniature totem poles, each about waist height and intricately carved. These were wooden poles, traditional and fierce looking, each with painted white teeth inside a grinning mouth and an odd crest upon each head.

The drumming changed. Two drummers kept up the irregular beat of the dragon's hearts, but the others began a more measured tempo. I was not surprised at all when more of Peter's cousins appeared, also in regular clothing except for a few stylized pieces of jewelry that indicated they belonged to the Haida nation. They danced in a line, bobbing their heads, and I realized that they were meant to be in a canoe. I remembered what Peter had said, about safe shores, and that the Haida had been known up and down the west coast for their prowess as a sea-going nation.

The lead dancer stood straighter, like she was bracing herself against the bow of the boat, and held up a rope in her hands. At the end, there was a large ring, like an inflexible lasso. The canoe stalked the dragon through the motions of the dance. I realized that there had been a singer performing too, in the Haida language. I hadn't even noticed him, so entranced was I by the drumming. Peter wasn't translating, and I was glad. I liked figuring out music by myself.

Three times the dragon slayer in the bow of the canoe cast the ring towards the dragon, and three times she missed. At last, she made a successful throw, and the dragon began to writhe on the end of the line. Before I could wonder what exactly one did with a dragon on a line like a fish, the dance changed again. The irregular heartbeat of the dragon increased in tempo as the beast struggled and tried to get away. The beats representing the dancers in the boat quickened too but didn't fall out of step. A third rhythm joined in, and the singer's voice changed. It had to be the ocean, I could tell, even though I didn't understand the words. We watched as the dancers in the boat pulled the dragon down, not towards the boat, but towards the water.

The dancer-dragon came to where the totem poles lined the performance area, and lay down across the front of them, defeated at last. The singer finished, and the lights returned to normal as the rest of the dancers broke the formation of the canoe. We all clapped, and not just politely. I know a polite clap when I hear one, having had years of experience playing classical music to people who don't know Bach from Bartok. These were enthusiastic responses.

"Did the dragon drown?" I heard Owen murmur beside me. He said it quietly, but loud enough to be overhead by those around us. Porter laughed.

"No," Peter said. "The orcas took care of it."

"The whales?" Owen said.

"They're not called Slayer Whales for nothing," Peter reminded him. "They didn't get that name just because they nab moose swimming between islands."

"They do that?" I said.

"Oh, yes, and dragons too," Peter said. "They're vicious creatures."

"Do you still slay dragons that way?" Courtney asked, her face alight with interest.

"We use deep-keeled motorboats and a synthetic compound instead of stone," Peter said. "But more or less, yes."

Owen was looking at Peter with a speculative expression on his face. Porter rolled his eyes.

"We're not on holiday, Thorskard," he said.

"I know, sir," Owen said. "But if there's something nearby, I'd love to observe."

"I'll ask my mother," Peter said. "This time of year, there's usually one or two Aleutian Salties swept off course in a storm that wash up on the beaches and cause trouble."

"Tomorrow, Peter," Porter said, and there was no time to reply, because Peter's uncle was back at the mic.

"Again, welcome," he said. "Please make yourselves at home here, for however long you stay."

With that apparent dismissal, the younger members of Peter's family came to see him in a throng, and it was all introductions and handshakes until we began migrating to where there was a buffet set up with enough food to feed most of Peter's town, all of the newcomers, and us as well. I couldn't balance my plate in one hand and serve myself with the other, so I waited while Davis got me a plate.

"Peter tells me you would like to learn to drum," said Peter's mother, appearing near my elbow.

"I would," I told her. "But I don't think we're going to be here long enough."

"Your Owen hopes to see a slaying," she said. It wasn't exactly a question.

"Yes," I said. "Frankly, so do I. From a safe distance, if possible, but he likes to see how other people work, and I have to write about it, so it's best if I see it with my own eyes."

"We don't hunt dragons," she said. "There is a balance in nature, and the orcas slay many dragons on their own."

"Doesn't that pollute the water?" I asked.

"Most saltwater dragons need fish from the ocean to survive," she said, shaking her head. "It would make no sense for them to poison their own food source. Their bodies break down in salt water, and cause only a little damage."

"What about non-ocean dragons?" I said.

"They are a problem," she replied. "Which is why we don't slay them unless we have to. That's what the dance means, at its heart. We can protect ourselves and those we welcome to our homes, but we don't slay indiscriminately."

"I suppose that's a good policy." I said it as diplomatically as I could. I was hardly one of the people who believed we should be actively seeking dragon extinction—to start with, I was pretty sure the human death toll would be too high—but I wasn't exactly keen on just letting them have their own space, since they tended to infringe on *my* space. I was also, of course, responsible for the damage on Manitoulin Island, which she must have known, but if she chose to judge me for it, she kept it from her face and manner.

"It was easier, before," she said. "There are more dragons now, and more people. And fewer fish."

"I like the totem poles," I said. "Fort Calgary's are striking, but they are plain."

"The Oil Watch didn't want to make their dragon slayers superstitious," Peter's mother said. "So they didn't decorate their totem poles the way we do. But we learned how to slay dragons from the orca, so we put their image on the poles to remind us."

I looked at the totem poles again, and now that I knew they were supposed to be orcas, I could see it.

"Some have other designs," I said. "Do they all mean something?"

"Of course," she said. "You have songs to tell your stories, and we have these. Each is a chronicle of a famous Haida dragon slayer. I can tell you about them, if you want."

Before I could answer, Davis appeared with my plate, and I had to juggle it, my cutlery, and my glass towards one of the long tables that had been brought into the community centre.

"Maybe tomorrow?" I said. Our shortened schedule ensured we'd make our train but left no time for the tour Peter had originally suggested. "Before we leave?"

"That sounds like a plan," Peter's mother said.

The only thing we talked about at dinner that night was how we imagined dragon slaying from a canoe would work. Courtney went through about eight napkins trying to sketch a plan for a canoe with enough ballast to hold together under the strain of a dragon pulling on it, and she and Aarons spent most of dessert arguing about the math involved. Porter watched them with a fond expression but quickly turned away when he realized I had seen him.

Peter sat with his family, or at least the closer members of it, for dinner. I could tell he was glad to be home. I never had asked why he'd gone to Alberta, or why he thought wheat farming was a good alternative profession for a man from a forestry family. Of course, he'd never asked me why I wasn't a doctor or an accountant, so I supposed that was fair. He looked different here, though. And the banjo voice that had been out of place on the flat of the prairies seemed to fit better with the ocean as a backdrop. He was so different from Nick and Owen, both of whom were instruments meant to be featured. The banjo did better as part of the whole, like I did, with countermelody. We were more alike than I had thought, but we were also tied to homes in very different places. If I had ever thought of him in a "maybe someday" sort of way, those thoughts ended when I saw the way he sat with his cousins, the way he fit into the music here. The way his rhythm matched the beat of the drums.

Those drums weren't for me, but I could still feel them in my blood as I sat and ate, for once not in any hurry to finish with everyone else. I watched Owen and Nick talk animatedly to each other, presumably wondering if they were strong or accurate enough to get the lasso around the dragon's neck. Aarons had tried to get Nick's engineers on his side, but Courtney's argument was prevailing, and one of them had finally cracked open a drafting book so that the rest of us could have something to wipe our mouths on when we finished eating. Asking the professionals probably occurred to them, but they were obviously having too much fun to do that. It wasn't home but it was home-like, and I was glad we had this much time, even if tomorrow we were getting back on the train for more days of monotony.

I knew it was foolish to wish for dragons, but in that moment, I found myself hoping we would get to see one slayed while we were here. The drums were in my blood, and I wanted to see if I could write the song to go with them.

THAT LOVELY YOUNG WOMAN
WHO PLAYS THE PIANO

Owen did not get to see a pod of orcas slay a dragon. I'll admit to being a little disappointed as well, if only because I wanted to see Peter's cousins pilot the canoe. (Six of them were dragon slayers, though only two were official enough to have served in the Oil Watch.) Instead, we spent our morning in Port Edward watching the dragon slayers practice marksmanship. Eventually, Peter offered to show me the larger totem poles down on the seafront. I'd seen about all I wanted of Nick trying to explain to Owen how to follow his shot, so I agreed. Laura raised her eyebrows at me as we left, but I had already figured out how I felt the night before, so I wasn't as unprepared as I might have been.

The beach was freezing and more than a little treacherous for walking since the rocks were coated with frozen spray. The sea ice, heaved up on shore by angry winter waves, proved to be an obstacle worthy of the most grueling course at Basic

Training, and by the time we reached a good vantage point, I was winded and sweating inside my coat and gloves.

"You really slay dragons out there at this time of year?" I asked, pointing at the roiling grey ocean.

"Well, no," Peter admitted. "This time of year we either leave them for the whales or try to get them on shore. But Owen looked so excited, and I didn't want to break his heart."

"He's tougher than he looks," I told him.

"He looks pretty tough," Peter said. "He's enormous, for starters, and when he's in uniform, he looks very authoritative."

I considered it. I was still used to thinking of Owen as the weedy kid I'd gone to high school with. But he had changed a lot in the last two years. I looked down at my hands, soaked inside my gloves.

"I wanted to thank you," I said. "For helping me with the music. It's been hard for me, for the past while, and you made it fun again."

"I had fun too," Peter said. There was a cautious hope in his eyes.

"I kind of wish we would be able to keep doing it," I said, doing my best to pretend I was Sadie and actually good at this. "But with you on this side of the Rockies and me on the other . . ."

"Yeah," he said, and the hope fizzled. I felt something in my stomach unclench. He didn't look angry, or even particularly sad. More wistful, I guess. I could handle wistful. "I guess that's always going to be a problem."

"They are pretty substantial mountains," I pointed out. "Plus, you know, Chinooks. If I ever see one of those again, it'll be too soon."

"They're going to keep you in Alberta for a while," Peter said.

"Ugh, don't remind me," I said, and laughed. "Tell me about the totem poles, please. It'll take my mind off it."

Peter grinned and launched into story after story of the dragon slayers who had protected his family's lands. Some of them were people Peter had known, and others were figures out of legend. It was fascinating to hear the two types of stories together. And always, there were orcas.

"They taught us how to slay dragons," Peter repeated. "So it's seems only fair to honour them."

My hands had gone from overheated to freezing in that awkward winter way, and I rubbed them together, blowing air, though that did little to help.

"We'd better get back," Peter said. "Your train is leaving soon, and I think your squad might miss you if you're not on it."

"You're probably right." I looked out over the ocean one last time. I might never see it again. There was something odd in the water out towards the island where I now knew the bulk of Peter's family lived. "What's that?"

Peter looked where I was pointing and smiled.

"Orcas." As soon as he said it, I felt silly for not realizing immediately.

We watched the pod play in the waves, their six-foot-tall black dorsal fins cutting through the water like a sword cuts through a dragon's hearts. One of them even breached, and I saw its white markings, a sharp contrast to the black flanks. On the totem poles, they were often painted red too, which made them look fierce. Seeing them in the ocean, I decided that they were fierce enough without the red on their sides. They were sleek, and when one opened its mouth, I saw teeth that would put a soot-streaker to shame.

"I'm glad they're on our side," I said to Peter as we scrambled over the ice back towards town.

"I think you might be surprised to find out how many people are on your side," Peter said.

"I didn't mean a real side," I said. "I meant against the dragons."

"Well," said Peter, holding out a hand to help me down the side of a particularly steep piece of ice, "there are dragons and there are dragons."

"That doesn't make any sense at all." I slid down and landed beside him. He squeezed my hand through the glove and winked.

"My cousins slay dragons," he told me. "I've sat in the canoe while they do it."

"Don't tell Owen that," I said. "That will actually break his heart."

"I'm serious, though," he said. "I've helped slay dragons. We all have. We work as a team, like your Guard does in Trondheim."

"It just seems practical," I said, more to myself than to him. I thought for a second that he might say something else, but he tripped on an outcropping of ice and I totally failed to catch him, so he tumbled down onto the rocky beach while I followed as quickly as I could.

"I'm fine," he said. "Just a stupid trip."

"If you're sure," I said. "Ilko can look you over, if you like."

"No, I'm good," he assured me. "I just didn't see that one in time."

I pulled him to his feet, and he didn't let go of my hand. Most people were so careful with my hands when they knew my injury, like it would still hurt, but Peter was never like that. He held my hand like it was totally normal.

"It's not like we can't talk to each other," he said, after a moment. "The mountains can't block the Internet."

"True." I didn't pull away.

"And we can still do songs," he said. "I'll try to record an orca slaying on video, if I can."

"Owen would appreciate that," I said. He smiled ruefully, and let go of my hand at last.

The ride back under the mountains was peaceful and dull. I spent much of it listening to the recordings that Peter's mother had given to me, of her drumming and some of the other Haida songs. I could hear a mandolin in some of them and knew that it was Peter playing. I would always have that much of him, anyway, which was as much as I really needed.

"You're really okay?" Owen said quietly, for about the fourteenth time since we'd left Port Edward.

"I'm really okay," I told him. Again.

"It's just that Sadie said she thought you might actually like this one." Owen didn't even look uncomfortable when he said it. It was very annoying.

"No," I said. "I mean, I like him. And I'll miss him, because I'm not likely to get across the Rockies too many more times in my life, let alone up to Port Edward, but there was nothing beyond music, I promise."

"Music might have been enough, once," Owen said. "Do you think?"

I thought about it for a second before answering. Before Sadie, before Owen, I thought I would be "that lovely young woman who plays the piano" forever. I wasn't particularly lonely, though I knew my parents had worried that I never got out. I had crushes on dead composers and pieces of music, and the occasional opera singer, but nothing tangible. Then I'd met Owen—and Sadie, who seemed determined that I was going to be astonishingly popular if it killed her. To my surprise, I found I liked it. That last year of school, no longer under my own pressure to be so dedicated to practice, I had eaten in the cafeteria and found that there was something to be said for the experience. I didn't think about Alex, Heidi, or the others very often, but when I did, it was fondly. For so long, I had sat out—playing solo instead of ensemble. I was good at it, it was true, but when I turned out to be good at ensemble as well, that didn't make my solos any less proficient.

"Yes," I said finally. I looked straight at him when I said it. "But that was before."

"Before you were famous on YouTube?" He smiled.

"Well, I'm not sure I'm famous on YouTube," I said. "But I meant before that. When we started working together."

"It's the kind of work best done with friends," Owen said, and I knew from his tone that they were Hannah's words. "You know, I was worried at first that you would just think we were using you because you were talented. But I really do like being your friend."

"Likewise," I said, leaning into his shoulder. It was broader than I remembered. "Well, except I was worried you'd think I was working with you because I wanted Lottie to stay and keep dragons from burning my house down."

"I swear to God," said Porter from the seat behind us. If I craned my neck and pushed up as tall as I could, I could almost see him. Owen only had to turn his head. "If the pair of you don't shut up, I am going to break the window and throw myself from the train."

"Apologies, Lieutenant," I said, doing my best not to giggle. "We thought you were asleep."

"Not for lack of trying," he growled.

"We'll keep it down, sir," Owen said, which I thought was ridiculous because we'd been talking fairly quietly. The fire crew was a few seats ahead of us, crammed in around one of the folding tables that were theoretically for paperwork, and trying to teach the Americans to play Cheat, with middling results.

"Are you going to write a song about the whales?" Owen whispered.

"I only saw them for a minute," I said. "And I think it will take me some time to get the drumming down."

Peter's mother had given me a small drum, along with an oversized stick that would be easier for me to grasp, but I figured it would be a while before I tackled learning to play it properly, much less incorporating it into songs.

"I think I'll write instead about the way Port Edward works together," I said, after a moment's consideration.

"Please tell me it's going to be a sea chantey," Owen said.

"Probably," I said. It would be hard to get around it. It was almost impossible to separate my feelings about Port Edward from the sound of the waves crashing on the icy rocks. Between the sea and the dragons, it was no wonder the Haida had such excellent drums. The cold water and warm houses, the family and the sense of home, would be best put to folk music, and not my usual tendencies towards classical.

By the time we got to Hinton, I had the beginnings of it in my head. We had thought that Owen and Porter would be leaving us there and returning to their desolate watch over the forests. Instead, we found new orders for all of us to return to Fort Calgary. There was no elaboration, and I did my best not to be concerned about it. But for some reason, the shadow that the mountains cast upon the prairies was much, much more menacing than it had been when we were on the western side, and the shelter offered by those cold, unadorned totem poles seemed less protective, now that I had seen real ones with my own eyes.

ONE MILLION

Fort Calgary was as we had left it, except there was a hum of activity in the corridors that had been absent since the snow had started to fall. Spring came slow to the prairies, but it could be prepared for, and prepare we did.

We were being deployed—all of us together, including Nick's and Kaori's squads—to the forests north of Grande Prairie. We were not being sent to slay dragons. Each plot of forest, carefully zoned out by the companies who had the logging rights, was carefully bordered by firebreaks, and every spring it was necessary to go north and clear them again. This year, we would also be widening many of them to keep the fires from jumping into populated areas. It would be cold and hard work—I'd finally be able to put to use all that exercise I'd gotten since Basic—but at least we would be together.

Before we left, I was summoned to General Speed's office. The orders came only for me, and I knew as soon as I saw Courtney's face that I was probably in trouble, but there was nothing for it. Annie and Laura helped me get into my dress uniform and made sure everything was perfect. From the way we tucked my short hair under my cap to the laces on my boots, I was the picture of an officer in the Oil Watch, low-ranked as I was. Inside that uniform, it was easy to stand up straight. It was easy to remember that I was good at my job and loyal to my duty, whatever my philosophical differences with the Fort's commander might be.

"Don't take the bait," Courtney said, pulling on my collar before I could leave. "Whatever he does or says, don't take it. That's what he wants. You haven't done anything wrong yet, but he'll try to goad you into something. That's how he operates. Don't let him."

"I won't." I didn't want to know how Courtney knew these things, though I had some suspicions. "And thank you."

The general's outer office was occupied by two desks for the general's aides (both absent—probably by design). His door was heavy and, surprisingly, made of wood. Everything else in Fort Calgary was concrete or steel, and seeing something flammable was odd. If dragon fire managed to get this far, a burning door was probably the least of our worries, but it still struck me, and it took me longer than it should have to raise a fist and knock.

"Enter," said the general, and it was then that I saw the knob on the door was the sort of handle that I found the most difficult to manipulate. I refused to panic and got it open as quickly as I could. I walked to the front of his desk and stood between the two chairs I would certainly not be invited to sit in.

"Reporting as ordered, sir," I said, saluting crisply.

"Bard McQuaid," General Speed said. He did not say "at

ease" so I remained at attention. "It has come to my attention that you have been chronicling our exploits in the Oil Watch to promote your own fame."

"Excuse me, sir?" I said, when it became apparent that he was waiting for an answer.

"Your Internet activity. On YouTube," he elaborated, looking like it caused him physical pain to say the words. "You have written more songs about the support squad and about the Fort than you have about your dragon slayer."

Apparently General Speed had done his homework and read all of the old regulations pertaining to the role of a bard— as I had done before enlisting.

"Sir," I said. "My dragon slayer was not here for the bulk of the winter. I chronicled what I could, as outlined in subsection D."

"So you did," the general said. "But at the same time, your followers online seem to think that you are the hero of the tale, not young Thorskard."

"Sir?" I said, now legitimately confused. That had never been my intention.

"You honestly expect me to believe that you have no idea how many followers you have?" General Speed demanded. "Or what they say about you?"

"No, sir," I said. "I don't read the comments."

The general sat back in his chair, steepling his fingers and looking at me like I was something to be considered anew.

"Well, then," he said, almost to himself. "Perhaps it's not as bad as I thought."

I didn't say anything. I could hear the snare drum beating out an unflinching rhythm. It would be marched to, and nothing out of step would be tolerated. I remembered what Courtney had told me. I wouldn't take the bait.

"You are prepared for your reassignment?" he asked after a moment.

"Nearly, sir," I replied. I wasn't sure what he was fishing for. "Our engineers are making lists and we expect to be ready within two hours, provided the materials they've requested can be found."

He didn't so much as flick an eyelid when I mentioned his daughter. He might as well have not even known who Courtney was.

"Very well," he said. "You're dismissed."

"Sir!" I saluted automatically, mostly on instinct. The dismissal had been a little abrupt. I fumbled with the door to get out, but he didn't look up from his paperwork.

I followed the corridors back to the barracks, much more slowly than I had on my approach, and tried to figure out what had just happened. Whatever the general had wanted, he'd clearly gotten from me, and it made me uncomfortable not to know what it was.

Perhaps he had genuinely thought that I was using my time in the Oil Watch to set myself up for some kind of post-service musical fame, and I had been able to convince him otherwise. I snorted, getting a glance from one of the caretakers as he passed me with a mop. He smiled at me and waved like he knew who I was. There weren't that many females on base and only one bard, so it was possible. But I didn't recognize him at all, and I felt a bit bad if I had forgotten meeting him.

In any case, it seemed unlikely that I had made General Speed feel better about my intention for my post–Oil Watch life. If anything, he seemed relieved about something more immediate. Something I had failed to notice.

I froze in my steps, heart hammering like I'd run a mile in full kit. He'd talked about my following, and I had misunderstood. Peter had given me a hint on the beach—that I had more people on my side than I imagined—and I'd been so distracted that I missed it. General Speed hadn't meant my followers. He was worried about something far more significant than clicking a thumbs-up icon on a Web page. He'd meant my *fans*.

It was late, but not so close to lights-out that I couldn't squeeze in an e-mail to Emily if I had to. I was in luck, too, because she was available to chat.

"Hey!" she said when I connected. "This is a surprise."

"How many followers do I have?" I asked. "The YouTube channel. How many followers does it have?"

"I miss you, too," she said, confused. "Um, we broke a million subscribers the other day. That was exciting. Do you want me to record a video thanking people? That seems to be trendy."

One million. One million people. And that wasn't even counting the casual viewers who hadn't subscribed. And they all heard me sing or play. They were all hearing the Story of Owen. But Owen rarely appeared in those videos. They were hearing his story, but they were hearing it from *me*.

"Siobhan?" Emily said.

"I—," I started. "There's not going to be new music for a while," I managed finally. "We're being deployed."

"All of you together?" Emily asked.

"Yes," I said. "Firebreak season."

"Sounds like no fun at all," Emily said cheerily. She was the indoor type.

"I'm sure we'll manage," I told her. "Look, I'm sorry to just randomly ask you questions for no apparent reason, but I'm kind of on my way somewhere."

"No problem," she said. "I should have mentioned your followers earlier. Did you want me to make that video? Thanking them?"

"Yes," I said, smiling. "I think that would be a good idea."

"Be safe," she said. "Take care of Owen."

"I will," I said, and signed off.

One million people. It wasn't just Trondheim and Port Edward. It was the world.

I walked back to the barracks and assured Courtney that her father hadn't done me any permanent damage. I'm not sure she believed me, given how distracted I was for the rest of the evening, but at least we got the packing done.

"Drum?" said Annie, looking down at what remained to be squared away.

"No," I said, "but the bugle for sure."

"Really?" asked Laura. "I mean, we're going to be in the middle of nowhere."

"Exactly," I said. "And sometimes the radios won't work. But you'll be able to hear this."

I tapped the case, and Courtney added it to her list. The bugle went in Aarons's kit, because he could carry it by the handle while we were walking. I couldn't, so I got the spare shovel and axe because they could be carried on my back.

It was the middle of nowhere, but at least we'd have each other. And thanks to Courtney, we would be very well prepared. Owen would carry mostly his own gear. There would be a few ATVs, but we'd do the bulk of our work on foot. To everyone's relief, it would be too hilly and too heavily wooded for the horses.

I fell asleep listening to Courtney recite where everything had been packed, so that she'd remember even if she didn't have her list handy. I'd write her a song too, I decided. She was as much a hero as I was, and apparently I had a million followers I could share her with.

THE STORY OF JOAN

It wasn't dragons that burned her, in the end.

But everyone remembers her name.

FORTY BELOW

The good thing about winter in northern Alberta is that it is so cold that the snow stays very, very frozen and remains light and fluffy for weeks after it has fallen. This came as a surprise to all of us but Laura, because in Ontario and Eastern Canada, snow tends to get heavy and gross after a while, and wading through two feet of it can be very hard. For the first day, even with our packs, it was almost like a game, wading through knee-deep snow like it was nothing. Of course, then we had to camp in it.

The military is nothing if not efficient, so we had a very well-appointed base camp. The tents had strong canvas sides, lined with a polymer that kept out even the fiercest winds, and the generators worked to keep us warm. Were it not for the ridiculous number of layers we had to put on before we went outside, it would have been almost like regular camping. I had done no small amount of winter camping with Owen and Aodhan, and sometimes Sadie, but those had always been short trips. Way out here and for this many days, well, let's just say we all got really good at going to the bathroom half-in and half-out of our fireproof snowsuits.

The actual work was grueling. Clearing the firebreaks wasn't too bad, because most of those trees were young saplings. The firebreaks that had to be widened were much worse, because most of those trees were much older. Generally speaking, logging wasn't done in this part of Alberta during the winter because the ground is too treacherous for heavy machinery, but this particular kind of logging couldn't wait for spring, because that was when fire season started.

It wasn't just dragon fire that we were working to prevent, although the fact that about sixty percent of Alberta forest fires were caused by dragons was what got the Oil Watch to do the actual labor.

In addition to our squad and Porter, Nick and his mentor, Kaori and Amery, and all of their squads were involved too. By the time you added in the five-hundred-odd regular members of Princess Patricia's Canadian Light Infantry deployed out of the base in Edmonton, we were nearly a whole company. All of us managed to get on well enough, mostly because Kaori was very well-liked by the Patricias. The only problem was that Amery's antipathy towards Owen and Porter was even more apparent now that they all had to live together in close quarters.

"I don't expect everyone to love me," Owen said about three weeks into our extended camping trip. "I just expect them to have a reason for disliking me."

"Maybe Amery thinks General Speed has the right idea about dragon slayers and their support crews," I suggested, trying to use a can opener on a can of beans. Owen let me struggle with it for a while, and then he just took it. I didn't say anything. I was hungry too.

"I don't think so," Owen said. "She didn't complain when Kaori suggested it was time to cut everyone's hair again."

"I still don't think that was a good idea, by the way," I told him, running a hand over my scalp. "My neck gets cold."

"It's forty below," Owen said. "I think your neck would be cold anyway."

Since there were almost six hundred of us, we worked a rotation of field and camp jobs. The regular troops were divvied up with the dragon slayer squads, and we all worked on week-long jaunts out from the main base camp, returning each night to smaller, less permanent camps. Saturdays and Sundays were spent in the main camp, redistributing work for the following week and attempting to thaw out. So far, Owen had worked with Nick's mentor twice, and once with just Porter and some extra troops from Edmonton, but he had yet to go with Amery.

I had spent the first week in the main base camp with the big radio, a map, and a metric ton of straight pins, which I used to keep track of where everyone was and how many firebreaks they had cleared. It was kind of fascinating, and I learned the geography of the river valley pretty quickly, but by the second week Porter had decided that he wanted me in the field with them, because they were headed for a hilly region where they didn't think the small radios would work. They didn't, and I spent five days in camp freezing my ears off, blowing bugle calls so that everyone would know when it was time to eat. I'd be lying if I said it wasn't the most fun I'd had since Christmas. Porter made sure to talk about how useful I had been, so the next week, I went out again with Nick's crew and did the same thing. Our next assignment was with Amery, and all fourteen members of Owen's crew were going together.

"Do you really think we need this much stuff?" Laura asked, looking with some dismay at what Courtney expected her to carry. "The Patricias will have a lot of spares, you know."

"That may be," Courtney sniffed, "but I like to know that you'll have what you need."

"The only fires we've seen have been for cooking," Laura said under her breath as she lifted her pack by its strap with a mournful expression on her face.

Privately, I rather agreed with her. But at the same time, I couldn't deny Courtney's point. During the week I'd spent with Nick, Kaori and Amery had found a nest of Wapiti eggs, and we'd seen signs of 'Bascan Longs—trees bent over with slashes from their tail spines, not to mention the burns on the tree bark—though none of the actual dragons themselves. I suppose it never hurt to be prepared.

"You should try lifting one of the Patricias' packs," Courtney said. "We just have to carry fire stuff. They have to carry everything they would if they were in Afghanistan."

"What, in case of insurgents?" Annie said.

"For practice," I said. "Like how the Redcoats all had the same kit, whether they were boiling to death in India or freezing to death in Quebec."

"'Cause that worked out so well for them," Laura muttered.

"Well, you're carrying that pack, so stop moaning about it."

"Yes, ma'am," Laura saluted. She didn't even look that sarcastic.

My alarm beeped. Time for taps. Even though we were in camp and everyone could use the radio just fine, it had become customary for me to play the main calls of the day: reveille, meals, and taps. It meant I had to get up first and was always late to meals, because the best spot to be heard from was also far from the commissary, but I didn't mind. It helped that we weren't rushed through meals and that someone else always got my plate when they went through the line to get their own.

I pulled the bugle from the case and polished it off with my shirt.

"Why do you always do that?" Annie asked. "It's not marked up at all."

"Comfort, I guess," I told her, making sure the spit valve hadn't frozen shut. In this cold, the bugle was nearly impossible to tune, but so far no one had complained. It probably helped that I was the only person who could hear the instruments the bugle had to be in tune with.

"She likes to know where everything is too," Courtney said, and I smiled at her. It was true.

I set the bugle on my cot and stood so that I could pull on my snow pants. I was still wearing my boots—the pants had a zippered leg—and the clasp was big enough that I could do them myself. I put on my thermal and then the fireproof coat. I was already sweating, but I knew it would be worth it as soon as I stepped outside. Last came the balaclava, toque, and thick mittens.

At least we'd yet to experience a skin-exposure warning.

I picked up the bugle and headed for the tent flap.

"See you in a moment," I said, and ducked out.

I walked across the camp by myself. There weren't a lot of people out. This call was almost entirely unnecessary, except it told everyone that the kitchen was closed and let the nighttime radio operator know it was time for his or her shift. Still, it was my favourite song of all the calls, so I didn't mind in the slightest.

The thing about taps is that it wasn't written for the woods, but it could have been. Each note gets held as long as you want. There are pauses for effect. It's a song about going to sleep, but it's also a song filled with joy, or at least with contentment for a day's work done well. The words were added later, and unlike those added to reveille, they match the profound nature of the melody. I went to stand by the flag pole and licked my lips under the balaclava. I pulled the hood down and raised the bugle to my mouth.

It's odd to play for so many people and not have any of them actually watch you do it. I couldn't see another soul, but I could feel them all pause. Such is the nature of taps.

I finished the song—it's not a long one—and headed back for my tent. On the way, I saw that I did have a one-person audience, and I'd missed her because she had been standing in the shadows.

"You're very good," Amery said when I saw her. She had a more delicate drawl than the other Southerners on her crew and Nick's crew.

"Thank you, Lieutenant," I said. "I'm fairly new at the bugle."

"I prefer it when it's jazz," she said. "But you need valves for that."

"I'm not so good with valves anymore," I admitted, wiggling my fingers inside my mittens. "And I was never much for improvisation."

"I can imagine that," she said. "I didn't get to see much of the good part of New Orleans when I was there, but I did like the jazz."

"Katrina?" I asked, as politely as I could. This was the closest we'd ever had to an opening with her, and I was determined to take it.

"The aftermath, mostly," she said. "Not exactly the best place to start your tour with the Oil Watch."

"We say the same thing about Alberta back home," I said. "But I guess it's for a different reason."

"I'll bet," she said, and then she seemed to remember that since I was technically under her command for the week, I couldn't leave until she dismissed me. "Don't let me keep you out in the cold if you've got a place to be."

"Good night, Lieutenant," I said, and walked back to the tent.

IN FRONT OF THE HORIZON

"Katrina explains a lot," Owen said when I'd told him about my very short conversation.

"How so?" I asked. "Is this one of those dragon slayer honour things?"

"Kind of," Courtney said. She sat on the foot of her cot and watched as I peeled off my layers. Owen sat on my bed and folded things as I handed them to him, unless they were wet and needed hanging. "Katrina was the first time that the Americans brought in Darktide instead of just relying on the Oil Watch. The 'consultants' only slayed dragons on orders from the corporations they represented, only put out the fires they were paid to put out, and completely turned a blind eye to any flooding, because it wasn't part of their job description."

"I remember my mother swearing at the TV a lot," I said.

"I remember Hannah having to restrain Lottie from getting on a plane so she could go south and bash heads together," Owen said. He took my snow pants over to the drying rack and laid them over a bar. "She doesn't get mad often, but when she does, she's pretty mad."

"I still don't understand what that explains about Amery," I said.

"Well," Owen said, "Lieutenant Beaumont doesn't like consultant dragon slayers."

"We're the Oil Watch," I pointed out.

"Yeah, but Lottie's not," Owen said. "Not anymore, anyway, and when I'm done with my tour, I am not going to be any more accountable than she is. Plus, we did kind of destroy the ecosystem of the world's largest freshwater island last spring."

"I guess that makes a little bit of sense," I said. "When you talk to her, be sure to stress how dependent you are on the goodwill of the people who live in Trondheim."

"Thanks, Emily," Owen said, grinning.

"Get out of my tent, Thorskard," I said, but couldn't even muster pretend anger behind my words. "We're tired and we have to walk tomorrow."

He laughed, but he did leave us alone. When he was gone, we pulled our cots as close to the space heater as was safe, and prepared for our last warm night until next Friday.

"You know, even with the cold, this is still kind of fun," Annie said. "It's been more like what I thought I was signing up for."

"I know what you mean," Courtney said. "Siobhan, will you sing us taps? I like the words."

Voices carry pretty well at night, even in the woods. I have no idea who else besides us could hear me when I sang, but I didn't try to be quiet about it. Taps was easy to play, and it was easy to sing too. I let the words fill the tent, and if they escaped out into the night, so much the better. Taps is, after all, hope for a good night's rest, and everyone in the camp earned that every day.

In the morning, we shouldered our packs and walked back into the bush. We would be picked up by helicopters on Friday. Usually, the routes were arranged so that you looped back by week's end, even if you had to spend most of Friday walking. This week, though, we were headed out so far that they had decided it was worth the risk to fly back. It was a larger group than usual too, with Nick's squad in addition to ours, Kaori's, and Amery's, and a whole platoon of Patricias, so that they would match the Watch numbers nearly one to two. Of the dragon slayers, only Nick's mentor and her squad would stay behind to protect the main camp.

As a rule, helicopters were less risky than airplanes when it came to air travel. For starters, they were more manoeuvrable and could be landed much more easily. Oil Watch helicopters had special blades which could, in a pinch, decapitate a dragon, though that was a last resort because it tended to kill the helicopter in addition to slaying the dragon. If the pilot wasn't able to eject in time, things could get very messy. Still, it was kind of exciting. The idea of it, I mean. I left slaying-by-helicopter to Courtney and her sketchbook.

Our first two days were spent working on a ridge line, clearing trees so that the landform could be used as an outlook for both fires and incoming dragons. From the height, we could just make out the low blue line of the Rockies in the distance.

When it got dark, we could see the lights of Grande Prairie in the other direction, even though it was some hours away.

"That's nothing," said Laura. "You can almost see the lights of Regina from Saskatoon, if it's clear."

"That is just insane," Amery said. She had taken to eating with us because Kaori liked to, though she still wouldn't sit close to Porter. Her conversation with Owen was strained, but at least they were both making the effort.

"Lieutenant, tell them about the dragons in Texas." Professional as always, Kaori somehow managed to make that a polite request.

Amery began to recount a story about the time she and a couple other dragon slayers from the National Guard, a sort of pre–Oil Watch organization the Americans had, took down what was apparently the largest dragon in North America.

"Bigger than a Chinook?" Nick asked at one point during the tale.

"Nothing is bigger than a Chinook," Porter said flatly, and it was as if the cold wind blew the fun right out of the tent. There was a long silence, and the camaraderie of the evening was entirely broken.

"Aarons, you wanted to see my swords?" Owen said, finally. I looked at him with a smile.

"Yes, if you've got time," our smith said. "It's been a while since we've really inspected them, and it's cold out here."

"I've got time now," he said. "Nick? Courtney?"

They all filed out with Nick's smith trailing behind them, and I turned to Kaori to ask her about her time in Edmonton. She hadn't done a lot of dragon slaying there, but she had gotten to see how a regular prairie city functioned. Edmonton had no totem poles because it was outside of the Chinook range (though some environmentalists pointed out that every year that range was increasing). It did, however, have the second-largest shopping mall in North America.

Porter disappeared from the tent a minute later, and Amery relaxed as soon as he was gone. It was probably out of line, but with everyone distracted, I couldn't quite help turning to her after I had finished talking with Kaori.

"What is it that you don't like about him?" I asked. "Is it just that he's rude?"

"No," she said. "I don't like that he's a career officer who doesn't follow orders."

"He follows orders," I said, a bit defensively. He was my commanding officer after all. And he was involved with one of my very good friends.

"The ones he likes," she said. "And the ones he doesn't like, he follows grudgingly. And every now and then, he disobeys entirely. He is exactly the sort of person who shouldn't mentor Owen."

That was more or less exactly what Lottie had implied at Christmas, but I got the distinct impression that the two women had different reasons.

"What, because he'll ruin Owen's reputation?" I asked. Technically, I was probably being insubordinate, but I figured in for a penny, in for a pound, and pressed on anyway. "Because I'm pretty sure that happened before we got here."

"Maybe," Amery said. "But he's not helping."

"I think he's helping a lot," I said. "He's helping Owen become a better dragon slayer, and that's what's important."

"You say that now," she said. "But someday you'll be

watching his court-martial, wondering how the hell you all got there."

I wasn't entirely sure we were talking about Owen anymore.

"So you knew Porter before?" I said. "In Kansas?"

"Of course I did," she said. "He was the best. We were all so excited, Americans in general, I mean, when he was assigned there. This heartthrob of a British SAS dragon slayer. And then he destroyed an entire state because he didn't feel like honouring the oldest rule in dragon slaying."

"Less than two percent," I said, remembering what Courtney had told me.

"What?" She finally looked dangerous now, like she would report me to General Speed, and I would have to face whatever reprimand he could come up with. In that moment, I found I didn't care. I was through with stories. It was time for truth.

"That's how much of Kansas is on fire. Less than two percent. And he saved hundreds of lives. If you're going to make a career of this, you should probably stop listening to all the stories. I tell a lot of them, and I'll tell you something: I lie all the time. I lie for effect; I lie to protect people. But I lie. And so does everyone else, whether they are bards or not."

She stared at me while I stood up to leave. It's difficult to make a dramatic exit when you have to put on four layers of winter gear between your seat and the door, but I did my best anyway. She didn't try talking to me while I was leaving, at least. Maybe she finally understood what I was trying to achieve.

Out in the cold, I realized that we had lingered over dinner for much longer than usual. We didn't have an official lights-out, but we did have a very early wake-up call, and most of us were pretty possessive of our sleeping time. I pried my glove off to check my wristwatch and saw that it was nearly time for taps. I put my glove back on as I was walking for the tent, and got my bugle without any of the ritual I'd so happily told Laura about only a few nights before.

I didn't want this to be the rest of my life. Not the part where I was in the woods in Alberta, but the part where I had to defend the people I loved from people who didn't know the whole story. I guessed it would be easier once I got home, back to the people who actually respected us. I would be able to ensure that our side of the events was told, and since I was apparently famous on the Internet, there was going to be a pretty receptive audience. It was the next few years I was worried about. The ones I'd spend out here.

And yet. It wasn't just Owen that our comrades were coming to respect. It was me, too. The cleanup crews in Fort Calgary all waved to me when I walked past them on the base. Most of the guys in the Patricias seemed to know me on sight, like they'd heard about me before we'd arrived. Kaori had kept her head shaved while she was in Edmonton, as had the rest of her crew and Nick's crew as well. Maybe it wouldn't be so bad.

Reaching the ridge top, I looked out over the vista and sighed. There were so many freaking trees, and we had to cut down so many of them, and it was hard work. I knew it was important, but that didn't make it any more fun. I was about to start the call when something caught my eye.

The sun had set hours ago—this was winter in Alberta— but to the west there was an orange glow on the horizon.

No. My blood ran cold. Not *on* the horizon. In front of it. The stars above me shone clear, but those to the west were covered by a darkness that was no cloud. It was smoke. Smoke and fire to the west. And I knew what that had to mean.

I raised the bugle, but it wasn't taps that I played. It was the dragon call, with the special code, the one I had never wanted to play.

Chinook.

GOOD PAYLOAD, DECENT RANGE

The first thing we did, of course, was fight. Or rather, the mentors fought with each other, and with the infantry commander who was theoretically in charge of the whole operation.

"How are we even sure it's a Chinook?" the commander said. "She just saw fire near the mountains and panicked."

"Siobhan McQuaid does not panic," Porter said, his voice absolutely steady. I was grateful for his vote of confidence, but to be honest, I was pretty close to panic.

"Chinooks don't come this far," Amery said.

"They've gone farther," Porter reminded her. The mood darkened considerably, and I saw Porter and Owen lock eyes. They both seemed to deflate for a moment, and then straighten as they reached some agreed upon purpose. I was jealous. I had worked for a long time to be able to do that with Owen. Porter had only had those few weeks in Hinton. Still, this was hardly the time and place for that. I turned my attention back to my dragon slayer.

"This is going nowhere," Owen hissed in my ear. "Come on, let's go."

We hadn't been dismissed, but I didn't think they'd miss us too much. Nick and Kaori, standing behind their own mentors, followed us out of the mess tent. Annie, Aarons, and Davis were waiting outside, obviously eavesdropping, while Courtney stood beside them. She at least pretended to be going over a requisition list. They didn't look remotely abashed when we got close. I didn't blame them.

"What are we going to do?" Nick asked. "We've got some time, I know, but it's headed for Grande Prairie, so they're in big trouble."

"They should be able to evacuate," Kaori said.

"To where?" Nick said. "You can't just turn sixty thousand people into the woods at night in the winter. At Fort Calgary, we've got the whole base, and Edmonton and Moose Jaw have emergency tunnels, but Grande Prairie just has regular shelters, and that won't be enough."

"What if we shot it?" Courtney's face was white in the dark, and her voice scraped out as she said the words, like it was the hardest thing she'd ever said.

"With arrows?" Nick was nearly hysterical now. "I'm good, but there's no arrow in the whole world—"

"With an SAM," Courtney said. The words tripped out now, like she was afraid that if she stopped talking, the words would stop coming. "Surface-to-air missile."

We were all shocked into silence. Three dragon slayers, raised from the cradle to cringe from the very idea, a firefighter who could see better than anyone the damage in her mind, a medic who could smell burning flesh and imagine leukemia for generations, and one bard who knew all the stories. Only Aarons, the smith, looked less than stunned.

I shook my head. That was the one thing we couldn't do. I could see the map in my mind, clear as if it were in front of me. We were too close to where the Wapiti River joined the Smoky. If we shot the Chinook here, we could contaminate the entire northern Alberta water table, and that was before you considered the part where we would set a large area on fire.

"I think she's right," Owen said after a very long moment. He had locked eyes with Courtney, which was not normal. Usually he and I made decisions together.

"Owen, are you insane?" I asked.

"No," he said. He still didn't look at me, though. Maybe it was the light, and I just couldn't follow his eyes. "They'll have time to barricade the Peace River, and most of the Smoky will be upstream of the damage. Even if it gets as far as the Lesser Slave, they should be able to contain it."

Apparently I wasn't the only one who had been studying the map.

"What about the forest?" Kaori said. "Not to mention the oil and gas in the ground here. It is the livelihood for the region, and it will not grow back in a hurry."

"At least they'll be alive," Nick said. "I think they'd rather be alive."

"Fine," I said. I could feel the instruments assembling—rustling sheet music, settling in, looking to the conductor for direction. Except I didn't know who the conductor was, so I didn't know where to look. "Where are we going to get a surface-to-air missile?"

"We'll take it from the stores," Courtney said.

"We have that with us?" Now I was feeling hysterical too.

"The Patricias travel like they're in a combat zone," Courtney reminded me. "Artillery included."

I tried, but there were too many pieces in play for me to deal with, too many parts and me behind on my own sheet music. I couldn't see everything. I couldn't see enough. Courtney was the planner. If she knew where something was and how to use it, I would just have to trust her.

"Fine," I said. "Are you just going to steal it?"

"Pretty much," she said.

"I'll come with you," Owen said.

"No, just me," Courtney said. "They won't court-martial me if they catch me poking around in the stores."

"You're as much in the army as I am," Owen pointed out.

"Yeah, but I know my dad pretty well, having spent most of my teenage years trying to provoke him," Courtney said. "The only thing he holds in higher regard than the dragon slayers of the Oil Watch is the dragon slayers in his own family, and he would never, ever let my court-martial cast any dirt on our image. If I get caught and I can't talk my way out of it, he will."

"At least let me go with you." Owen finally looked at me, but only briefly. "Once you give it to me, I can just disappear into the brush and no one will be able to stop me."

Courtney looked at him for a beat too long, and then at me. I was thinking about fire, and horns, and didn't see what I should have seen.

"Fine," she said. "Let's go."

They disappeared into the dark, and we stood around, breathing steam and trying not to think about the inferno that was about to settle down on our heads.

Porter stuck his head out of the tent and saw us.

"Where's Owen?" he asked.

"Busy," I said. It was not my best lie. Mostly because it was the truth.

"When he gets back, tell him I want to see him," Porter said. "We have to arrange the camp for low emissions to avoid catching the Chinook's attention. It'll be a cold night."

"I will, sir," I said.

"I'm sending down to Calgary for some of that chemical the Japanese have been working on. It's still experimental, but we're about to have a perfect testing ground, I'm afraid." His eyes narrowed. "Where's Courtney?" he asked, his voice much quieter.

"Also busy," Nick said. He was a terrible liar, so it was fortunate that he was telling the truth too.

Porter's face hardened and then softened in an instant.

"Stick together," he said to me. "No matter what."

Then he was gone. Annie and Aarons went to marshal the rest of our squads and pack up in case we needed to move in a hurry. After a moment, Davis followed them.

"Stick together when, exactly?" I said, to no one in particular. "Does he mean huddle together for warmth?"

Neither Nick nor Kaori had an answer, and we shuffled our feet in the snow for what seemed like hours until Courtney came back.

"It's done," she said. "We got a Stinger. Good payload, decent range. Can be put on an ATV for transport. It was the biggest MANPADS we could manage."

Basic Training was a while ago, so it took me some time to remember exactly how the Stinger worked. One person. Unguided range. And Courtney had come back by herself.

"Where is Owen?" I rounded on her.

"He's gone," she said.

"He's gone where?" Nick asked.

"I'm not telling you which way he went. You'll never catch him anyway."

Then Nick's eyes widened, white showing in the dark. "He can't. He can't."

"He's going to," Courtney said. "We have to get ready for the fires. Get the others. Get everyone."

"Courtney," I said, my voice flat as my mind raced. "It's a close-range weapon."

"I know," she said. Her hands were still. Her hands were never still.

"You know," I parroted. I wanted to fly at her, to rip off my gloves and sink my fingernails into her face. But I couldn't feel anything.

"Siobhan, we have to move," she said. "There is going to be a fire."

I couldn't drive the ATVs, because my hands weren't deft enough to squeeze the throttle or the brakes. I don't think I could have driven anyway. My mind was too busy sorting parts, trying to stall until the ending was ready. So many things I could do now. And so many things I couldn't. Technically, ATVs are one-person vehicles, but I rode behind Nick anyway. We tied my hands around his waist, which was also dangerous, particularly in the dark. At least we would be on a cut line, and it was one we had just cleared, so we knew that it was straight and relatively free of surprises. Nick drove as cautiously as he could in the darkness, but we were still jarred and shaken when we got to the coordinates Courtney had selected.

The stars were all obliterated now, and an orange glow surrounded us. We could only guess how much fire the Chinook had laid down as it came out of the mountains. Usually, they liked to hold off until they got to their targets, and then they breathed fire until they had no fire left to breathe. No one could guess the range, though. The Chinook that Porter had slayed in Kansas had held off burning until it got there, and no other Chinook on record had traveled that far.

Courtney was on her radio when Nick and I arrived, the last to do so because he'd been going slowly. And I listened while she told Porter what we were doing. What Owen was about to do. I waited until she was done, until Porter had told her to be careful, and meant something entirely different, before I went over to her.

"Does he have a radio?" I asked.

"Yes," Courtney said. "But he's on the other side of that," she waved at the forest. "I don't know if he'll hear you."

"Give it to me," I said.

I took off my gloves so I could press the buttons properly. The cold bit at my fingers.

"Owen?" I said. "Owen, can you hear me?"

I tried a few more times, but there was only static.

"We don't have much time," Nick said, looking up. "It'll be on top of us soon."

"How do we know it'll go for him?" Kaori asked, as delicately as possible. Her eyes shone, and I knew it wasn't just reflected light.

"He took some extra munitions," Courtney said, watching me carefully. "And there's an active oil rig. He's going to light it on fire."

"Courtney," I said. "You don't just walk away from—"

And then the look they'd shared before they stole the SAM fell into the harmony, and the song made awful, awful sense.

Trees produce oxygen as part of their life cycle, and I was in a forest. I tried to breathe in, to move to the next measure, but I couldn't do it. I tried and tried, but the air was gone, and I was stuck until Nick walloped me in the stomach and instinct took over.

"Nick," I said, after I finished gasping. "I need you to help me climb a tree."

Nick nodded and took the floodlight to see which tree would be the best. The one he selected was not the tallest, but it had the widest branches at the bottom, and it was one that even I could climb. At last we were as high up as we could safely go, the cold wind pulling at our coats and the heavy scent of dragon smoke all around us.

"Try now," Nick said. He pressed me against the trunk as the tree shifted in the wind. "Don't worry about falling," he said, his hands solidly on either side of me, holding on for both of us. "I've got you."

I let go of the trunk and fished the radio out of my pocket.

"Owen!" I yelled. "Owen Thorskard, you answer me!"

There was a crackle, and then his voice.

"Siobhan!" he said. "I'm sorry. Don't be angry with Courtney. It was my idea."

"I'll be mad at whoever I want," I said into the radio. Nick buried his face in my shoulder, and I wondered if he was crying, like Kaori was.

"Okay," he said. "Be mad. But don't be so mad that you forget the story."

"Fuck the story. We're supposed to go home together. We're supposed to live in Trondheim, and you're supposed to have adorable baby dragon slayers with Sadie."

He laughed at me, then, but it was hard to tell because there was a roar above us as the Chinook drew close. It was hard to see in the dark and through the tree branches, but its presence was unmistakable. In the distance, we saw the orange flare of an explosion, and I knew that Owen had lit the rig. I screamed, not bothering to muffle the sound, and above us, the dragon keened and turned, wings splitting the air. As it headed towards the new source of carbon dioxide that Owen had so thoughtfully provided, I had a flash of memory—a classroom and an imaginary canal and a girl who could casually change the course of history because it was over, and the fire couldn't really hurt anyone. This one could.

"Siobhan?" It was Owen, through the radio. He sounded so calm.

"Don't," I begged. "Run."

"Siobhan," he said again.

"Stop it," I yelled. I wanted to reach through the radio and grab him. "Please, you can still run."

"Siobhan, I need you to tell Aunt Hannah—" he started.

"SHUT UP!" I screamed again. It must have hurt Nick's ears, he was so close, but he didn't let me go.

"Tell her that I'm sorry."

"Owen."

"Tell her that I love her."

"Owen."

"Tell her—" He laughed. "I don't know. Tell her a lie."

We could hardly see, except for when the Chinook passed

between us and the fire. Then, there was blackness, but all other times, there was just orange. He must have waited until the very last moment, until he couldn't possibly miss. Chinooks don't have many weak spots. He was only going to get one shot.

Across the valley, the sky and ground lit up with fire. It took a moment for the sound to reach us, but when it did, it was deafening.

"OWEN!" I screamed into the radio one last time.

But there was nothing after that.

VERY WELL TRAINED

There was fire, and plenty of it, but I wasn't afraid of it anymore. The forest around us burned, despite the efforts of Annie and the others. The Patricias reached us—not just the squads that had come out with us, but a whole company from base camp. Kaori helped out where she could, but I kept losing sight of her in the dark river of people. The engineers were on standby to fix, replace, or stand in as necessary. The medics had water for drinking and every kind of burn dressing you could imagine.

I don't remember climbing out of the tree.

Nick must have done it for me, somehow got both of us safely back on the ground. As though safety mattered anymore. I sat down and lost track of him. My hands were bleeding, and someone wrapped them with a light gauze, but I didn't feel it any more than I felt fear. If I was lucky, I would never feel anything again.

I couldn't imagine telling Hannah, telling Sadie, that I'd be coming home alone. Then I remembered that I wouldn't have to. Some officer they didn't know, probably, would bring them the news. Sadie might hear it through the grapevine, but Hannah and Lottie would get a knock on the door and two officers in perfect uniforms. Hannah would know, of course, as soon as she saw them. But they had words they were supposed to say.

They'd have to call Aodhan home. Someone would have to tell Catalina. And they wouldn't be able to take any time to grieve properly. There were always other dragons. Always other fires. And there was no one to take Aodhan's place. And now there never would be.

"Siobhan?" I realized that Davis had been saying my name for a while. I forced myself to pay attention to him, to a person who was here and breathing.

"What?" I said.

"Don't touch any of the chemicals." His eyes were wet. I wondered if it was water or snow or tears. Probably tears. "You might get an infection."

I wanted to tell him that I didn't need my hands anymore, that it didn't matter if they got infected. I couldn't tell the Story of Owen. There wasn't anything to tell. It would end in a crash of cymbals and drums and one fading note from the horn.

"All right," I said. "Tell Courtney to find me something else to do."

It was like my words had gone on without me.

Nick still hadn't let me go. "You should go back up the tree," I told him. "They'll need you to see what's happening."

"I gave Courtney the radio," he said softly. "She's getting orders from on high."

Above the fire, I heard the sound of helicopter blades.

One passed overhead, and a large crate fell into a clear space. Courtney was on it immediately, distributing new supplies with efficiency, but the steady beat that usually accompanied her movements and her organization was gone. The helicopter passed over us again, much lower this time, and I saw we had more backup. Amery jumped, landing hard in the snow, but she rolled to her feet quickly enough and waved off Davis and Ilko when they converged on her. She went to Courtney and began issuing orders.

I looked at Nick. His face was covered with tree sap and scratches that had come from fingernails not bark. I had fought him when he brought me down from the tree. I hoped that I would remember to apologize later. Now, though, all I could focus on was the great nothing that surrounded him. His fingers moved, twisting at his sides, but there were no whispering strings. No promise of a backing orchestra.

"Nick," I said very seriously. He leaned closer to hear me. "Why do you do that with your fingers?"

"What?" He sounded confused.

"Your fingers," I repeated. "Why do you twist them?"

He looked at his hands like they didn't belong to him. I knew how that worked. There was the slightest ghost of a smile, and then: "It's what I do to check the fletching on my arrows," he said. "It's a habit. Like how you always check the slides before you play."

I didn't think I was ever going to play again. There was too much quiet, even with the fire raging. If I tried to find the music, I would have to find everything else too.

"I can't hear the music," I told him.

"It'll come back," he said. "I know it. It'll come back."

"No, he won't," I told him. "The fire took him."

"You had music before Owen, didn't you?"

"Yes," I said. "But it was different. It wasn't as much fun."

"It's not gonna be fun for a while," Nick said. "But it'll come back."

"Siobhan!" Courtney appeared beside us. Nick finally let me go. "They've brought us that compound I was talking about, the Swiss one."

"How did it get here?" I asked.

Then I remembered: Porter had sent for it. They must have flown it up, and then he'd given it to Amery.

"We need to go and put it down on the fires," Courtney said. She was talking to me like I was a child. I was grateful. It was easy to understand her. "We're going to use the usual equipment, but we need Nick to help. Amery is going to stay here and run the operation. Will you be okay with the medics?"

"Of course," I told her. "The dragon's slayed."

Ilko came over and took me to where he and the other medics were set up. They wrapped a blanket around me, even though I was wearing a snowsuit, and then I remembered that blankets are what people get when they are in shock.

We waited for hours. Every now and then, someone would return for more supplies, and Ilko or Davis would get up to help them, following Amery's orders to the letter. One of them always stayed with me. They talked about everything. Ilko told me more than I ever thought I'd learn about the Toronto Blue Jays. Davis told me about his plans for medical school, and how he was hoping to be a GP in a small town, like my mother.

And the fire burned.

For the first while, I didn't answer them at all when they

spoke, but eventually it seemed rude to just sit there and not contribute. Without realizing it, I found myself telling them about how I'd drawn music as a child without realizing what it was. I told them about my house in Trondheim, about the piano and my grandmother's hymnal. I told them about the high school, that St. George was our mascot. And I told them about the time a family of dragon slayers had moved to our town.

"Everyone's been so happy," I said. Ilko wasn't looking at me, but Davis was. He looked a bit concerned. "Since they came, I mean. Livestock deaths are down by almost thirty percent, and we've only lost three barns in two years, not counting what happened to Saltrock, of course. That was a little different."

Davis's hand was on my arm under the blanket. I wondered if he thought I was going to run away, or if I was going to break.

"We wanted them to stay," I said. I realized that Amery was standing very close by, her own medics attending to a fresh scrape on her face. Tree branches, I thought. "We wanted our own dragon slayers. They helped us, and we fed them. They don't have to stay, but they stay. They made Trondheim their home, and now they protect it."

I met Amery's eyes, and she nodded.

"It's a good plan," she said. "For the right kind of town."

"Trondheim's a good little town," I said. "We're lucky to have them. The Thorskards."

But we wouldn't have all of them anymore. I pushed the thought away even as it occurred to me, but it was no good. I couldn't talk anymore. I just sat there and listened while Ilko went on about baseball and Amery answered calls on the radio. At some point, Porter arrived, landing no more gently than Amery had. He looked at me, and I stared blankly at him. I thought for a moment he might take me by the shoulders and shake me, but instead he turned away towards someone who had crashed back into the cut line.

On it went. Things fell from the sky every time the helicopters came close. Before, I would have noted the pitch of their blades as they cut the air and how it harmonized with the roar of their engines, but not now. I heard the noises, but I didn't make them into music the way I used to. I couldn't find the hidden notes the way I always had. I couldn't make them sing.

"Siobhan." It was Courtney again, at my elbow. I hadn't heard her come back.

"What time is it?" I don't think I was sleeping. I was just completely out of touch.

"It's almost dawn," she told me. I looked around. The sky was a bit more grey. And the smoke was clearing, even though we still couldn't see any stars above our heads.

"Is the fire out?" I said.

"As much as possible," she said. She coughed, and Davis pressed a bottle of water into her hands. She drank it obediently. I tried not to think about what we might have inhaled all night. "The smoke jumpers are going to come over from BC and do the rest of the drops from planes."

"How bad is it?" I asked.

"It'll be okay," she said. "Trees grow back, and they were able to block off the Wapiti River before it joins the Smoky. He picked a good spot."

"He's very well-trained," I told her. I didn't even want to think his name. I knew as soon as I did, I would never be able to stop.

The others drew closer. They were burned and covered

with dirt and sap, but they were whole, and I was glad to see them. That feeling of gladness stirred and worked up all the other feelings with it, so I tried to tamp it back down, but I couldn't. Underneath, I thought I heard something familiar. Something I loved. Something I thought I had lost.

"Siobhan?" It was Nick. He was holding the bugle.

"You brought the bugle?" I said to Courtney.

"We'd been having problems with the radio," she said. "I packed it in case we needed to call for each other in the woods."

That wasn't what I was going to use it for now, though. I could call muster all I wanted. All of us who could respond were already here.

"You should do it now," Amery said. She pointed up. "They'll be here soon."

They would. And when they did, he wouldn't be ours any more. We'd have to share him with everyone who wanted to hear the story.

I was still frozen. But when Nick set the bugle in my hands, I felt cold brass and remembered. The familiar thing I heard was the horn. It was Owen's horn, in spite of everything. He had one more song. And I would find the music to write it.

"Siobhan?" Courtney asked, but I nodded.

I was clumsy, even more so than usual, because of the gauze. Courtney helped me put my fingers on the bugle and then stepped back, giving me space. I didn't know if I had the breath, if I had the air, but as I raised the horn, the squads fell into their lines, and the bard came through.

Day is done,
Gone the sun
From the lakes, from the hills, from the sky.

It was the wrong song for this time of day. But it was the first song that came to mind. In Canada, they play the last post on Remembrance Day. But in the Oil Watch, we play something else. Taps is not just a song to play for the setting of the sun.

It's the song we play for the dead.

All is well
Safely rest
God is nigh.

The last note hovered in the trees, and then the helicopters started to land.

TRADITION

We were airlifted back to Fort Calgary as soon as the sun came up. We could see the smoke jumpers' planes, and the jumpers themselves, or at least their parachutes. I hadn't even noticed them last night, but of course they had been brought in. They could cover more of the fire from the air than we could on the ground. For a moment, I envied them. They only had to come in when the dragon was dead, and most of them must have stayed aloft to disperse the chemical. From that high up, the fire damage didn't look as bad.

I was taken straight to the infirmary, where they re-bandaged my hands. The gauze they used was much heavier; I could barely move my fingers at all, but the doctor told me that I'd be out of the wrappings soon enough.

"And if you feel any twinges, anything you think might be an infection, tell them to bring you here immediately," he said, and I was escorted back to my quarters.

I was staying in officers' quarters now, presumably so I

couldn't compare stories with any of my fellow squad members. I wondered if we were all being held separately. The base didn't have that many unoccupied single rooms, but it did have a lot of storage closets. If General Speed wanted us to be isolated, he could do it quite easily. At least I hadn't been taken to the brig.

I had no access to the news, and I was profoundly glad of it. If I had been able to turn on a television or go online, I knew I wouldn't have been able to resist the temptation to do so. I shuddered to think what they were saying about us now. Last summer, they had called us ecoterrorists, and we'd only ruined an uninhabited and relatively worthless island. This time, we'd done far worse.

Except it hadn't really been "we." Well, it would be "we" as far as General Speed was concerned, but Courtney had set it up so that it looked like Owen had acted alone and we had immediately gone into damage control. That made me angry. I didn't know how the rest of the squad felt, but if they thought I was going to sit by quietly while we let Owen take the fall, they had another thing coming, and I didn't care what it did to our future prospects.

I took a shower, mindful of the gauze. It was the first true shower I'd had since leaving the base all those weeks ago, even if I couldn't really wash the smoke from my skin. Then I had to put on the uniform I'd arrived in, which almost entirely negated the shower. I decided to take advantage of the bed, because my adrenaline and second wind were both well-spent, and I was exhausted. I lay down and did my best not to think, but a tune pulled at my mind. The more I listened to it, the easier it was to relax, and at last I fell asleep.

Hammering on the door woke me later. For a bleary moment, I couldn't remember where I was. Then it all crashed in on me, and I dragged myself out of the bed. I was horribly rumpled and still in the uniform I'd been wearing under my snowsuit, but there was nothing for it. I hauled the door open.

"McQuaid." Porter nodded sharply. Then he looked at my uniform. "You look terrible."

"They didn't give me anything to change into, Lieutenant," I told him. "They just bandaged my hands and left me."

"Stay here," he said, and stalked off muttering to himself. About ten minutes later, he came back with a clean uniform and an MRE. He sat down on the bed—there was no chair—and gestured for me to sit beside him. "Food first," he said, peeling back the tinfoil and unwrapping the fork for me. It was the first time he'd ever done anything like that. I swallowed hard around the lump in my throat and ate as fast as I could.

"What's happening?" I asked, speaking around a mouthful of something I was pretty sure was chicken. Porter wasn't really the type to complain about me talking with my mouth full.

"The usual bullshit," Porter said. "They're arguing about who, if anyone, to blame for all of this. The regular army is furious with us for going above their heads, but mostly I think they're embarrassed that three green dragon slayers and their fire crews acted before they had a chance to."

"How bad do you think it'll be?" I didn't think my parents would care too much if I was dishonorably discharged, but I would go down fighting anything less than full honours for Owen.

"Well, Amery is speaking on your behalf." Porter sounded surprised, understandably. "And they like her a lot more than they like me. Also, your training sergeant from Basic has agreed with her, and he's well-respected too."

"Won't it just look bad for them if we get in trouble?" I asked.

"They can't get you in trouble, Siobhan," he said gently. "They can punish you indirectly, as you've seen done, but they can't come out and do anything officially. He saved too many lives."

I thought about that for a moment while I finished my dinner, or lunch, or whatever it was.

"So what happens next?" I asked.

"Well, first you get changed," Porter said, passing me the uniform.

I went into the bathroom. It was an unmodified uniform, which usually meant that Annie helped me with the buttons and bootlaces. Annie wasn't here, though, and I was damned if I was going to ask Porter for help. It took me a while, but I managed, though I couldn't do the tie. I had no idea why bootlaces were something I could do and neckties were not. Maybe it was the angle. At last I gave up and went back out with it undone around my neck.

"You'll have to talk to the general," Porter said when he saw me. He stood and tied my tie without fanfare. He looked down at my feet and must have decided that those knots would hold, because he didn't move to fix them. "But I'll be with you, and so will Amery."

"And Courtney?" I asked.

"Yes," Porter said. "He's refused to let her out of his sight since she got back. I think it scared him more than he's willing to admit, her being that close to a Chinook."

"She was closer to the one that came here," I pointed out. "But I guess she was in the shelter for that."

"Well, whatever the reason, I'm glad," he said. "She seems to calm him down a bit, somehow."

"That's probably good for me," I said.

Porter handed me my hat, and we went out into the hallway. It might have been my imagination, but I swear that everyone we passed straightened. They didn't come to attention, not quite, but they stood a little taller. Like they were proud. We passed a cleaner, the same man I'd seen before we'd gone north, and he bowed his head as we walked by.

It was Owen, I realized. He was gone, and this was how they remembered him. By doing their jobs but taking time to honour him in the process. I could do that.

Both of General Speed's aides were at their desks, but they didn't say anything as we passed. In the office, I saw that not only were Courtney and Amery present, but so was our entire squad. Wilkinson and Anderson, who had sustained the worst injuries, were sitting in the chairs while everyone else crowded around them. It was a tight fit, but we managed.

"I realize that this is not a happy time," the general said after I gave my oral report of what had happened. He looked at his daughter before turning to look at me. "But there are things we must discuss. About your future within the Oil Watch."

I twisted my hands, but when I looked at Amery, her face

was calm. Whatever the general was talking about, it wasn't necessarily a bad thing.

"Tradition dictates," he went on, "that when a dragon slayer is killed in the line of duty, his support squad is offered a choice."

I recalled that, vaguely, from Basic. And Speed had said "in the line of duty." That boded well.

"You are all entitled to retirement from the Oil Watch with full honors and benefits," General Speed said.

Parker shifted the leg he'd burned, but no one else moved. I'm not entirely sure anyone else breathed.

"You may also request reassignment as individuals," Speed said. "And your final alternative is that you are able to select another dragon slayer to follow as a squad. The dragon slayer you pick must not have a crew and must accept you."

I felt everyone in the room shift to look at Courtney. She was the one with the lists. She knew where everything was, and I knew that everyone would follow her lead, even though I wasn't sure I could. The look she directed at Porter was speculative, and when he nodded, the barest of smiles appeared on her face. The rest of the squad straightened as best they could and shifted, ever so slightly, in Porter's direction.

"We will support Lieutenant Porter, sir," Courtney said.

There was not an ounce of familiarity in her voice as she spoke to her father, but neither was there any hint of disrespect. I watched as he softened, just a little bit, and Courtney dropped her gaze.

"Very well," the general said. His voice was absolutely as professional as hers, but there was something new in his eyes. Fear, I thought. With just the right amount of regret. "I will have the appropriate paperwork done up. You are all dismissed."

We walked back to the barracks quietly, Porter in the lead. It wasn't exactly cause for celebration. Reassignment of the crew by the crew's choice was supposed to suppress any rumours of bad luck, but the truth was that most people took retirement. Losing a dragon slayer was hard, and I wasn't sure if I wanted to go to work for Porter as I had for Owen.

He must have known when he came to get me, for all he pretended not to. He'd been much nicer to me than he had before. Presumably that would wear off eventually, but maybe it was also an audition. He'd tied my tie, knowing that I was about to go to a meeting where I'd end up his bard. I didn't know if I could write for bagpipes. They were much less user-friendly than the horn.

"It'll be different," Laura said at last when we got to our room. All the guys had followed us in, even though that wasn't really within regulations, and Nick was waiting for us, sitting on the foot of Kaori's bed.

"But we'll all be together," Annie said. "At least until our four years are up."

They were all nodding. They would do this as a group. What we had started with a Singe'n'Burn on the banks of the St. John River we would finish together, or at least as together as we could.

"Siobhan," Courtney said hesitantly, "when you were telling the general what happened, you were using your story-telling voice."

I hadn't even realized it, but of course I had been. It was easier that way when I was telling a story. I could even pretend I hadn't told one great lie to ensure that the people who most deserved the truth from me would never, ever find out what it was. It hung there, for a moment, and I almost cracked. But then Nick stood up.

"No, she wasn't," he said, coming to sit beside me. And he had been there with me, so everyone believed him.

"You don't have to, Siobhan," Porter said. So gently. He was sitting on Courtney's bed near the wall, and yet somehow, he was still the centre. "You can go home, retired, full honours. And if you stay, you never have to write a note about me. You've got your own story to tell, and I'm happy to be a part of it, if you want."

My own story. That was the one thing I had barely allowed myself to consider. It was always Owen's story that I told. But I thought about the cleaner who waved at me in the corridor; the men of the Patricias, the one million followers who watched my videos, our crews with their shaved heads. Maybe it had been my story for longer than I thought.

"Will you come with us?" Courtney asked, her heart in her eyes.

"Yes," I said, and I did my best to smile at them. I'm not sure how well it worked. "Yes, I'll come with you. But first—" I paused. "First I need to see him home."

Porter's smile was soft. I nearly didn't recognize him, but his voice was still the same, even with the gentle overtones. There was familiar music in it, and I would write it, even if he didn't realize the story was about him. Apparently, that's what I was good at. I would write one last song about Owen. I could hear it as clear as ever on the edges of my soul. But I would tell his story for the rest of my life, because it was my story as well as his.

"That's tradition too," Porter said.

Then Courtney took both of my hands in hers, and for the first time, I cried for Owen Thorskard.

THE HIGHWAY OF HEROES

It was a very small container. The smoke jumpers had taken what they could from the ruins of the ATV, but the Chinook had been all over everything. I heard Porter tell Courtney that from the photos, he was pretty sure Owen had practically been on the beast's tongue when he fired. I hoped those photos were heavily classified and kept somewhere where even Emily would never find them. I certainly never wanted to see them.

They'd cremated what they found and put it into a box for us to carry home. I had no idea how large an urn usually was, but this one seemed small. I had only just gotten used to thinking of Owen as a giant, and now I could carry him around in one hand.

We landed in Trenton, having flown back. Sadie arrived shortly after we did. The Oil Watch did not customarily allow girlfriends compassionate leave, but her mentor had supported her application and made it out to look more like she was his training partner—which happened to be true—and the leave had been granted. We sat together, just the two of us, while they arranged the motorcade, and I told her most of what had happened in my own unadorned words. We both cried, and then I hummed the main theme of the song I was composing for her so that she could hear it. It would never have words, I had already decided, but that didn't mean it would be hard to understand. Sadie had tears in her eyes again when I finished.

"It will be beautiful," she told me. "I know it."

It usually takes two hours to drive from Trenton to downtown Toronto, where the coroner's office is. It took us three hours that day, because we drove the whole way below the speed limit. There were two police cars in front of us, lights flashing but no sirens, and then the hearse with its tiny urn. Then there were three black limos. Sadie and I rode in the first one with Davis and Ilko, and everyone else was in the other two. Last came one more police car.

Every member of the Canadian Forces who is killed in the line of duty makes this trip. They land in Trenton and drive down the 401. The coroner's office receives and registers them, and the official death certificate is made up. Then the body is released home for the funeral. That is the official procedure. What happens on the 401, however, is entirely beyond military protocol.

It started in 2002, when four soldiers made the trip at the same time. People came out to line overpasses, to pay their respects. It expanded to involve local firefighters and police officers for crowd control, and soon they had to close the roads whenever a hearse was coming through. By the time Owen made the trip, it was an expected, but no less meaningful, ritual.

"Look," said Sadie when we got close to the first bridge.

I craned my neck to see out the window. There they were, hundreds of them, on this overpass and all the ones I could see. They stood above us and let the flags they held hang low over the railings. I had assumed I'd run out of tears eventually, but I hadn't yet. Sadie took my hand, crushing my hat in the process, and we watched until we left the bridges behind.

"I came to do this once," Davis said once we'd exited the highway. "To stand on the bridge, I mean. We had to walk for more than a kilometre, there were so many people. I think there were more today."

"There's always more for a dragon slayer," Sadie said.

"It's not really about the numbers," I said. "It's that they come at all."

We drove the rest of the way in silence.

The Trondheim memorial was long, and I don't remember most of it. I didn't sing or play. I sat with the support squad, though my parents sat directly behind me, and afterwards they took me home before I had a chance to speak with anyone.

I didn't really mind. I had work to do and not a lot of time to do it. I wanted to compose this song myself, or at least do most of the work before I called in Emily for help, but a couple hours after the memorial, Courtney showed up at the house. She was still in her dress uniform, though I had changed into my civilian clothes, but she didn't look uncomfortable.

"How is everyone?" I asked.

"I think they're sleeping," she said. "We've been stressed."

That was an understatement.

"You're not?" I asked. "Tired, I mean."

"I'll live," she said. "Besides, I thought you might need some help."

"You write music?" I asked.

"No," she said. "But there are a lot fewer letters in music than there are in the alphabet, and I can write that just fine."

I laughed in spite of myself, and we set to work. Courtney had no idea what she was doing, and she couldn't make the same helpful suggestions that Emily often did. But she was a quick study, and since she was mostly just manipulating notes on the computer after I sang them in, she did just fine. Mum made us stop to eat at one point, but by the time it got dark, the song was more or less done. It had been in my head for so long that actually writing it down was almost the easy part.

It was longer than I had expected it to be, and it had a lot of parts. I hadn't set out to incorporate every person we'd worked with that night, but they had all crept in, one by one. Most of them were hiding in the general orchestra, but a few had features in the main part that I hadn't been expecting. I didn't fight it, though, even if it sounded odd at the start. By the time I had assigned instruments to all the parts, and multiplied the ones that needed to be duplicated, it felt like it was nearly done.

"I should go," Courtney said. "I think you're just going to poke at it forever, and Porter will be worried if I'm not back soon."

"You've been a huge help," I said. "This would have taken me forever if you hadn't come over."

"Honestly, I kind of wanted to see how you worked," she said. "You get to watch me all the time."

"It does seem fair," I said.

"I can't believe you have all that noise going on in your head, all the time," she said, putting her coat back on.

"I can't believe that other people don't," I said.

"I guess it's kind of like blueprints," she mused. "You just read them differently."

"It's exactly like blueprints," I told her, and we went down the stairs.

"You're sure you don't need a ride back to the motel?" my dad asked as I saw Courtney out.

"No, thank you, Mr. McQuaid," Courtney replied. She'd called him 'sir' over dinner, and he'd laughed so hard he'd almost choked. I think he was feeling a bit emotional. "I don't mind the exercise."

"She really doesn't," I said. "We don't have any green space in Fort Calgary, so the air's always a little weird."

"I'll see you tomorrow, Siobhan," she said, and then she was gone.

"Are you done for the night?" Dad asked. I must have looked as tired as I felt.

"No," I said. "There are a couple of things I need to tweak on the song. And before that, I need to go to the Thorskards."

Mum and Dad both froze for a moment.

"Does it have to be tonight?" Mum asked.

"Yes," I said.

It was an easy drive to the Thorkards' house. I could probably do it in my sleep. I'd done it so many times. Hopefully, I'll be doing it many more.

When I pulled into the driveway, there was smoke coming out of the forge and the van was gone. I couldn't really judge, I supposed. I had gone straight from the funeral to recording music. We all had work.

I turned off the engine and walked towards the forge. I rang the bell—more of a gong, really, so that Hannah would hear it—and a few moments later she opened the door.

Her face was red from the heat, but her eyes were red too.

"Hi," I said, not sure what else to say.

She pulled me into her arms, wrapping them so tightly around me that for a moment it was hard to breathe, and then she let me go.

She took me inside and made me tea, and we sat for a while without saying anything. I hadn't known exactly why I needed to come here, what I needed to say to her, or what I needed to hear. Only that something had been pulling at me, the way a song did sometimes, and I'd decided to follow it.

"It all happened really quickly," I said, finally. "I mean, Owen and Courtney had figured it out, but I hadn't. I wasn't thinking that far ahead. I didn't even get a chance to stop him."

"You couldn't have stopped him," Hannah said softly.

"What will you do now?" I asked. "Will you stay in Trondheim, now that Lottie's plan is broken?"

Hannah laughed. It was a hard, ugly sound. The kind of laugh you make yourself have because the alternative is screaming and breaking through the walls.

"This *was* the plan, Siobhan," she said, her voice harder than I'd heard before. "This was always the plan."

My heart froze. She loved Owen. There was no way . . .

"I don't understand," I said.

"It was supposed to be Lottie," Hannah continued, in that same dark tone. "But she fell. After, when she woke up and I realized she was going to live, my first reaction was abject relief. I thought I got to keep her. I got to keep them all."

She stirred her tea, even though there was nothing in it.

"But they don't stop," she said. "They are out there right now, defending some helpless barn from a soot-streaker. They never stop. It couldn't be Lottie, and it couldn't be Aodhan. And Owen—he was the only one left, in the end."

I felt my heart thaw to a quiet horror then. This had been the plan. Yes, they had probably hoped for a longer game, more years, more stories, but the outcome had always been the same. To sell a tale, you need a hero. And there are very, very few ways to sell a hero.

"Why didn't you tell me?" I asked. Why hadn't they told me that I was going to be his friend? That was I was going to go with him to his death? That was I going to survive and have to tell everyone in the world about it, over and over and over again?

"Would you have stayed?" Hannah replied. Her voice was soft again, more like her normal one. "Would you have followed him?"

I didn't know. So I told her a story instead.

"He said to tell you that he loves you," I said. "He said to tell you that he always thought of you as his mother."

At least that was the truth, though Owen hadn't said it.

Hannah put her face in her hands, but she didn't cry again. She just heaved, her shoulders going up and down like she was pulling on the bellows, until she recovered.

"Will you write his story?" she asked me, like Lottie had done before. "Will you sing his songs?"

I heard it then, like I always did. Lakes and islands. Old vans and red barns. Prairies and mountains. And fire. Always fire.

"Yes," I said, and the melody soared. "I will."

And I do.

THE STORY OF OWEN

This is the Story of Owen.

It starts out slowly, as small towns do, with small notes and small parts, split between flute and strings. It grows, like wheat in spring, through small adventures that bind the town together. When it grows too big, it leaves, but it will always remember where it came from.

It thrives on the prairies, where drums and pipes add volume and depth. But danger lurks, looking down from the mountains, and when it strikes, it strikes with deafening blasts from the horns and crashes from the percussion.

It struggles next, using all the pieces it has gathered thus far. It ranges high and low notes against a faster tempo, until at last, the music is overwrought and stops.

But that isn't the end.

The horn is a difficult instrument to learn and even harder to master when you have broken hands. But it climbs out of the ashes with the main theme, strong sounds in its bell and notes that hang like golden keys in thin air.

The other instruments find their way back in—strings, clarinet, flute, trumpet—until once again the orchestra swells together, following the rising and falling hands of the conductor to the triumphant finish.

It took me a long time to figure it out, the Story of Owen. I thought I was composing it, observing it from the outside and chronicling it for those who would follow in his footsteps, but I was wrong. I composed music, it was true, but that was not my role.

Burned hands will struggle to hold a lot of things, but a conductor's baton fit as easily into my hands as if I had been born with one clasped there. I stood in front of the Oil Watch Ceremonial Orchestra, made up of players from all around the globe. Most of them had only seen the music a few hours beforehand, and we hadn't had a lot of time to rehearse. I wasn't nervous, though. I knew what I was doing.

We were playing on Parliament Hill, the full Oil Watch orchestra, as part of the Canada Day celebrations. It was sunny and too warm, the way Ottawa got in the summer, like it was making up for being so cold in the winter, but I didn't care. My support squad and Porter had seats of honour in the boxes reserved for the NDP. Everywhere I looked, I saw red and white T-shirts, and flags with the Maple Leaf in the centre.

The broadcast system activated, and the crowd hushed as we were announced.

Everyone knew the Story of Owen. They'd seen it on the news and read it on the Internet, but today they were going to hear the version I had written. The sheet music was in front of me, rustling gently in the wind, and the eyes of the crowd and of the musicians, were fixed on where I stood.

I raised the baton.

And the story began again.

Da Capo al Fine

ACKNOWLEDGMENTS

Two books! Which is about two more than I ever thought I'd get to see on a shelf somewhere. Who'd've thunk?

Big thanks to Agent Josh, who was very understanding when I told him I didn't want to write a second Owen book and then sold it when I wrote one anyway, and to Editor Andrew, who learned almost as much about Canadian history and infrastructure as I learned about the publishing industry.

To my ever-expanding writing group (Emma, Laura, Faith, RJ, and Tessa), some of whom I surprised with the ending: I love you all the most. We should work on the whole geography thing. To the Fourteenery: you got me through book one AND book two, which I think is over and above for a debut group. Ditto on the geography, though. Marieke Nijkamp gets massive bonus points for volunteering to read the sequel without having read part one, and Dot Hutchison read it and told me everything was going to be okay when I most wanted to light the manuscript on fire.

Huge thanks to my family, especially my sister, who put up with me visiting for the weekends only to disappear for hours, and totally fail at child-minding (though I thought Eli did a great job duplicating Brett Lawrie's tattoos! And the markers were washable!), and to EJ and Jen for offering up their cottage as often as I needed it.

And special mention must be made here to John, who got married to my friend Emma while I was finishing up the first draft, and who was down with me sending the last ten chapters to her while they were on their honeymoon.

The music of Heather Dale was a great inspiration to me, both for *Owen* and *Prairie Fire*, and I am very grateful to be able to use the lyrics from "Joan." Heather is a true modern bard with great music . . . and a Web site: heatherdale.com.

Finally, a shout-out to end all shout-outs to the staff at Chapters Kitchener. You have hand-sold my book like it was on fire, and I am so, so grateful for your hard work!

Prairie Fire was born under blue skies on a windy hill over-looking the Athabasca River, begun on an airplane bound for Texas, and written in at least six different area codes.

ABOUT THE AUTHOR

Emily Kate Johnston is a forensic archaeologist by training, a bookseller by trade, and a grammarian by nature. Someday, she's sure, she's going to get the hang of this whole "real world" thing, but in the meantime she's going to spend as much time in other worlds as she possibly can.

When she's not on Tumblr, she dreams of travel and Tolkien. Or writes books. It really depends on the weather.